Chasing Karma

Terry Shepherd

Ramirez & Clark
PUBLISHERS

For Dänna, who believed, even when I didn't.

Introduction

If I've learned anything as a cop, it is this:

The universe doesn't take sides.

*The goal is to survive, until Karma favors you in her
own time... and in her own way.*

*Your only hope is to have enough strength to emerge
from the maelstrom, neutralize the bad guys and
stay one step ahead of destiny's wreckage.*

— Jessica Ramirez

Chapter One

5140 Dennis Street - Paloma, Illinois

JESSICA RAMIREZ

When normal people face the barrel of a gun, their eyes dart between its infinite darkness and the corneas of the person tickling the trigger. Sweat beads above upper lips. Sounds and smells amplify. Seconds elongate into hours. Whatever bravado may be part of their act vanishes and even the least religious conjure up a prayer, pleading with God to give them the gift of one more day.

Psychotics simply smile.

Ted DeSalvo pressed the blade harder against the girl's carotid artery. The black, Halloween costume-variety dye coloring all but the roots of her brown hair slithered down the tanned forehead like a half dozen minuscule earthworms. It mingled with gothic black eyebrows, and half circle onyx eyelids, equally fabricated to go with the obsidian leather that accented the most appealing features of her lithe body.

The tip of the blade moved in and out against the tiny arterial

1

pulsations I estimated at nearly two-hundred beats per minute. Despite its razor's edge the compression didn't break the skin. The coiled potential was enough to tell me he was in control.

"Guns down, ladies, or you'll be responsible for two deaths today."

Ladies? That was the ultimate insult. My partner, Alexandra Clark and I are cops, with a decade of compartmentalized PTSD and distrust for anything male. Hanging that on us was an invisible spear DeSalvo loved to plunge into other people's souls.

"I hate being called 'ladies,'" Ali growled. "Let's kill him."

I ignored my partner. "Make a good decision for once, Ted. Prison is a target-rich playground for someone with your intellect. Death only confirms you're a loser."

DeSalvo's dig did nothing to change the accuracy of our aim, Ali's on the upper right quadrant of his chest, mine between his unflinching eyes, nor the intensity of our concentration.

Perhaps we were psychotic, too.

Ted's high-pitched giggle trilled the mating call of some unidentified species of bird. He stuttered the words between the annoying screeches. "You... You ladies always entertain. I... I hate to leave the performance."

I could see Ali's temperature rising, "He said it again! Let's kill him. Aim for the head. I'll ping his brain stem and he'll drop the knife like it just came out of a deep frier."

"Focus, Alexandra," I said. "That's a living being at the edge of his blade."

"Yeah, and she reminds me of your twin sister. I'm sick of this. He's nuts. Her only chance is if we split his skull like a watermelon before he kills her."

Our victim didn't like this strategy at all. From beneath a layer of gothic face paint I could see her sweat.

"I don't have a twin sister, Ali. And women cops de-escalate. You're not helping."

"I'm a lesbian, Jess. We don't de-escalate. On the count of three."

DeSalvo pressed the knife harder against the victim's neck. "She has security cameras. You are being recorded."

"Good," Ali said. "I washed my hair today. One."

I stole a quick glance at my partner. "You're just as psycho as he is."

The slightest cloud appeared on Ted DeSalvo's horizon. "Her family will sue you, sue the department and the city. Maybe even murder one for the both of you. Know how inmates treat girl cops in prison?"

That triggered me. "Did you hear that, Ali? He called us 'girl cops.'"

Ali nodded. She was enjoying this far too much. "Yeah. 'Two.'"

The victim's sweat was a river of black tributaries. Her face pleading. It didn't affect my focus.

"Sorry about this ma'am. But it appears that you and I are the only two sane people in this house."

DeSalvo made his decision.

"It's truly been real, ladies." Turning his head toward an end table he barked a command. "Alexa, turn on Cronus."

Ali, shouted "Three,"and the lights went out.

* * *

Ted DeSalvo planned this one carefully. He drew us to an abandoned 911 call at an innocuous residence of an invisible woman named Katrina Reid, so we wouldn't arrive with backup. A nosey neighbor told us she liked to cosplay with a preference for Malia Nurmi. "Vampira" to her small legion of fans earned an odd immortality thanks to her role in Ed Wood's "Plan 9 From Outer Space." The film is always in contention for number one on every list of the worst movies ever made.

There was more to the father of the god Zeus than just blackout curtains on a sunny afternoon.

I heard a bang somewhere nearby and a hissing sound as Ali and I fired into the darkness. The muzzle flashes revealed brief images of DeSalvo running to his right toward a door. We could hear his victim falling to the hardwood floor. I tried to bracket the hissing sound and caught sight of a canister on the floor near the kitchen sink, spewing gas among the flashes. Another gunshot illuminated our victim grasping her neck as blood flowed between her fingers.

The blackout curtains over every window were not solely for the mood. They insulated the interior to give whatever poison wafted our way the greatest effectiveness.

I holstered my weapon, not sure what to do next. "Alexandra. Help me with the lights, please."

They call Ali "Gates" for good reason. Her mind works faster than a Microsoft millionaire. She blew out a breath. "Am I the only one with technology at my apartment? Alexa! Lights on."

The Echo did her thing. Every light in the house snapped on. A door at the far end of the room swung shut. The Reid woman lay on the floor, blood coursing from a tiny puncture in her neck, with just enough intensity to delay our exit, attempt to save her life, and succumb to what I deduced was an airborne extermination agent.

Working with the same partner for ten years has its benefits. We each reflexively grabbed an arm. I pressed a finger into the incision to slow the flow of death. We dragged our victim toward the door Ted used for his getaway.

It was locked from the outside. What garage doors do that?

Alexandra cursed, un-holstered her Glock and fired her remaining lead into the mechanism as a gray cloud of demise inched in our direction. On the other side we heard an engine, the squeal of rubber against concrete and four evenly spaced gunshots.

A shoulder against the wood shattered the remaining resistance and we were in Ms. Reid's garage. I could see a convertible BMW blow down the street in the direction of the freeway.

I ran to the curb and emptied my mag in the Beemer's direction. He turned right at a corner next to a yellow street sign that said, "Go Slow. Children at Play."

"No respect for the law," I muttered.

"I should have shot the bastard on the count of 'Two'," Ali said keying her handheld. "Ten-David-Fifteen. Shots fired. 5140 Dennis Street. One victim with a neck laceration. Requesting EMS and back up at this address."

Dispatch whispered an acknowledgement. "I got this, Jess. Go get him."

That's when I saw what the gunshots had done. The four tires on our Tahoe were flat. "Dammit. That guy can shoot. Four Flat tires. I can't do that on a 'good' day."

Seconds were burning distance between Ted DeSalvo and me. I would have given my meager life savings for an EMT and a ride.

Our victim was unconscious. My ever-confident partner pressed a blue body-substance-isolation glove over the woman's neck. Ali stroked her forehead with a free hand. "She does look a little like you. Ever thought of dressing like a Goth for Halloween?"

"I need wheels, Ali. Time is wasting."

I scanned the neighborhood for a fast car with an owner at home.

"The garage," Ali said.

In our haste to exit, we missed it. A pristine MTT420R, the fastest street-legal crotch rocket ever made. A set of keys dangled from the ignition. Whoever this Reid woman was, she had class.

Ali waved me toward the blue, two-wheel beauty. "Try not to have too much fun while I'm saving this woman's life. What's her name, anyway?"

I bent over our victim. The make up made her face impossible to decode. "Reid. Katrina Reid. Gothic hooker, I'd guess."

Alexandra Clark pressed some gauze against the wound.

"We've all gotta make a living. Go put Ted DeSalvo out of his misery."

I snapped a finger an inch away from Katrina Reid's face. The noise caused her eyes to flicker open for an instant. "Don't you dare die on us, Katrina." I nodded toward Ali. "It will ruin her day."

The bike had juice. I shot out of the garage in pursuit, the adrenaline rush I loved flowing through my body.

"The chase is on, Teddy boy! Hell hath fury and her name is Jessica Ramirez!"

Chapter Two

Paloma, Illinois

JESSICA RAMIREZ
My motorcycle and I placed a bet on the freeway. The first clue that we were getting warm was an overturned SUV near the southbound on-ramp. The likely driver stood by the side of the road, one hand holding a cell phone to his ear, the other pressed against a shoulder dripping crimson. I slowed to a stop long enough to ask, "Silver BMW?"

"He shot me!"

The driver's voice could barely compete with the 420's whine, but his nod was all I needed.

The MTT had a rated top speed of 199 miles per hour. "Faster than you'll ever dare to go," the website says.

They didn't know me.

I've been a motorcycle enthusiast from the day I borrowed Antonio Rojas' mini bike without his permission. The intimacy of being one with the machine and the adrenaline rush of unprotected speed were almost better than sex.

7

Almost.

Ted DeSalvo still had options. Ahead was the junction where the road peeled eastward toward Springfield or west in the direction of the state line. Or he might jump off onto a back road and get lost among the amber waves of corn and soybeans that rotated between a dozen different farms in the vicinity.

Before I could process my irritation with too many choices, his intentions became clear. This time it was a pickup in the median. A tall, weathered man with a farmer's tan and biceps to match was just emerging from the vehicle. There was a bullet hole in the windshield. Another six inches to the right and the slug would have lodged in his skull.

DeSalvo was Westbound on I72, headed toward Missouri.

MTT isn't lying about their crotch rocket. With the throttle about halfway home, I was approaching one hundred and thirty miles per hour. Every twenty seconds, I had to thread around another disabled vehicle with bullet holes in the windows.

My psycho was intent on killing people.

* * *

ALEXANDRA CLARK

The palpations of Katrina Reid's sliced carotid artery weakened. Her heart raced in a futile attempt to pump oxygenated blood to her brain. Despite my best mitigations the woman had lost a ton. I worried there might not be enough to sustain her crucial organs.

I tried to keep my voice calm and professional as I pressed dispatch for an update, failing miserably. "10-David-15, what's the ETA on the medics? We're losing a patient here."

The silence while they jumped frequencies to talk with the ambulance unnerved me.

"Less than two minutes out, 10-David-15."

"Tell 'em to put the spurs to their horses, dispatch. I don't think this one's gonna make it."

Right on cue, the tiny palpations I could feel against the palm I rested on Katrina Reid's chest chose that moment to disappoint me.

"10-David-15 to Dispatch. The patient's heart has stopped."

* * *

JESSICA RAMIREZ

A silver speck at the mirage confluence of asphalt and horizon grew into a car. The top was down and a sub-human form I recognized was pumping slugs into every vehicle he passed.

The law of averages said he would eventually hit somebody where it hurt.

I unholstered my Glock, hoped I could control the 420 and drew a bead on the bastard.

He must have seen me in his mirrors. I was a nano-second from firing when he slammed on his brakes, wrestling the Beemer to a stop as I flew by on the left. Traffic behind him swerved. When I was certain the inertia of a chain reaction crash would engulf DeSalvo's vehicle, he jammed the accelerator to the floor, leaving an inch of smoking rubber on the pavement as he shot forward.

* * *

ALEXANDRA CLARK

The EMTs burst from the back of their red rolling breadbox, dark blue bags filled with lifesaving implements in hand. I could sense them unfavorably critiquing my CPR skills.

I spit out the ABCs between compressions.

"Likely 35 year old female with a single laceration to the left carotid artery. Airway clear, breathing regular but weak until just now. The incident happened approximately ten minutes ago. Significant blood loss, over two pints. Pressure applied to the wound after about ninety seconds. Lost the heart beat two minutes ago."

The senior EMT took over the compressions as her second handed me a saline bag. I remembered one of the medics explaining that its loss of blood volume, not loss of red cells that can kill.

"I'm IV trained." I said, feeling more helpless by the minute.

"Left arm," the senior barked, "Start the line, Officer. Nate get out the paddles."

Nate, who looked way too young to be playing with grown up defibrillator gear, powered up the unit, ripped the woman's shirt open, measured the targets with his fingers and greased the paddles in less time than it took me to find a vein. The sinus rhythm screen drew flat line across its green crosshatch.

Nate's boss must have had confidence in him, motioning me away from the dead body the kid yelled, "Clear."

Bang. The usual upward thrust of a chest hit with several thousand volts of electricity.

Flatline.

"Hit her again."

Bang. Another involuntary undulation.

Flatline.

"Another one."

Bang. This time I could hear the lungs press some air out of Kartrina's mouth. It sounded a lot like a death rattle.

Flatline.

"One more and then we call it," The senior EMT said. Her voice was without emotion. I reckoned she had seen too many of these and was well inoculated against watching a person die before her eyes.

Nate squeezed the triggers.

Bang. The pulsing heartbeat was weak but registering on the screen.

The supe exhaled. Nate exhaled. I exhaled. "Grab the stretcher and transport," she said

As an afterthought, she shot me what passed for a thin smile.

"Good work, officer. If she pulls through, it will be because you saved her life."

* * *

JESSICA RAMIREZ

By now I was a good mile and a half ahead of DeSalvo, nearly losing control of the bike as I skidded into a one-eighty at the foot of the Mark Twain Memorial Bridge. Revving the turbine to maximum rpm, I released the clutch.

Our rate of closure was easily two hundred miles per hour; two knights with semi-automatic lances on a collision course.

I had one shot, a buffeting crosswind, and a five percent chance of hitting my target before his BMW turned me into a strawberry stain. In the distance I could see Ted DeSalvo bracing his own semi-auto on the dashboard in my direction.

My life has never flashed before my eyes in the valley of the shadow of death. The peaceful calm that has always been an advantage in moments of mutually assured destruction engulfed me. The sound of the wind and the whine of the turbine faded into silence. I put DeSalvo's forehead in my crosshairs, said a prayer to my father and squeezed the trigger.

* * *

ALEXANDRA CLARK

The breadbox skidded into the ambulance lane at the Paloma General ER entrance. Since our vehicle had four flats, I grabbed a ride to keep Nate company. I was glad I did. We had to shock the woman twice more on the way.

Junior Engler was waiting. Our least favorite resident MD was flanked by the code-blue team. "Take her into the ER on the stretcher," he shouted adding sarcasm to his next command. "Clark, we don't need you. We try to save lives in here."

I swallowed a response and decided to wait outside. The cardiac needles in the code kit were big enough for a horse. I didn't like sharp things.

A nurse I knew patted my shoulder as she helped rush the wheely inside. "You probably gave her a second life today. Let's hope she does something useful with it."

JESSICA RAMIREZ

I felt the sting of the weapon's kick against my wrist, picked an evasive vector and leaned the 420 into it. DeSalvo sailed past before I could gauge whether the nine-millimeter slug had found its target.

The chain reaction crash cleared the highway of traffic, giving me a wide field of cement to execute another one-eighty. Squinting into the afternoon sun, I watched as the Beemer drifted to the right. A fender caught the guard rails at the edge of the bridge. The vehicle became airborne spinning a lazy circle before rolling on its top and parting the waters of the Mississippi in a giant rooster tail of foam.

I guess I should have expected someone to alert the Missouri state cops. Six cruisers blocked the West side of the bridge at the point where my jurisdiction ended.

The Beemer submerged, undulating as the currents carried it under the bridge. There was no attempt to jump into the water and try to save Ted DeSalvo's life. In the bike's rear view mirrors, I saw two Illinois State Police vehicles skid to a stop behind me. Four troopers ejected from the doors; guns drawn.

Some macho man yelled, "Drop the weapon. On the ground. Spread eagle."

I held the butt of my pistol between the thumb and forefinger of my left hand, displaying my shield with my right.

The man with the voice shook his head and the boys slowly lowered their guns.

"Jessica Ramirez." It was a deflated recognition. A disappointment.

I grinned; my gaze still focused on the river. "At your service, Gentlemen."

Chapter Three

Portland Oregon – The Same Day
Armand Castillo unlocked Portland Place Apartment 204 and stood back to let the cops do their work. It didn't pay to follow them in. When some anonymous phone call led to a welfare check, that usually meant a dead body or shaky trigger fingers.

His complex reeked of drug dealers and addicts. But this tenant didn't fit either description. She kept to herself and paid on time. Armand hoped she was simply on another of her long vacations and the place might be empty.

The pungent odor of putrefaction disabused that notion.

Curiosity overpowered caution. Armand followed the two uniformed blues and a third man who wore an expensive suit, perfectly shined shoes and a Rolex watch into the single bedroom at the far end of the sparsely furnished unit.

Her bloated head rested on the silk-covered pillow she told Armand she had bought in Beijing. Arms extended atop matching sheets and a carefully arranged comforter. The contents of her intestines discolored the area below the waist. Rivulets of red foam painted trails from the edges of her nose and mouth, creating small crimson pools on the mattress.

And yet, the tableau had a mortician's touch, not at all like the contorted sprawls Armand was used to seeing from behind crime scene tape.

One of the cops called in the 10-54. "No need for lights and siren. This one has marinated."

"Got a name?" the man in the suit asked.

The apartment manager felt an uncharacteristic lump in his throat. You kept emotional distance when the relationship might end in eviction. Somehow, this one had insinuated herself into his heart.

"Susan. Susan Molinero."

"Can you identify her?"

Castillo swallowed the bile his gag reflex tried to eject. The body looked only vaguely like his tenant. It was the bracelet and the one polished fingernail that gave Susan away.

"The jewelry and that blue fingernail on her right hand. She told me about the bracelet, purchased in China. And who could miss one blue fingernail? That has to be Susan Molinero"

The man in the suit put a hand on Castillo's shoulder. "Know who we should call?"

"Diana somebody. I'll get Susan's rental application for you."

"This happens all the time, Agent Meredith," one of the blues said. "People vanish, reinvent, and die alone where you can't decipher their past. It's getting to be a normal thing."

Richard Meredith of the Central Intelligence Agency lifted the lifeless hand to study the nail polish. "Susan Molinero's resume is anything but normal, officer. It's critical that we get this identification right." The hand at the end of the wrist with the Rolex pointed to Castillo. "No offense, my friend. But I'll need more than an apartment manager's intuition to put a name with this face."

Meredith leaned over the dead woman until his head was just

inches from hers. "Just who are you, young lady? The person I was sent to terminate, some unlucky body double?"

The putrefaction didn't seem to bother Meredith. He sniffed the sickening odor emanating from her body as if it were a bouquet of daffodils. "One way or another, I'm going to find out."

Armand Castillo retreated. Between the smell of death and the revolting picture of Meredith's proximity to Susan Molinero's distended expression, he knew he was in for some sleepless nights.

Chapter Four

Playa del Muerte - Colombia

The brass knuckles were a nice touch, Michael Wright thought. Don Alejandro telegraphed the punch, knowing his victim could do nothing to stop it. The sound of contusioned skin and cracking bone was familiar to the FBI agent. So was the pain. By now, almost an hour into his interrogation, its intensity was beyond any medical scale. Michael had to fight the natural desire to faint. The Don wouldn't get that satisfaction.

"Only one other man of your profession a has ever tried to infiltrate our operation, Agent Wright."

This wasn't the lyrical Spanish in tourist YouTube videos. It was the guttural grunts of someone who had come from the lowest caste in a poor country, fighting his way to the top in its most dangerous game.

"He warned us there would be more... before I disemboweled him with the claw of a mountain lion."

The Don ran an index finger across the bloody mass where the brass had done its work. He studied the red droplets with scientific intensity before licking the digit clean with his tongue.

"American blood tastes different. Not nearly enough iron. Perhaps an example of your poor constitution?"

Michael calculated the time. He needed perhaps five more minutes.

"You're still a loser, Alex." Michael used the familiar contraction to anger The Don. "Your own men would kill you in a heartbeat without the false bravado."

That triggered another punch, this one to the gut.

Michael's head lolled from side to side as he tried to take in the feng shui of the drug lord's beach-front mansion. "And your taste in interior design. What cheap hotel is missing furniture?"

The Don turned to a small table where the tools of his interrogation trade were arranged in medical precision. The mountain lion's claw lay there, the bones of the leg melded into the grip of a hammer.

"Your usefulness is at an end, Agent Wright. You have utterly failed your country and are now nothing more than an unpleasant distraction. I shall enjoy ripping out your intestines, one foot at a time."

Michael heard the sound first; the rhythmic thump of whirling steel blades slicing the humid air. He let his head roll backward in the wooden chair where his arms and legs were restrained with duct tape... and laughed. It began as a low chortle, growing louder until it was almost insane in tone and intensity.

"YOUR usefulness is at an end, Alex. The Book of Amos, chapter four, verse twelve."

Michael Wright locked eyes with his tormentor. The laughter was gone. Through a haze of blood and flesh The Don could see ice-cold resolve.

"Prepare to meet thy God."

The sounds were louder. Spanish echoed from the beach to the balcony where Don Alejandro's cadre of bodyguards kept watch.

"¡Helicópteros!"

The blue sky was black with the aircraft, perhaps a dozen or more converging.

With a single lunge, Michael ripped free of his bonds. An uppercut stunned The Don. The mountain lion claw flew from his captor's grasp. Michael plucked it from the air like a ninja warrior grasping a fly.

"Never restrain a victim with duct tape, Alex. The adhesive will be a bitch to get out of my clothes."

Michael Wright twirled the weapon in the air with a majorette's precision, catching it on the fly and swiping the razor-sharp talons across the Don's neck, severing both carotid arteries in a single thrash.

* * *

The strike team was in and out of Playa del Muerte in less than fifteen minutes. The human remnants of Don Alejandro's drug empire lay lifeless, lined up side-by-side in the main house amid the hotel furniture and poorly executed copies of famous paintings.

One of the Marines assigned to the mission wrote, "Death to Drug Runners" in Colombian blood at their feet.

* * *

The carrier based MH60 choppers returned to their floating home. Michael Wright found himself aboard an MH-47G Chinook, headed for San Jose, Costa Rica, surrounded by medics, engulfed in the powerful decibels of the helicopter's power plant.

"You must be Irish," one said as she cleaned the contorted skin where the brass knuckles had done their work. "Most patients who get kissed by brass break bones and need reconstruction."

Michael was about to respond when a familiar face emerged from the flight deck.

"Michael Wright, that's the last time I loan you out to the CIA."

FBI Associate Director Terry Taylor's voice easily cut above the howl of the engines. His million-dollar grin took Michael's pain down a notch. "Since when do you show up in the field, Director Taylor?"

"After almost twenty years, you could call me Terry, ya punk."

"Respect for my superiors, sir. And I'll be just fine concentrating on bad guys within our borders. Want to tell me why you're here?"

Taylor nodded to the chief medic. Wordless instructions passed down the chain and the group disbursed, leaving the two men alone. Taylor produced a pair of noise canceling headsets, not connected to the chopper's comms systems.

"Much better," he said as the active circuitry quieted the deafening decibels down to a cool hum. "How did you like Colombia?"

Michael raised an eyebrow. The move made his entire face hurt. "Not a retirement destination, sir. Something's up, or you wouldn't be anywhere near putting yourself in harm's way."

The slightest bit of wind fell from Taylor's sails. He slumped forward, hands resting on his thighs. "There's some fallout from your little adventure in Moscow. We have intel that The Triumvirate is targeting your girlfriend for assassination."

Despite the shot of pain, Michael frowned. "Jessica? Why?"

"We live in a political world, Michael. Even the oligarchs who pull the strings behind the scenes become vulnerable when they fail. The Triumvirate has failed twice. The Vega matter and The Captain. Jessica is a symbol, a poster child for their weakness. As long as she lives, The Triumvirate's status is in danger."

The radiating discomfort of Michael's injuries was eclipsed by cold tendrils of fear. He was aware of the power and ruthlessness of The Triumvirate. When they made decisions, people died.

"What do we do, sir?"

Taylor avoided eye contact. Never a good sign. "As bad as our three musketeers are, they have a vested interest in international stability. If a power struggle erupts it could lead to worldwide disaster. The Administration believes Jessica is expendable."

Anger tightened Michael's throat. There was no "sir" in his question. "Are you prepared to allow that to happen?"

Taylor's gaze was earnest. Either he was about to tell the truth or a lie. Michael never knew which. "No, Michael. I am not. There is a wrinkle that has turned up the heat. Excalibur was involved."

Michael caught his breath. "X?"

"The deadliest assassin in the business. For the last two decades X has been linked to everything from regime change to organized crime. Until recently nobody has ever seen or spoken to X."

Michael parsed Taylor's words carefully. "You said X *was* assigned to kill Jess?"

"For two-million bucks. Sometimes Karma favors the prepared, my friend. Every anonymous threat must have a go-between. X had one and we flipped him. He provided a name and a location. But someone beat us to Excalibur. She's dead."

"X was a woman?"

Taylor grinned. "You of all people should know that a woman can be a superhero or a super villain. X was one of the worst."

Michael's confusion grew. "If X is dead, doesn't that make protecting Jessica easier?"

Taylor exhaled. "Jessica Ramirez seems to be the six-degrees-of-separation for The Triumvirate. Guess who found Excalibur's next of kin?"

Michael was already calculating flight options from San Jose to Chicago, O'Hare. Taylor must have deduced it from his darting eyes.

"We screwed up, Michael. The coroner released her body for cremation before our man could intervene. And the only positive identification was the manager of the apartment complex where she was living. There's a chance she smelled the flip, faked her death and is still out there looking for your fiancée. Your next duty station is Paloma, Illinois."

Michael felt his heart race. A thought made it race faster. "But what if X is already in Paloma?"

"Meredith was on scene when the local law found the body. He is on his way to Paloma right now. He'll connect with Jessica and keep her covered until you arrive."

Michael knew Rick Meredith well. The common bond of combat in Afghanistan cemented a lifetime brotherhood. "Rick's a good man. How much can we tell Jess? She deserves to know what's happening and why."

The Associate Director put a hand on Michael's shoulder. "Use your judgment, Michael. But don't let personal feelings cloud it. I'm burning a ton of personal capital to convince a bunch of politicians one little Latina does not need to make the ultimate sacrifice for her country."

Taylor motioned to the medics to return. "If Excalibur is still alive, kill or capture her and all sins are forgiven."

Michael gritted his teeth. "Do you have a name for me, sir?"

"Susan Molinero. And there is another link to Detective Ramirez."

"Let me guess. Susan and Jess have friends in common."

"It's worse than that, Michael. They went to school together."

Chapter Five

Paloma, Illinois

JESSICA RAMIREZ

"Silent" Susan Molinero was so good at being invisible that few of us who graduated with her remembered who she was.

The Paloma High School Class of 2002 had a Facebook outpost for our 20th reunion. I occasionally trolled the page to see how much weight the popular girls had gained since graduation.

Silent Susan briefly took on a roommate in Oregon where both found jobs at a Portland semi-conductor plant. Diana La Pierre was that roommate. Diana posted a plea for next of kin on our reunion page.

That's how I got involved. Diana and Susan stayed nominally in touch after Susan found a place of her own and took off on one of her trips.

Diana told me she did that often, working long enough to earn a plane ticket and some spending cash, and then disappearing. Several months later, she showed back up at work, tanned, tired, looking "rode hard and put away wet," and not saying much about where she went or what she saw.

I turned to my yearbook and contemplated the angular face and the tight-lipped expression. I get paid to remember details. Susan was an enigma.

A single exchange on Susan's sparse profile page began to unravel the mystery.

* * *

It was Roberta Steele who sent a brief birthday greeting around the time Susan moved to Portland. I chased Robbie down in the trailer park she shared with the high school sweetheart she married. He was not at home when I knocked on Roberta Steele's door.

The face that answered it betrayed a moment of stunned surprise before bracketing who I was. "Jessica Ramirez. Damn, you and Susan could be sisters."

The voice was familiar. Robbie added a few pounds to her five-foot-nuthin frame. The limp I remembered from high school was more pronounced. A pair of drugstore reading glasses balanced on the edge of a prominent nose. She still looked like the senior picture I carried to confirm her ID. Her place reeked of cannabis.

We shook hands with the detachment of strangers. "Sure is weird how people age," Robbie said, reading my mind. "I bet you couldn't pick me out of a line-up thanks to the mileage on this body." She was right. "And as I think about it, you and Susan grew up to share the same coloring and bone structure. From a distance you could be twins."

She ushered me in, motioning to a couch across from a pair of recliners with a clear view of a flat-screen television that was way too big for the room. An angular cat who radiated adoption sat on one of the recliner arms judging me.

Robbie wiggled an ample caboose until it found the right spot.

She retrieved a joint from a candy jar between the chairs and lit it, before considering my probable concern.

"I've got a card, Jessie. I'm legal." She inhaled a second drag and took my measure. "I figured you would be a swimming coach by now. The cop stuff was a surprise."

Everyone knew me as the jock who owned the state freestyle records, expecting I would get a full ride at a Division One university. Few were aware of how my father dashed those dreams. Everybody knew he was dead.

"I was sorry to hear about your dad. I had my husband check our LP tank after your house blew up."

That was the Robbie I knew. Totally direct with zero sensitivity to others' feelings. I've never been good at small talk, so I got to the point. "I guess you knew Sue back in school."

"Sure did. She was the closest thing to a best friend. Her grandmother had money, owned a horse farm and a swimming pool. I spent every free moment out there. Sue would hoist me on top of her most compliant mare, grab a stallion for herself and we explored the county until the streetlights came on.

"The girl could shoot, too. Carried a Lone Ranger style pistol. I saw her pick off vultures eating road kill at fifty yards.

"Lost track of her after graduation until we found each other on Facebook. But that's the kind of person she was. Didn't say much and appreciated the fact that I didn't ask."

"You sent her a birthday wish a couple of years back?"

"Right after she moved to Oregon."

I stole a peek at the screen shot of their exchange on my smart phone. "Looks like she didn't respond."

"Sometimes she did. Sometimes she didn't. I never forgot her kindness in high school and felt bad that I had so little to offer in return."

Robbie regarded me over the tops of her cheaters. "You're here because something has happened to her."

I shifted into cop mode. Compartmentalization is a survival

skill. "She passed away last month, Robbie. Nobody can find a relative. I thought you might know somebody."

Robbie sucked in another cloud of THC and slipped deeper into the leather recesses of her recliner. "I was afraid of that. Her parents are dead. All that's left is a brother. They don't talk."

A vague image of a kid a couple years ahead of us started to form in my mind. He looked like Sue, only taller. There was a name. "Mark?"

"Good memory, Jessie. Yeah. Mark Molinero. My hubby bought a pick-up truck from him a few years ago. Still lives in Paloma."

Robbie balanced the joint between her lips the way they used to do it in the movies. She produced a small purse from a pile of magazines that formed a Berlin Wall between her chair and a twin embossed with an imprint of her husband's ass. Thumbing through a pack of dog-eared business cards, she found the one she was looking for and passed it to me.

"M and M Landscaping. He has a backhoe and a trailer. Digs the graves at Paloma Glen Cemetery. Kind of appropriate considering the conversation."

That was the extent of our mutual interest.

I thanked her for the business card. "Mark can be a jerk," she said. "I could see him abandoning Sue. The guy spends what little money he has on booze and bowling. I would hate to see her end up in Potter's Field. Hope the Class of 2002 has a Plan-B when he lets you down."

I had no dog in the fight. Diana would be the one to confront Mark Molinero. I tried to think of something kind to say. "Will I see you at the reunion?"

Roberta Steele dipped her head, looking up at me with a cultivated cynicism perfected over years of rejection.

"Let's not kid ourselves, Jessica. Neither one of us will be there. You left them behind when you put on a badge. They didn't have to work hard to forget Sue and me." She scooped the cat into her arms. "We were invisible."

I let the "invisible" line go and was halfway out the door when she shot me one last question. "What does the coroner say caused Sue's death?"

I didn't know.

"The girl was always as healthy as her horses. Natural causes doesn't fall into Susan's lexicon. Do a high school classmate a favor, Detective. Check it out."

Chapter Six

Paloma Glen Cemetery

JESSICA RAMIREZ

Diana made the call. Mark Molinero claimed Susan's remains from the County authorities. The mortuary bill was paid as was the tab for a small, tasteful headstone and a square of grass next to Susan's parents at Paloma Glen.

Her ex-roommate didn't make the trip for the brief graveside service. Roberta's last question stuck in my craw. And I wanted to make sure someone besides Mark and his wife showed up for Sue's send-off, so I did.

The padre I knew well from Our Lady of Guadalupe parish officiated. Since I was uninvited, I stood at a respectful distance, trying to place names and faces with a trio of grounds keepers waiting to fill the hole that Mark Molinero likely scooped with a single swish of his backhoe.

The plot overlooked a gentle slope of symmetric monuments carved with the names of long discarded human beings. I could imagine the subtle subtext of the salesman's burial pitch. The view of the Mississippi might draw an occasional inquisitive soul after future generations no longer cared about who you were or what you did.

In a world where cancel culture often erased the living, perhaps some granite with your name on it was the best slice of immortality the dead could hope for.

Father Pablo's remarks were brief; appropriate as could be for a someone nobody really knew. "In her own way, our sister, Susan Mary Molinero made her mark on the world. Even though we may not know her story, somewhere, someone's life was forever changed because she lived."

I wondered how many of my mothers Catholic friends added "Mary" or "Maria" to their daughters' birth certificates. In her spiritual mind, we were all born virgins worthy of the biblical handle. Hate, inadequacy and fear are learned from others. Job security for people like me.

Mark and wife declined to toss a trowel of dirt into the tiny hole where Susan's urn would forever rest. I wanted to slap him for that. Father Pablo signaled the shovel crew and the three mourners drifted toward the parking lot.

The groundskeepers and I converged on the tiny excavation. I held out a palm and took one of their implements into my hand, tossing a shovel full of dirt onto the nondescript urn.

"Godspeed, Susan. Wherever you are, I hope it's a better place."

I saw him when I gave the scene one last visual sweep. The cut of his suit and the spit-shined black shoes were out of place. A cashmere coat clashed with a Jerry Garcia tie. The clean-shaven face and close-cropped haircut screamed military.

He stood at the entrance to the mausoleum, about thirty yards beyond the interest of anyone present but me.

I had no reason to find out who he was. More clean-up in the wake of the DeSalvo affair awaited me back at Paloma Police Headquarters. I reckoned that even my partner, the nosey Alexandra Clark, would have let this guy drift back into anonymity.

But detectives are supposed to be alert to things that don't belong. He didn't. I stalked Spit Shine to his vehicle.

"A friend of Susan's?"

My query caught him in the nearly empty parking lot, next to a nondescript piece of rented American iron.

He turned to face me. The eyebrows telegraphed recognition.

"Jessica Ramirez. Michael Wright told me you might be here."

The accent was as American as Apple Pie. Even without mentioning my FBI boyfriend, I would have guessed that this manicured mass of masculinity was Federal.

He had my attention. "Why would the Bureau dispatch someone to Susan Molinero's send-off?"

Spit Shine shifted his linebacker's weight from one shoe to the other. "I could say that I was passing through and Agent Wright asked me to look you up."

"What's your name, sailor? And why are you giving my classmate Paloma's version of the Arlington treatment?"

Spit Shine extended a grin and a paw, revealing French cuffs, gold cufflinks and a Rolex GMT Master that was a little too tight for his wrist. "Rick Meredith." The smile seemed genuine, and the teeth were perfect. "Michael will be disappointed if I don't at least buy you a beverage and ask after Maria and your mother while I'm here. It's almost five p.m. Are we close enough to quitting time for a round of margaritas?"

He seemed to know everything about me. And I was beginning to get the uncomfortable sense that the demure Susan Molinero was not the invisible person we had written off for the last two decades.

My world had changed since our return from Europe. Michael got a promotion and was quickly sucked into another assignment. I could deflect his proposal to act like married people a while longer. Instead of being hometown heroes for fifteen minutes of international fame, Ali and I seemed to be more alienated than ever from our fellow Blues. Only the slowly growing cadre of minorities and women who fought their way through the gauntlet smiled at us. The old guard averted eyes and conversation stopped when we entered a room.

What was most discomforting was the civility of both the chief and my supervisor, Captain Batavia. They were the lead dogs in the pack of old-guard jackals and their behavior was one-hundred and eighty degrees in opposition to their minions. Ulterior motives almost always hide behind smiles.

Mom and Maria came back from Mexico smiling and sunburned. Even my grandmother was pleased with the new house she shared with them, and she always found fault with everything.

The time bomb I felt ticking came into stark relief in the reflection of Spit Shine's Cole Hahns oxfords. As I gave him directions to *The Vine and Barrel*, I could feel the minute hand advancing toward midnight. I texted my partner.

Jessica

Hey, Ali. Meet me at our usual watering hole but keep some distance. I may need a witness.

Alexandra

Give me about twenty. Running some prints on a dead body somebody found in the river. Male model material but no shoes and no timepiece. The things people steal!

Despite, or perhaps because of the danger that lurked in every corner of my life, the addictive rush of adrenaline was irresistible. Every fiber of my being screamed I was headed for trouble again. I couldn't wait to find it.

Chapter Seven

CONNECT TO SIGNAL SECURE MESSENGER

Jess
Do you know Rick Meredith?

Michael
Yes. He found you?

Jess
One of your Band of Brothers?

Michael
Yes.

Jess
What are you not telling me about Susan Molinero?

Michael
(Pregnant Pause)

Terry Shepherd

Rick knows more.

Jess
You're being evasive, Michael. Come clean.

Michael
Not here and not now.

Jess
Not a good sign. I am inclined not to be nice to your friend.

Michael
He's a good man. He'll fall in love with you just like I did.

Jess
Can the sugar, Michael. Why does he want to talk to me?

Michael
Trust me, Jessica. Do as Rick says.

Jess
A lot of help you are. Can you tell me ANYTHING about what
you're doing without violating national security?

Michael
Only that I want to continue the conversation we started on the
plane.

Jess
And move in together? If I were listening to my inner voice, I would
be breaking up with you, Michael Wright.

Michael
Just don't pawn the ring until we can play house for a while.

Jess

I'll consider it, Mr. Wonderful. Whatever the H you are doing, be careful, ya big lug.

Michael

I love you to the moon and back, Jessica Ramirez.

Jess

Behave, you horny macho man. And send Ali and me a headshot of this friend of yours. You know my thing about talking to strangers.

Michael Wright

Sending now... Ex-Marine. Shiniest shoes you've ever seen. Rolex watch. Return the favor and have Alexandra send me a pic of you bench-pressing twice your weight. Seeing you in workout clothes lights my candle.

DISCONNECT

Chapter Eight

The Vine and Barrel

JESSICA RAMIREZ

The tree trimmers took over the cop car parking spot the friendly manager of *The Vine and Barrel* reserved for us. Two public works guys fed thick limbs of the dendrological victim of a recent Illinois windstorm into the whine of a wood chipper. They waved.

"Wanna play with our toy, Jess?" one asked over the scream of the pulverizer. "It's a great stress reliever."

"Keep it down, will ya?" I said, pointing to the bar entrance. "People are praying in there."

The hard hat pressed his palms together and looked skyward as his partner slammed a thick slab of tree trunk into the chippers steel jaws.

* * *

A pitcher of margaritas and an order of nachos were waiting for me when I found Spit Shine.

"How do you rate?" I said when the door to the bar closed behind me, dimming the roar outside. "It's Friday happy-hour, SRO, and you have a table and snacks waiting for you."

"Got a flight to catch, so I called ahead."

The man calling himself Richard Meredith motioned to the other side of the booth and pushed a glass of my all time favorite cocktail in my direction with the fat end of a fork. I held up a hand.

"Thanks for the offer, but it's soda for me. Paperwork."

Never accept a drink you haven't seen poured by the bartender. I've had experience with that.

The man with the Spit Shine shoes ignored my rejection. "How does your family like their new place? I hear they build nice homes in Paloma Acres."

I tried to remember if I had ever mentioned the name of the new subdivision to my FBI boyfriend. "We were attached to the old place. So many memories. Sounds like you are on a schedule, so how about filling me in on why you are here?"

Spit Shine left the salt dip untouched and poured himself a drink, sipping the cocktail as if it were fine wine. What margarita lover does that? His upper lip twitched. Not used to the taste.

He rubbed the wrist where the too tight Rolex band cut into his skin. "Any indication the Molinero woman may have been ushered into the hereafter by someone other than Mother Nature?"

I shook my head. "Not that I know about. You FBI people have the instant connections to the Oregon authorities. You tell me."

He pushed his drink away. "Our working hypothesis is that she was watching TV. One or more criminals held her down while another pressed a pillow over her face. Death by suffocation. Local police said she looked like she fell asleep in her chair. Are you sure you won't join me for one round? These margaritas are delicious."

If they are so fricking delicious smart guy, why aren't you drinking yours?

I felt the vibration of an incoming text message. The inconsistencies in this man's story had my attention, so I didn't check the screen. I egged him on.

"Motive?"

"No idea. It happens all the time in apartments where drugs are bought and sold. Witnesses told the police she did both."

Wrong again, buster. Knowledge is power.

Spit Shine fingered the Rolex again. "How long does it take to get to the airport from here?"

"Less than ten minutes. What's your flight number? I can check the line at TSA for you?" The phone vibrated again. I figured it was something important.

It was.

The first text was Michael's promised photo. It looked nothing like the subject sitting across from me.

The second text was from Ali.

Alexandra

The DB prints match Richard Meredith, CIA. One bullet to the back of the head. A pro hit. Your date is not who he portends to be. ETA two minutes. Watch yourself.

I had already deduced the unmistakable print of a semi-auto pressing against the left breast pocket of Spit Shine's suit coat.

Right-handed. Shoulder holster.

"I wish I could be of more help, Mr. Meredith. If you are in a rush, I'm happy to cover the tab."

Spit Shine stood. He left his suit coat unbuttoned; right arm relaxed. He was one move and about two seconds away from his weapon. I followed suit, resting my hands on my hips. The normally painful press of my Glock against the ass-carry Kydex holster I carried when in plain clothes felt reassuring. I reckoned I had a half second on him if he made a move.

"Sorry we didn't have more time, Jessica. I would have loved to learn what Michael sees in you."

"I often wonder about that, too... whatever your real name is. Susan Molinero died in bed. And Michael says Richard Meredith isn't FBI. Was that your slug they found in the back of his head when my colleagues pulled Meredith's body from the Mississippi?"

The eyes tell tales. His were blank slates. "That shot on the motor bike. It was nice theater. But you missed by a mile."

That small detail wasn't in the papers. My cheek twitched. That's what they call a "tell" in Vegas. I hate when it does that.

"Who the hell are you?"

He moved. I moved. But he didn't go for the gun. The bastard anticipated my draw. He blocked it with his left elbow, peeling the weapon from my fist with his right hand, gaining control and pointing the barrel against my temple.

"Moscow's compliments," Spit Shine said. The voice was no longer American. The Cyrillic consonants brought back memories I was trying to forget.

I flexed. My fist knocked the Glock clear of my skull as he pulled the trigger. The lead found one of the row of pitchers that hung above the long mahogany bar, shattering it into a constellation of glass shards that took out the entire row like tumbling dominos.

Whoever this guy was, he was fully briefed and well trained. He read my backspin kick, grabbing a leg as it flew by his face. I had to jump to keep him from breaking my ankle. My right foot caught his cheek.

That had to hurt. But he three-sixtied into cat stance and fired a front kick at me as he went for his weapon.

The closest thing I could find to match it was a chair. I smashed it against the arm that held the gun. The familiar cough of an SR-2 Vektor sang out. Another bullet lodged in an oak beam that supported the roof of the place.

Spit Shine didn't lose his grip. But he lost a precious second that gave me the opportunity to use his body weight against him. I'm smaller than most men, but you don't need height or bulk with Aikido. Patrons at a long table next to us scattered as Spit Shine landed on his back in the center.

The familiar voice of *The Vine and Barrel* manager sang out my name. I looked his way in time to see him toss my Glock back to me.

I caught my service weapon in mid-flight, swinging it toward the long table where Spit Shine was shaking off a concussion and trying to decide which image his uncoordinated eyes sent to his brain was the right one to shoot.

His aim bracketed me in a hail of lead to the left, slowly swinging right until he was empty.

He wanted me dead. I wanted him alive.

Dodging the fire was easy. Anticipating his resilience was not.

Spit Shine rolled off the table, threw one of its original occupants in my path and ran for the door. I cleared the human obstacle in time to see Ali, in full uniform and sunglasses, standing next to the covered truck that was receiving the pulverized forestry remains.

"Freeze comrade," she yelled above the cacophony. "You're under arrest for the murder of Richard Meredith. Spread-eagle on the ground, please. Or should I say it in Russian?"

The two hard hats scattered. They knew our reputation and valued their good health.

Spit Shine nodded to Ali in respect and turned to me, dispensing a half smile. "Do svidaniya, Detective Ramirez. There will be others."

Then he dove headfirst into the jaws of the wood-chipper.

His weight knocked the machine free of the trailer ball that aimed its output into the truck. Inertia forced the feed pipe downward. My partner was instantly covered with mulch-sized particles of human blood and bone.

Ali shook a layer of goo off her hands, keyed her soaked radio and ordered Hazmat to the scene. She spit a colorful constellation of cuss words as she removed her sunglasses to regard me.

"I should have shot him when he came out the door."

"Hold that pose, Alexandra," I said, pulling up the camera app on my phone. "And smile. This one's for Instagram."

Chapter Nine

Paloma General Hospital

JESSICA RAMIREZ

"Your victim needed four units of blood," Junior Engler told us in the ICU hallway. He nodded to my partner. "If you had not given her first aid, she would be on a slab at the morgue. Not bad for a couple of rank amateurs."

Doctors can turn bedside manner on and off like a light switch.

"Alexandra handled things just like you would have, if you had been there, Junior," I said. "Any luck with your attending applications? These overnight shifts must be tough on your social life."

Everyone knew "Junior" Engler was with us for another year because he couldn't make the cut at any decent hospital with an opening for an attending physician.

"Just let the girl heal, Jessica. No cop questions until I say so."

A nurse materialized at Junior's side. "Dr. Engler, 406 lost his catheter. The balloon broke and I'm afraid his bed is quite a mess."

Ali jumped in. "Remember, Junior. The cath goes in the little hole in front, not the big one in back."

Junior was halfway down the hall. That didn't stop him from firing back. "Should be easy if you ever need the procedure, Officer Clark. You're the biggest asshole I know."

When he was out of sight, we both dissolved into laughter.

"Extra points, Ali. That was classic. Wanna take a look at the life you saved?"

* * *

Katrina Reid slept. Her face was obscured by a swath of bandages.

She was about my size. She had trim, almost masculine features, the body of a sprinter with hands that were a little too big for the rest of her well-proportioned frame.

"Who are you, Katrina Reid?" Ali whispered as we stood at the foot of her bed. "They say you were renting the house on Dennis Street and had just moved in. And why the black-out curtains? Light sensitive eyes like the guy from U2? Or are you doing some Goth kink business on the side?"

"What would a world-class nut job like Ted DeSalvo want with a tiny stick of dynamite like you?" I wondered.

Ali pulled a scan of the woman's rental application from her pocket, unfolding it under the dim LED fixture that cast a blueish glow over the proceedings.

"No work history or previous residence info. Not even a cell number. But paid a year's rent and double the security deposit in cash for a set of keys."

I blew out a stress breath. "What woman in that neighborhood owns a BMW and a MTT420R motorcycle."

"A very successful hooker just might, partner." Ali murmured. "So many questions. It feel like we're grabbing at straws, Jess."

Straws were my life. "I depend on straws, Ali. They always deliver the tastiest cocktails."

"Perhaps the most important question has nothing to do with you, Katrina," Ali said to our slumbering victim. "Ted DeSalvo never leaves a victim alive. So, why did he spare you?"

Chapter Ten

Police Headquarters - Paloma Illinois - The Next Morning

JESSICA RAMIREZ

We inhabit one of the patriarchy's last bastions, an apelike culture, barely evolved from our simian ancestors. Alpha males compete for dominance and females contend with binary brains that define us as either sex partners or enemies.

Alexandra and I had long ago put our stakes in the ground as adversaries. We were moving targets for an escalating hail of insults whenever we showed up at roll-call.

"Hey, Fargo. Is that Steve Buscemi I see dripping from your earlobe?"

Ali spread her arms to take in the crowd of blue testosterone in the squad room, beckoning for more with up-turned palms.

"Bring it on."

"Get any of that Russian in your big mouth, Gates? I hear that's the only way a guy has a shot at those gorgeous lips."

"Hey, JRam," another voice sang out, holding up a sheet of

paper. "Email from Classmates dot com. They want you to be their cover girl for the next issue of Dead Alumni Magazine?"

"I hear they are hiring at Public Works, girls. Ever thought of a career in landscaping with human mulch?"

Disgusting. I raised a middle finger, pointing at each tormentor. "I bet you guys stayed up all night thinking up your witticisms. And that's the best you can do?"

My sometime colleague, Detective Lou Harrison, weighed in. "Got a warrant for your arrest, girls. Improper operation of a crematorium without a license."

"Ice-creamatorium," a voice in the back added. "Ben and Jerry called. They want a name for the new flavor you two invented."

Another one. "I'll have a White Russian, Ramirez. Shaken not stirred."

"OK, guys. Enough one-liners. Open mic night is over."

Bruce Sokolove's growl silenced the troops. The day shift command sergeant could slice you in two with a withering glance. Nobody wanted to be on the receiving end.

"Ramirez, Clark, the new Medical Examiner wants to see you both."

A muffled voice erupted from the back of the room, "Yeah. He wants to check Clark's hair for a missing toe."

Sgt. Sok pointed a finger in the sound's direction. "I know that's you, Marquette. Shut up." and then to us, "Detective Ramirez, Officer Clark. You're excused."

* * *

"Well, that was interesting." Ali scrunched her lips into a half circle, usually a precursor to some witticism. "I expected a little more creativity."

My mind was already elsewhere. "That Russian guy knew about my joust with DeSalvo. He claims I missed. How would he know about that?"

Ali pressed a finger against her cheek in mock thought. "Tarot cards. He impressed me as the kind who gets his intel from tarot cards."

My partner could have cared less about a bad guy who was now a hamburger patty. I decided to let my question marinate. "Any intel on the new M.E.? The City sure took its time filling that job."

Ali raised an eyebrow. "Who besides us would work in a nondescript Illinois college town like Paloma if they didn't have to?"

It was a good question. "Someone either on the way up or the way down."

We knocked on the opaque glass with the words Adams County Coroner painted on it.

"Don't bother me while I'm working."

There was no mistaking the voice. I swung open the door to reveal the half smiling face of Doctor Joey Price, lately medical examiner for Coconino County, Arizona, our partner in crime when Ali and I were chasing Vega.

"Your uncle sends his regards, Detective Ramirez. He wants a copy of the picture you shot of Officer Clark covered head to toe in Russian Dressing."

I was delighted. "Joey! What in the name of Jesus, Mary and Joseph are you doing here?"

Ali fist bumped our friend. "Yeah. You left a brand-new facility and a hand-picked team for this Mississippi cesspool?"

"Ailing parents in Champaign," Joey said, his eyes averted as always. "This is close enough to get to them quickly if I need to, but far enough so the assisted living people won't call every time they spill a bed pan."

A fist bump wouldn't cut it for me. I circled the desk and wrapped my arms around Joey, planting a smack on his cheek. His discomfort with the proximity was palpable. "Seriously, cowboy. It's great to see you. How long have you been here?"

"Long enough to identify Agent Meredith and have a look at

the tomato soup Officer Clark brought me from that wood chipper. Do you two ever kill a bad guy with bullets like normal cops?"

This was Joey Price at his most loquacious. Living on the spectrum made social interaction problematic. But we both knew that behind the emotional disconnect, lay a brilliant brain and a good heart.

Ali must have sensed Joey's discomfort with my public display of affection. She let him get back to business. "Still too early to ID the comrade who tried to ice Jess?"

"He's like many of them. A stolen identity, no prints or DNA on file. A cipher."

"A lingering associate of the late Vladimir Prokofiev?"

"Can't speculate without data," Joey answered. "It's a likely conclusion." Joey turned his non-attention to me. "I would expect an in-person encounter with Agent Wright."

The edge of Joey's mouth twitched. It constituted a grin in the visual language of autism. "All we need is your uncle and Dr. Bob for a family reunion."

That covered it; most of the cast of my adventure in the Grand Canyon. I sensed Joey's true message and wished we were all together again, too.

"Did our ground beef kill Agent Meredith?"

"Ballistics confirms it was his gun."

That was Joey. Careful to stay with the facts without drifting into the theoretical.

Ali pressed. "Sergeant Sokolove said you want to see us."

"I had a feeling you might be the butt of inappropriate remarks this morning. I hope you were dismissed before having to endure the worst of them."

I knew Dr. Price better. "Something's up, Joey. You don't bring two cops out of roll call to protect us from a few insults."

Joey handed me a manilla folder. "Susan Molinero's personal effects from Portland. Not much. Driver's license, passport, social security and a couple of credit cards. The sum total of her estate I'm afraid."

I popped the folder into my gym bag, the closest thing to a briefcase I carried.

"You could have put that one in my mailbox, Joey. What don't you want to tell us?"

Joey Price fingered a printout on his desk. "I got the autopsy report from my counterpart in Hannibal. Your psycho friend in the BMW was killed by a single bullet to the brain. He was dead before his car hit the water."

Ali clapped her hands. "That was one shot in a million, Jess. And on a fricking motorcycle no less. I bet there's not a cop on the planet who could have hit a bullseye on an eight-inch target from a crotch rocket at over two-hundred miles-per-hour rate of closure."

Joey nodded. "You're right, Officer Clark. There isn't a cop on the planet who could do that. The entry wound was in the back of DeSalvo's head. And ballistics says the shell casing the state cops found on the highway wasn't from Detective Ramirez's weapon."

"Spit Shine," I muttered. "But why DeSalvo and not me?"

* * *

Ali's eyes glazed as we left the new medical examiner to his work. "Joey Price in Paloma. I wonder how long that will last."

My mind was elsewhere. "Not my weapon? The way DeSalvo faded into that guard rail told me I hit my damn target."

Ali gave me one of the smirks that always pissed me off. "Are you certain about that, partner? You had so many endorphins coursing through that body of yours, I'm surprised you could hold a gun, let alone shoot one."

Spit Shine. There was a bridge. I guessed he was on it with a deer rifle. But I wasn't ready to concede the point. "What was old Ted doing at the Reid woman's house anyway? And what was up with the custom-made black-out curtains in a residential neighborhood? This isn't London in 1943."

"It's still our case, partner," Ali said. "I say we check up on our victim to see how she's faring after her near-death experience."

"JRam! Gates!"

The thundering bloat of Captain Ben Batavia's baritone cut through the hum of cops heading to their cars after roll-call.

He stood outside Chief O'Brien's office, like the brown-nosing hang dog he was, arms folded, back ramrod straight in an attempt to look taller. I'm sure it unnerved our supervisor to have to look a couple of five-foot-eight women straight in the eye.

"Missouri is taking DeSalvo," he said it with his usual abruptness. "The dirt bag has more warrants there and an FBI agent is on the way to consult with their team. You're off the case."

Consult with their team? The Hannibal cops were just as short staffed. And it was unlike old Ben to let someone else get the glory. To hear him tell it, it was Ben Batavia who encouraged us to go after our bad guy in London.

I couldn't let it go. "We were the officers who initiated the bust, sir."

"And Jess contributed to neutralizing the threat," Ali added.

The captain must have been waiting for that one. "She nearly got people killed in that chain-reaction accident on the interstate, Gates." He consulted his notes. "Discharging a service weapon in a residential area? And the new M.E. has a report that shows the entry wound on an angle not consistent with JRam's position at the time of the shooting."

A nervous tick danced on Batavia's cheek. The boss had not meant to share that last bit of intel. He backtracked. "The most conclusive evidence is the ballistics report. The slug was not a 9 mil. It was a high-powered rifle, likely a Missouri State Police sniper on the bridge."

The entirety of the chase took less than ten minutes, barely enough time to position cop cars on the Missouri side of the river, let alone deploy a sniper. And Joey's report said the bullet came from behind DeSalvo. This stunk. I was about to say so when Batavia added a postscript.

"Turns out the brother of the Oregon dead girl you helped find has a warrant. You know him by sight so he's all yours. No more contact with anybody involved in the DeSalvo matter. Grab the paperwork and go get me Mark Edward Molinero."

Our boss slid behind the safety of the chief's office door. Conversation over.

"Go get me Mark Edward Molinero. No more contact." Ali imitated Batavia to perfection. "Those orders came from far above Ben's pay grade. This feels like politics."

A wave of fatigue enveloped me. The high from our adventures during the previous forty-eight hours was dissipating. What remained was the pulsing ache of the PTSD that filled my emotional wheelbarrow to the brim.

I felt the vibration in my pocket. We had no imminent work to do, so I pulled out the cell and read the screen.

Michael
Guess who's coming to dinner? I'm free of my assignment and will be in Paloma in time for some delicious Mexican sustenance. Know anyone who might be able to oblige my appetite?

Chapter Eleven

The Ramirez Household – That same evening

JESSICA RAMIREZ

The left side of Michael's face looked like someone had hit him with a baseball bat. I was both annoyed and worried. I wished we were alone and anywhere but here.

"Would Agent Wright care to sit at the head of the table?"

I didn't like the formality with which Mama invited Michael to sit in my father's chair in the family dining room. As long as I lived, Papa's place at the table would aways be empty out of respect for the family patriarch and in the hope that his spirit might come back to visit us someday.

Tonight, I was outnumbered.

Maria, flirtatious as always, wore her most revealing dress. The black lace pattern of a bra purposely one size too small pressed her cleavage above the neckline. Her dip to pull back the chair was much deeper than necessary, leaving little to the imagination.

Mama, and the rest of us stood out of respect for the male in the household. She bent a palm in Maria's direction.

My grandmother bowed almost imperceptibly, raising her sangria glass in a toast motion before enjoying a significant swallow.

Alexandra stood next to Mamacita, arms folded, her cocktail balanced on an elbow. A wicked smile aimed in my direction as if to say, *"You asked for this."*

Michael stared at me for guidance. I shrugged in resignation and nodded toward the chair.

"What an honor to meet you all at last," Michael oozed. "The *Carne* aroma is captivating, Señora Ramirez." He bowed in Mamacita's direction. "And to have the pleasure of knowing the wife of Luis Ramirez-Hernandez is a moment I will treasure forever."

His perfect rendering of my grandfather's proper surname scored points. I think my grandmother actually blushed.

"And Maria," My sister was running her hands up and down his right bicep as if it were a hunk of freshly barbecued spareribs. "Jessica told me of your beauty, but mere prose is incapable of appropriate expression. *Muy Hermosa, querida.*"

Jesus! What a suck-up! I bet he practiced those three Spanish words for a week so he wouldn't screw them up.

They had the intended effect. Maria turned red as a radish, melting her body against him. "I like this guy, Jessi. He's the best *guapo* you've ever brought home."

"The only *guapo* Jessie has ever brought home," Mama added. Noticing my rising temperature, she decided to move the proceedings along. "*Por favor, sientese.* Please, sit."

He did and we did.

Mama passed each dish his way first, happy to have a man in the house again. "So tell us, Michael," she said. "What does an FBI agent do?"

I couldn't let that one pass. "He keeps secrets, even when they might be important for someone he cares about to know."

"That's so..." Maria reached for the right word. "Patriotic. How many of the Ten Most Wanted have you personally captured, Agent Wright?"

Michael held up a hand. "Please, Maria. It's Michael. And I don't often get involved in those cases. I'm a liaison between the Bureau and the Central Intelligence Agency. There are times when what we do at the FBI crosses boundaries. I'm the guy who makes sure both sides of the fence know what's going on."

I scooped a blob of carne asada onto my plate and gulped a dose of sangria. "That's the first time in the three years we have known one another that Michael has actually explained his work." And then, with ineffectively veiled sarcasm I added, "We need to invite him to supper more often."

Ali could see where this was heading. But instead of bailing me out, she dug me in deeper.

"So, Jess. Why aren't you wearing your ring?"

Every eye at the table laser beamed to the third finger on my left hand.

"Ring?" Maria exclaimed. "Michael gave you a ring?"

Ali threw more gasoline on the fire. "An engagement ring, Maria. The biggest rock I've ever seen."

"¡Mijha!" My mother's voice squeaked like a Kewpie Doll. "You never tell us anything!"

Mamacita leaned toward me, pulling the reading glasses that hung from a chain over her abundant chest to her eyes. "Jessica Mary Ramirez-Hernandez. Do you have an announcement?"

There was that "Mary" name again. I did not feel like a virgin.

It wasn't a question. It was a command. When Mamacita commanded, family law required obedience.

It was my turn to flush. I reached into the pocket of the cargo pants where I hid the ring whenever I was at home or at work, as if wearing it in front of friends and family might curse me. I held it up for inspection between my thumb and index knuckle, shooting Michael the angriest expression I could conjure.

"Michael thinks we should test drive marriage to see if we can get along."

If Papa was here, that would have triggered a tirade about family values and how co-habitation before marriage was the road to hell.

But Papa wasn't here anymore. Decades of repressed estrogen in the room exploded like Fourth of July fireworks.

"It's breathtaking," Mama said.

"Totally appropriate for my *nietaa*," Mamacita added approvingly.

Maria sighed. "I would do anything for one just like it. Do you have any brothers?"

I raised an eyebrow in Michael's direction. "And she totally would do anything, Michael. Watch yourself."

He ignored me. "No brother, I'm afraid, Maria. Just one sister. I was raised surrounded by strong women." The bastard winked at me. "And always dreamed of marrying one."

Alexandra tossed another dirt clod into the punchbowl. I wanted to punch her in the mouth. "He's asked for her hand twice and she's put him off both times."

The discontent was unanimous, expressed in a disapproving "Ohhhh!" that must have lasted twenty seconds.

"Put the ring on, Jessie," my sister said. "Show us what it looks like on that bony finger."

I]slid the jewelry into position. "It's not bony. And the only reason I don't wear it is because I'm left handed and it impedes my ability to hold a handgun."

Alexandra coughed.

I glared at her. "Keep messing with me, Ali, and I'll tell them you preferences."

"They already know that Jess. Everybody does. Stop evading the elephant in the room. Why haven't you given Michael an answer?"

This was my supposed best friend. The group leaned in, not wanting to miss a single syllable.

"Family comes first, Alexandra. It's a Latin custom. With Papa gone, I'm the oldest. There are no males in the household, so the family is now my responsibility."

Maria jumped to Michael's defense.

"That's crap, Jessie. We're just fine and you need to live your own life. If some boy gave me a rock that size, I would follow him anywhere and do whatever he asked."

Visions of her past exploits stirred an uncomfortably erotic picture in my brain. I lost my appetite.

"You already follow any man anywhere," I said. "In Paloma the bumper stickers say, 'honk if you haven't slept with Maria Ramirez.'"

My grandmother almost choked on her sangria.

Mama feigned disgust. "That's an exaggeration, Michael. Don't believe a word Jessie says."

I needed to blow off some steam and my sister was the easiest target. "It's common knowledge that Maria has kissed about every toad in the county. Not one has turned into a prince."

Maria shot a pleading look at Michael and daggers at me. "So, what's the truth, Jessie? Why didn't you accept Michael's marriage proposal?"

I looked to Alexandra for help. She slowly shook her head, way too happy for putting this weight fully on my shoulders.

I looked to Michael. He rested his chin on a pair of threaded fingers, looking sexy as hell.

I was on my own for this one. I gave it one more shot.

"Like I said, y'all. With Papa gone, I feel a responsibility to put family first. Marrying Michael would mean leaving Paloma and moving to Washington D.C. or Michael's relocation from the top of the pyramid to a small midwestern college town. My job, my responsibility and my friends are here. His are elsewhere. It's not fair to ask either of us to abandon our careers for love's sake."

My mother put her utensils in their proper places on the edge of the china donated to the family by our Catholic Parish friends, along with most everything else in the house. She placed her hands on her lap and faced me down with the stare I knew well. A lecture was coming and I had better pay attention.

"Jessica. We have all struggled to understand God's will since your father's death." She shot an appreciative look in Michael's direction. "Despite Michael's gringo background, I'm sure Papa would approve of this match." She paused, a minor dark cloud morphing her features. "You are Catholic, aren't your Michael?"

Michael gave a her a vigorous nod. "Born and raised, *Señora*."

If he didn't stop with the fricking Spanish, I was going to strangle him.

"We have a home," my mother continued. "We have our community. We have each built our own fulfilling lives."

I thought Maria might choke on her food after that last sentence. She was still very much a work in progress.

"It's time for you to do the same, *mijha*. Stop worrying about us. We will all be fine. God and your father want you to chase your own dreams. Write your own story. Everyone knows you are an extraordinary woman. Paloma is a small pond, and you are a big fish. Find an ocean where you can swim free. This is your Karma."

The Karma reference was new. But Mama was aware of how the aquatic metaphor would touch me. Points scored. She smiled at the man who was obsessed with being my fiancé. "Spend your life with a soulmate who shares your hopes and dreams."

"Yeah, Jessie," Maria chimed in. "Marry this hunk of perfection, or I will."

I turned to my grandmother, hoping she could quell this madness. She put down her drink and studied the thin gold band she still wore in memory of 55 years of marriage.

"No match is perfect, *querida*. But there is wisdom among the imperfections. *La cosa mas importante* is, do you love one another? If this is true, denying it is to deny God's will."

The pressure in my chest was suddenly strangling me. The claustrophobia of our conversation was more than I could bare.

A tiny realization began to come to me. A candle flame, quickly growing into a forest fire.

"OK. Since we are all sharing our real points of view, here's mine. I'm proud of my Mexican heritage. And I respect the choices my ancestors have made. But the world is different now. Everyone has been telling me what I should and should not do since I first punched Tony Rojas in the mouth in elementary school. Papa forbade me to swim with the best of the best, when I knew I could." I looked at Michael. "For ten years, men have been trying to convince me that a woman doesn't deserve to be a police officer. They keep secrets and either try to protect me or patronize me." I locked eyes with my mother. "Yes, Mama. I feel love. But I want a relationship on terms that benefit us both. I'm not sure that's possible when we each feel our careers are in different states." I reached across the table and took my grandmother's hand. "I want to be in love, Mamacita. But I won't be rushed. If this thing Michael and I have is going to last, figuring it out is going to take time." Finally, I spoke to Ali. "If you all truly care about me, stop criticizing me. I treasure your advice and wisdom. But this is my life and I have to live it my way."

I stood, bowed to each person in turn and said, "Excuse me, please. I need some space." A moment later I was out the door, gasping the freshness of the night air.

* * *

The long porch swing and the canopy of trees on Isbell Street were gone. Saplings from some contractor's nursery dotted our postage stamp front yard. Instead of a front porch, a pair of Paloma University lawn chairs dug permanent ruts in the grass.

Ali plopped into the empty one.

"Sorry about the cheap shots, partner. I guess I was a little over the top in there."

"A mile over the top, Alexandra. Are you trying to get me to dump Michael at the dinner table?"

Ali turned her chair so she could fire one of her serious stares at me. "Look, partner. Comrade Woodchipper wasn't some local gang banger trying to score points with his small-time boss. The Captain may be dead, but someone in his chain of command seems to think you're still a threat. Wouldn't it be safer for everyone if you were sleeping with an FBI agent in a city where they deal with these things every day?"

"How can I be a threat? You know more about what The Captain was up to then I ever will. Everyone around me is keeping secrets, especially that hunk of manhood who likes to hand out GPS jewelry to keep track of his girlfriends. Love has to be built on mutual trust. Besides you, who in the hell is truly in my court when the heat is on?" I pointed to the dining room window. "Certainly not mister 'seduce-my-mother.'"

Ali knew my moods. And she knew when to let things go until tomorrow. She pinched the bridge of her nose, pressing back a migraine. "Tell you what. Let's talk about this when we go bust Susan Molinero's brother. See what Michael has to say and keep him waiting for a couple of days. Even if you decide to give him back the ring, he'll ply you with some expensive restaurant meals and you can dance the nasty to your heart's content. What's wrong with that?"

Romance was the furthest thing from my mind. "I wish Silent Susan was still alive and right here with us. I'd love to send an introvert who only talks about horses and vacations out with Mr. Wonderful."

Ali stood. "No, you wouldn't. You and Michael might be a better fit than either of you realize, Jess. You have to find a way to see if you can live together day-by-day. This nasty habit of vectoring to the worst outcomes has been ingrained from a decade of crap from the gorillas at work. Meet Michael on neutral ground where you have time to really get to know one another. If it's supposed to work, that's the only way to find out."

I turned the spotlight on her. "And what about you and Lee? You left the love of your life in England six months ago and I haven't heard you say a word about her since you got back from that week-long boink-fest after our little adventure in Moscow."

Ali's eyebrows danced up and down like a middle school girl with a boy-band crush. "We FaceTime every night, smart-ass. I have standing job offers with Gerhardt at MI6, network security at British Telecom and the encryption division at Apple. I'm only hanging around here to watch your back, sister. So, get married and get out of my life."

My partner flicked my nose with her middle finger, spinning it upward into the universal salute that did not mean I was "Number 1." The feigned scowl melted into her Cheshire Cat grin.

"I love you, Alexandra Clark. If I weren't such a flaming hetero, I would consider becoming a lesbian and marry you myself."

Ali was halfway to her vehicle when she had the last word.

"Don't knock it till you've tried it."

Chapter Twelve

State Road 57 South of Paloma

JESSICA RAMIREZ

There were no ostentatious hotels for Michael Wright to seduce me to and no high-end rental cars in Paloma. I was already second guessing my agreement to show him my apartment. Gymnastics would be a given when we got there, and I wasn't in the mood.

"Well, at least you're still wearing the ring. I guess that means there is still hope for me."

"What happened to your face, Michael?"

"Temporary duty in Colombia. There is one less drug lord poisoning our kids. He found my intrusion irritating."

I wondered if this was the truth, or just another evasion.

"You should have let me follow you in my personal vehicle. I have to serve a warrant first thing."

"A calculated move to get you into bed, Detective. I want to know what it's like to make love to you without fighting."

"Why are you here, Michael? Certainly not to lay down that

suck-up performance at Mama's place tonight. Who was the real Richard Meredith? And why did the Russian whose guts are in the Zip-lock bag in Joey Price's freezer want to kill me?"

Michael's Waze app whispered a reminder to turn left into my apartment complex in one mile.

"Seems you are the one common connection between the Vega affair and our little Moscow vacation last year. You helped engineer two high profile fails for The Captain's bosses and they consider you dangerous."

I couldn't believe that. "Not just me, Michael. Alexandra was part of it. And so were you."

"The three rich boys behind The Captain would love to recruit Ali to their side, Jess. And I'm just another cog in the machinery who follows orders. You are motivated by a moral code. That's not in any international playbook. They don't understand morality and think you have some master plan to eliminate them."

"That's ridiculous. What's the saying, 'Blowing out someone's candle ultimately extinguishes your own?' I'm more than happy to live out my days chasing bad guys in a midwestern college town. They have nothing to fear."

Waze sang out the quarter-mile alert and Michael slowed the car to let a gasoline tanker pass.

"Not from their point of view. To quote Walter Scott, 'Vengeance to God alone belongs; But when I think of all my wrongs My blood is liquid flame!' That perfectly describes the love of my life."

I blew humidity on the passenger window and drew a K in the cloud with my finger. "Karma describes your love life, Michael. What goes around, comes around."

The tanker was two-thirds past us when the driver cut the wheel to the right. Michael's reflexes were fast. But he was driving a civilian vehicle without agility. The back wheels of the tanker caught the front bumper, forcing us off the shoulder of State Road 57 and into a cornfield. The explosive trailer popped free, teetered in our direction, threatening to crush the car and the two of us with it. The trucker floored his vehicle, killed the running lights, and disappeared into the night before we could get a plate number.

Michael's command voice shouted, "Bail!"

We did.

His rental continued to career into the knee-high field of corn. The tanker's top-heavy center of gravity did its work. Both the car and the trailer burst into an inferno of fire and light.

"In among the stalks," Michael yelled. "He may be coming back."

We crawled about twenty yards deep into the grain futures, lying side by side, eyes on the deserted highway.

I stole a glance at Michael's now dusty form. "Why do I always think I'm going to die if I keep hanging out with you, Agent Wright."

His eyes were locked on the road. We missed being dead by ten seconds, but he still had that damn million-dollar smile for me. "I promise you, Detective Ramirez. Life with me will never be boring."

While I bailed with only slight inconvenience, Michael had taken the brunt of the asphalt against the left side of his face. His breathing told me he cracked a few ribs.

"You look like a meat crayon. Are you hurt?"

He didn't answer, pointing south. In the reflection of the flames, we could see the truck. It crawled past the blaze; driver's side window rolled down. The face was familiar. In the adrenaline high, I couldn't place it.

"Our perpetrator," Michael muttered. The driver nodded and pulled away.

I went for my phone to dial 911. A strong hand closed over mine.

"No, Jess. We're close enough to walk it. It will be safer at your apartment."

Another man telling me what not to do. I didn't hide my indignance. "Someone just tried to kill us, Michael. You're injured and you want to *walk* away from a crime scene?"

"Trust me, Jessica. There are things I must tell you. Let's get away from this place before a civilian shows up and tries to help."

* * *

Paloma Estates Apartments

Michael must have had medical training in the service. He grabbed some ice from my fridge. After disappearing into my bathroom for about five minutes, he had most of the ugly stuff cleaned up. The bruises and contusions remained.

"Two percent milk and Cocoa Puffs?"

My "fiancé" described the complete contents of pantry.

"I eat most meals on duty and get take-out the rest of the time. The only other person who inhabits this place is my housekeeper. Why have stuff around that's going to go bad?"

"You're almost thirty-five, young lady, and you have zero domestic skills?"

"And damn proud of that fact, cowboy. Does that disqualify me as wife material?"

It probably was a strike against me, but Michael let it go. "No alcohol?"

I pointed to a boxy end table at the edge of my couch. "In there. Margarita mix, tequila, vodka for visitors and some Malbec that's probably gone bad. Help yourself."

With a bartender's dexterity, Michael found the lone pair of glasses above the sink, peeled some cubes out of an old-school ice tray in my freezer and poured us both substantial drinks, a margarita for me and straight Ukrainian vodka for him.

He pointed to my well-worn couch. "Graduation present?"

I plopped into the one spot that still felt comfortable. "High School graduation. Sit your ass down and tell me why we broke the law tonight."

He sat. Michael's tentative landing said his caboose was one of the body parts still hurting.

"The group who hired your Captain is known in intelligence circles as The Triumvirate. They are three oligarchs. One from India, one from China and one from Russia. Governments may feel like they control the course of history, but these three are the true power behind the power. Nothing significant happens in the stock market or on the battlefield without their involvement."

Michael took a breath and another dose of his vodka.

"It turns out that you foiled two of their biggest capers at great cost to their financial interests. And that, as we say in the biz, a huge blow to their reputation and credibility."

I wasn't following. "Why do ultra-rich guys who kill people care about reputations?"

"There are always contenders to replace those who hold the reins. And since your dance with Prokofiev in the Moscow subway, competitors have emerged who are angling to unseat our trio. The world survives on a razor's edge and anything that might tip the balance of power threatens to knock down the entire house of cards."

"You're mixing metaphors, Michael."

"And you're not paying attention, Jessica. There are people out there who believe that you secretly work for a competing interest and the events in New York, London and Moscow were carefully planned to discredit The Triumvirate's leadership. The easiest way for them to quell this unfounded belief and reassert their dominance is to snuff out the troublemaker."

I was beginning to get it. "To kill me."

"As long as you live, lives of those close to you are in danger. You saw how the Captain tried to kill Alexandra and Layanna. Your mother, sister, Ali, even your grandmother are in their crosshairs."

"And you, Michael?"

He rubbed a bruise on his cheek. "That drama played out a few minutes ago on Route 57."

I looked at the ice chips swimming in my cocktail glass. I felt like one of them; insignificant, existing for a tiny moment in time before being swallowed up by a maelstrom more powerful than I could imagine. "Who is doing the dirty work? It sounds like these guys farm this stuff out."

"We stumbled across some intel last week. There is a strong belief in Washington that The Triumvirate gave a two-million dollar contract to the X organization to liquidate you."

"Two-million?"

"Right up there with the rate card for drug lords and dictators. Kind of a compliment, in a perverse sort of way."

"And you came to town to tell me to watch my back until you catch this X person?"

"It's a long story. Some think X is dead. That body you helped bury? An informant told us that it used to belong to X."

"Silent Susan Molinero?"

"Yup. Every hit with X's fingerprints on it remains unsolved. And some of those hits are stories you've studied in school. Your friend Silent Susan is the best there is. And X's sole assignment at the time of her alleged death was to come for you."

I was still finding it hard to believe. "Woodchipper worked for her?"

"Director Taylor thinks so."

"So, what happens now? Does my family go back to Mexico with Secret Service protection?"

It was Michael's turn to stare at his glass. Whatever it was that was coming next wasn't going to be good.

"You didn't understand what I just said, Jessica. If you live, those around you will die. It will happen one by one. It will seem like a series of unfortunate accidents. But eventually your family, your close friends, anyone remotely associated with you will be dead."

The magnitude of his words and the calm way he delivered them shook me. And very few things in my life have ever shaken me. My father's murder and losing my Olympic dream were on that short list.

I wanted to find a pool where I could swim laps until I could wrap my head around it all. The night of romantic cardio I anticipated fending off had quickly morphed into a crippling terror.

I was Jessica Ramirez. I always found a way out of every corner. But this one had no exit.

The margarita lost its appeal. I set the glass on the end table and slumped forward. For the first time in my life, I felt defeated.

My voice sounded small. Helpless. I hated that sound. "What can I do, Michael?"

"If X is alive, she is close by. Her organization has many tentacles, and several are here in Paloma now. The man who killed Meredith was one of them. The tanker driver is another. The Triumvirate has commanded X to oversee the executions personally. So when things happen, she is not far away."

"You mean she could be outside of my apartment building at this moment?"

"It's possible. X will have to prove to The Triumvirate that you are truly dead. That means Silent Susan, if she is still alive, will come above the radar after you are killed to extract a pound of flesh."

"Quit talking in metaphors, Michael. What does Washington want me to do?"

Michael's eyes lost all emotion. I could imagine that this was the mode he kicked in before pulling a trigger.

"Washington wants to maintain the world balance of power. They say you are expendable."

Chapter Thirteen

Paloma Estates Apartments

JESSICA RAMIREZ

I ran. For the first time in my life, I ran away from the danger. I was out the door and into the back stairwell before Michael could launch his sore rear end from his spot on the couch.

I had no idea where I would go, but if this X was nearby, the bitch was probably out front. Perhaps even the dark figure in the gas company van that I noticed as Michael and I trudged up the driveway. Out of place sets off alarms. So many were ringing in my head after our encounter with the fuel tanker that one more didn't even register.

I was almost one hundred yards deep into the trees behind the complex when I felt a football player's grasp around my waist, tackling me to the damp forest floor.

"Listen to me, Jess. I'm not going to let you die. For Christ's sake, woman, I'm going against direct orders to save your life."

"I hate it when men call me 'Woman.'"

"Please shut up and listen."

As the words left his mouth, we saw the flash and felt the heat. A half second later the concussion bounced us into the air as if the earth were a trampoline. But not before we beheld the entirety of the Paloma Estates Apartments disintegrate into a volcanic plume.

The inferno expanded with the blast radius, consuming the first twenty yards of our forest protection. The night sky was illuminated by an ugly midday sun as the mushroom continued to boil upward. I could feel first degree burns bubbling up on every exposed inch of my skin. Michael contorted into a fetal position. I recognized the PTSD symptoms, perhaps from events in Afghanistan that populated a thousand nightmares, triggered as one at the front of his consciousness.

Then the rain began. But it wasn't rain. We were pelted by tiny droplets. Some felt like stones. Others felt like overheated gelatin. I realized in horror that these were the largest concrete, metal and human remains of what once was a twenty-unit apartment building and all that was human inside.

Michael's voice rose above the rainstorm. "This is what will happen to innocent people unless you do exactly as I say."

* * *

Paloma Regional Airport

I learned that night that Michael Wright knew how to hot-wire a car. I didn't ask where he picked up that skill. We were both glad to put distance between us and the tsunami of death intended to include me in its fiery wake.

We slipped unnoticed into the driveway of my mother's home so I could grab my gym bag from the trunk of my personal vehicle and change out of blackened clothing, into sweatpants and a hoodie.

Now we stood at the Paloma Regional Airport Executive

Terminal. A Cessna Citation X's ramjets howled behind us. It had no markings except for the tail number.

"You're riding in the fastest corporate jet in production, Jess. This thing can exceed Mach 1."

I could have cared less.

"The crew are carrying gear to the Army Golden Knights in Portland, Oregon. I was their original hitchhiker, headed that way to pick up the X investigation where Meredith left off. They have strict orders not to leave the flight deck for any reason and have been told they are transporting a top-secret undercover federal agent. They won't know it's you aboard. You won't see or hear from them, and they are to stay inside the aircraft until you exit at the end of the runway, before they taxi to the executive terminal. You'll be on your own from then on, but far away from X. We'll have Joey Price figure out how to identify a pound of flesh from that apartment mess and leave it where X can steal it. You'll get a heroine's send off. And we'll watch Joey and the funeral like hawks for anybody who is out of place."

I was still in shock, trying to process the magnitude of what Michael and I had witnessed.

"How will I exist without credentials or cash?" was the best question I could come up with. Michael had relieved me of my badge and ID.

He handed over what looked like a small Amazon shipping container. "There are ten thousand dollars in unmarked twentys and tens in this box, some false identification, and a Signal account credential you can use to communicate with me. If you can find an internet café, follow the schedule that's on the accompanying notes. It's random so most folks won't find a pattern. If I have news. I will ping you."

A microscopic beam of laser light escaped from the cop compartment in my head where I kept my emotions locked tight. My voice shook. "My family."

"It will be rough, Jess. But I'll watch over them."

"Will anybody know the truth?"

"Just Joey. He will need to identify you. I'll brief him."

"And what about you?"

Michael tried to find his smile and winked. It was not a convincing performance. "I'm headed back to the apartment. They have to find at least one survivor to confirm that you are a dead woman. That should placate Washington, too."

"You'll lie?"

"To save you, I would do more than that, Jess."

He looked at his watch and then at the aircraft. "First responders are probably already there. I had better go."

There was an awkward moment where neither of us knew what to say or do. The thought of our parting must have hit us both at the same instant. We flew into an embrace. I could sense Michael choking back sobs.

When we broke the clinch, his eyes were wet. Mine probably were, too.

My fiancé pointed to the aircraft's doorway. "I love you, Jessica."

I glanced at the dim interior of the jet. When I turned back, Michael Wright was gone.

Chapter Fourteen

Airborne

JESSICA RAMIREZ

The twin-engine Citation climbed into the Illinois summer night. Beside the two strangers on the flight deck, my only companions were a dozen parachutes, carefully packed between the seats at the back of the aircraft.

A quick inventory of my bag revealed the basic toiletries I used at the gym, a cardboard box with fake ID and ten grand inside, and the manilla envelope Joey Price gave me with Susan's personal effects in it.

Robbie was right. Our eye colors were identical as was the curve of our cheekbones and the way our long hair fell away from a widow's peak that made it so hard to part. I stuck her license, passport, and social security card in the zippered breast pocket of my hoodie as if its proximity to my heart might communicate some paranormal message.

Portland was where Michael said her story ended. If I had any purpose left, I should have been thinking about digging a little deeper into my classmate's death.

But the specter of destruction I caused back in Paloma swirled around me like a tornado. The prospect of some cop knocking on my mother's door to report that her oldest daughter was dead angered and terrified me. Mamacita was in her late eighties. I prayed the news wouldn't consume what little life essence remained in her soul.

I thought about Ali. This was just the trigger that could destroy her own quest for love and fulfillment. If she ever discovered that three men in some far-away place were responsible for my death she would kill them. I pitied anyone who stood in her way.

And then, there was Michael. His agency ordered him to sanction a murder. I guessed that it wasn't the first time he had heard the words. But tonight was likely the first time he defied them, risking everything to preserve one single life, a compulsive woman who too often let passion blind her to the cold calculus of reality.

That passion brought us together. It injected us into situations where our very existence hung in the balance, nearly killing him in Arizona and now putting his career and perhaps his life at risk again.

All because of me.

I've cried only three times in my life, the day Antonio Rojas beat the crap out of me in elementary school, the night my father dashed my Olympic dreams and the day he died.

Now, amid the white noise of an aircraft cutting through the thin air at 36,000 feet, I wept, angry, bitter, selfish tears.

My whole life had been a battle. At every turn people stood between me and my dreams. I always found a way to prevail until now.

Ten years of fighting for what I thought was right. Risking it all for a moral compass. And this is how karma rewards me?

I searched my gym bag for my cell, wanting to flip through every contact and commit a memory with every name. Somewhere between Mama's house and the airport, Michael had taken my technology from me, too, probably to plant among the cinders at my apartment.

I felt naked, vulnerable, and terribly alone.

Karma. You truly are a bitch.

* * *

Tears finally gave way to exhaustion and a sleep engulfed me with one nightmare after another. There was a common theme, a stage with me at the center, watching everyone I loved stand before me, eyes pleading for my help as a veiled figure used my own gun to put a bullet in each temple.

Their final words repeated over and over again.

"Jessica. Jessica. Jessica."

The voice deepened. The crisp midwestern accent began to change. The consonants became harder. The "Rs" started to roll, but not in the lyrical Spanish that was as much a part of me as my own name.

This voice was Russian.

Jessica. Jessica.

I felt something cold tweak my nose. It took a moment to regain my bearings in a darkened cabin where only a twin line of LEDs on the floor provided unsatisfactory illumination.

Jessica. Wake up. Time to die.

The words were emotionless. The cold, hard press against my nose had the smell of a familiar firearm solvent I knew well.

My eyes focused and a face came into view.

"The Chunnel Train in Paris," I said, recognizing at last the truck driver that looked for us in the cornfield from the cab of the fuel truck.

"You have a knack for failure, Detective Ramirez. I wonder why The Triumvirate is so concerned about your elimination."

The man who carried the Russian version of Dirty Harry's 44

magnum on the train from London to Paris, the man who shot Marie Culpado's traveling companion dead, the man who pushed us out of the door of a moving train was inches from my face stood before me. In his right fist a Taurus Judge revolver pressed against my forehead.

The most dangerous adversary is she who has nothing left to lose. I was that person.

My voice was surprisingly calm. Almost clinical. "Are you one of X's minions?"

The name colored his face with a dark mixture of admiration, fear, and irony. "Nobody has ever seen X. Some do his bidding. Others die by his sword."

He got Susan's gender wrong. My assailant knew much less about her than he realized. "Since we both know why you're here and you know who I am, want to tell me the name of my terminator?"

He pondered that one.

"Rupert. Let's go with Rupert this time. If you feel you need the familiarity, call me Rupert."

The smell of the gun solvent and the humidity of Rupert's breath snapped me out of my self-pity. The cool fire that always gave me strength in impossible situations coursed through my body.

If this was the end, I wasn't going to go quietly.

Rupert perceived the change. "You're getting ideas, Jessica. The eyes always give the mind away."

He cocked the weapon. I knew a thing or two about the Judge. It could fire a shotgun shell or an enormous hunk of lead that could stop a Grizzly bear. Either way, the weapon that jurists often hid beneath their robes in case the accused didn't like the sentence was an effective killing machine.

"Just waking up," I lied.

I liked the sound of my voice. The helpless child at the airport was gone. The powerful woman was back.

"If my end is a certainty, how about telling me how you got to me?"

Rupert's eyelids drooped. I hoped his ego would buy me time to think.

"We heard the entire conversation at your apartment, Jessica. Russians are very good at eavesdropping and your late housekeeper was kind enough to give us a key to install enough listening devices to detect a fly's cough."

An ugly grin cleaved his features. "I had hoped that your boyfriend would have his way with you before bursting your bubble. I wanted to hear you moan."

He pulled the barrel of the Judge away from my forehead long enough to caress my cheeks with it. "Perhaps you will moan for me soon?"

His voice went up into a question, but it was clear that this was an expectation.

"Focus, Rupert. This is about you, not me. How did you get onto a government aircraft?"

"Following you to the airport was easy. And crew members have accidents. Your copilot's was, unfortunately, fatal. It's amazing how much trust there is in the aviation profession. Our late captain didn't even question me."

"Late captain?"

"When they find the wreckage, there must be no evidence of a struggle."

Rupert showed me the butt of his weapon. "One strike to the right part of the head and endless sleep ensues. The radio is permanently disabled."

"Who is flying the plane if the captain is neutralized, and you can't?"

Rupert was tiring of our conversation. "The autopilot remains functional... for now. You ask so many questions, Jessica. And the time for my own departure is fast approaching."

From somewhere on his person, he produced a meat cleaver.

How do these guys get such big knives past airport security? Rupert slowly swiveled the blade before my eyes so I could appreciate its size and the damage the razor-sharp edge could do to my body.

"A pound of your flesh is what The Triumvirate wants, Jessica. And X is to deliver it personally." He pressed the tip of the blade against my chest. "I think your heart is an appropriate offering."

My peripheral vision sensed movement and that heart skipped a beat.

God bless you, Daddy, I prayed. *Please buy me another five seconds.*

Focusing my anger and pain in Rupert's direction I spat defiance at him. "Then do it, you Bolshevik bastard. Quit wasting my time."

The pilot must have still been severely concussed. He shouldn't have missed at that range. But instead of the head shot I knew had to be his plan, his handgun fired to the left, shattering the hand that held the cleaver.

A vertical block with my left forearm knocked the Judge away from my skull. A fist hammer to Rupert's throat set him off balance. As he fell backwards, the weapon discharged.

A bullet shattered a bulkhead window across from me. At this altitude catastrophic decompression would be fatal in less than 30 seconds.

Yellow masks deployed, just like in the safety videos. I pulled one free from its rubber band to activate the air flow and sucked in a breath.

Rupert tried to do the same thing.

I put all the energy a few cubic feet of oxygen could muster into a side kick. Rupert fell backwards, grasping for something to slow his fall. His finger was still on the Judge's trigger, reflexively firing the weapon again. The slug knifed through the fuselage parallel to the wing. Even in the darkness, I could see fuel begin to vomit out of the exit wound back toward the hot, spinning blades of the ramjet.

I grabbed another mask and filled my lungs. A heel to Rupert's jaw snapped his neck.

I bent over until my own face was inches from his. Rupert's mouth opened and closed like a fish out of water, the messages from his shattered C Spine no longer able to command his lungs to function.

"That's the last time you underestimate a woman, you son of a bitch."

Another breath of life and I went searching for the pilot. An inert body near the flight deck told me that my savior was in God's hands.

* * *

All I knew about flying could be put into a thimble. Aside from many skydiving trips, I had only flown in a private plane twice, both times with Ali.

With another lungful of oxygen, I stumbled into the cockpit and pulled the pilot's oxygen mask to my mouth, collapsing into his seat, trying to make sense of the glass monitors and dozens of buttons and switches in front of me.

Fire raged in the left engine. I wondered if the entire plane might explode at any minute. The instrument panel was ablaze with flashing lights and audible warning sounds.

Intuition told me to pull back on what looked like the port side throttle. A red light flashed on a fire extinguisher handle. A warning horn blared. The cacophony was distracting, so I pulled the handle. The wailing sounds stopped.

I wasn't sure what else to do, but I could sense a noticeable reduction in speed. With only one engine running and the autopilot working to maintain altitude, the aircraft's speed began to decrease. When I had flown with Ali in the tiny piston trainer she used to keep her private pilot's license current, gravity would pull the aircraft down and maintain airspeed.

The autopilot didn't want to let that happen.

I decided to pull the right throttle backward. I felt a definite reduction in forward thrust. I found the airspeed indicator and watched it decrease. Grabbing the steering wheel-like yoke I tried pushing it forward and felt resistance. The damn autopilot was attempting to hold 36,000 feet.

I started pressing buttons on the yoke, never a good idea in a high-performance aircraft. But Karma favored me and something called the electric trim deactivated the autopilot.

The nose began to respond to my forward pressure. It dipped and I saw the altitude indicator start to unwind.

At 24,000 feet, I looked for the one tiny radio I hoped Rupert had not destroyed. The Transponder. It was there, untouched. Normally, pilots set the numbers to 7700 in an emergency. An idea came to me; something that might send a message only my best friend would understand. I set the numbers to 5537. In a moment, every air traffic controller within radio range would record those four digits.

Unsure of how to re-engage the autopilot and wary of pressing any other buttons, I calculated there were just moments for me to don a Golden Knights parachute, open the bulkhead exit door and get the hell out.

Karma is a mercurial mistress. She can leave you just as quickly as she appears.

The vapor from the weeping fuel tank ignited. Seconds later the entire wing was engulfed.

Hooking into the parachute harness was pure muscle memory. Wrestling the bulkhead exit door open turned out to be easier than I expected. I didn't count on the impact of the blast of night air.

Ali's explanation of aerodynamics came rushing back to me with the hurricane force. Any modification of the surface area of an airplane impacts performance. I could feel the Citation tilt to the left. Ahead of me, the lights of Portland, Oregon were tiny grains of white rice tossed onto black fabric. Directly below me a line of orange dots marked a country road.

There were a thousand things I still had not figured out. But time was up. I pulled the goggles over my eyes, crossed myself and dove, headfirst into the slipstream, hoping the burning wing wouldn't slice my body in half, realizing a moment too late that I left my gym bag, false identification and Michael's ten thousand dollars in cash behind.

Chapter Fifteen

Paloma Estates Apartments

Ben Batavia stood next to the Paloma Fire Marshal, mesmerized by the football-field-sized square of glowing embers that was once a two-story apartment building. Fire hoses from three different battalions painted the remnants with parabolic arcs of water. Even under the downpour, the lava-like remains were still too hot to approach safely.

When Batavia felt the blast at his middle-class ranch home in one of Paloma's finer neighborhoods, he was certain the refinery had gone up. But the ugly glow south of town revealed the truth. He sprinted to his command car without changing out of his jeans and t-shirt, expecting the worst.

"Gas leak?" he asked, still hypnotized by the scene.

The Fire Marshal was equally entranced. "If so, it's the biggest one I've ever seen."

He pointed to a blob of metal with circles where four wheels had once been. "That used to be a Paloma Natural Gas van. You can make out the logo. Strange how a thin piece of plastic can leave it's mark even in the hottest fire."

A young street cop approached on the run. Clearly a rookie, he stopped to salute his superior.

"You can cut the formalities, Officer Brightmon. Report."

"We found someone, sir. Just at the edge of the woods. He's bruised up pretty badly and seems concussed. But I think he's alive."

"Any ID?"

"He's Federal, sir. Special Agent Michael Wright, FBI."

Batavia waved to a couple of paramedics, standing by their ambulance unsure of what to do. "Take us to him. Now, Officer!"

* * *

20 miles East of Portland, Oregon
JESSICA RAMIREZ

I pulled the ripcord as soon as I was clear of the aircraft. The smoking jet spun into an ever-faster corkscrew. Below, I could make out a field filled with circular white structures. They reminded me of the storage tanks at the Paloma refinery. The jet vectored straight toward them.

My hunch was correct. The Citation nosed into the center of the fuel dump, igniting its contents with a domino-like procession of fireballs erupting as each tanks' contents exploded in turn. The bright plumes illuminated the season's forthcoming wheat crop surrounding the storage facility, still green with youth.

Using the flames for guidance, I steered my chute as far away as I could from the crash and any other sign of civilization, still unsure what my next move might be.

I touched down on the run in a freshly plowed section of the spread. That would make burying the chute easier, perhaps deep enough that the planting machinery might never find it.

Within the hour, I was trudging toward the lights of Portland with no money, no technology and no idea what I might do next.

* * *

Paloma Estates Apartments

"He's stable. Banged up and possibly concussed, but stable."

The paramedic's assessment gave Ben Batavia the confidence he needed. He felt more than a little satisfaction breaking the smelling salts vial under Michael Wright's nose and slapping the agent across the face.

"Wake up, hotshot. It's the cop you threatened the last time our paths crossed."

Batavia watched the eyes roll and the slow, circular movement of Michael's head, classic signs of concussion. With consciousness came tears.

"She's gone, Captain. She was inside the building when the place went up."

Michael's voice was nearly a shout. Batavia deduced that the blast had deafened the FBI man.

"Who's gone, Agent Wright?"

The mountain of masculinity was a pitiful puddle of emotion. "We argued. She asked me to leave. I said I would wait outside until she cooled off and could find me back by the woods. I couldn't have been here more than a minute. Turned my back to look at the trees. There was a huge blast. That's the last I remember."

The paramedic interrupted. "We should get him to the hospital, Captain."

Batavia held up a hand. "When I'm done with him." He focused on Michael. "Who were you arguing with, Agent Wright? Give me a name."

Batavia new the name. He wanted his adversary to say it so it would hurt.

Michael Wright choked on the words. "Jessica. Jessica Ramirez."

Batavia nodded and motioned to the medics to load Michael onto a stretcher.

"You're lucky to be alive, Agent Wright. Everybody within one hundred yards of that complex is in line for St. Peter."

"I can't believe she's dead."

Michael repeated the sentence as if trying to get his mind to process what Batavia knew had to be true. "I can't believe she's dead."

The captain keyed his handheld. "Dispatch from 1-David-2. Get Chief O'Brien to the Paloma Estates Apartments immediately. And find Officer Clark."

* * *

JESSICA RAMIREZ

After about thirty minutes, the adrenaline rush began to wear off and I suddenly felt exhausted. The incredible stresses of the last twelve hours sapped whatever energy was left in my body.

The far-away lights of the city revealed the silhouette of a farm-house and the classical depression-era barn behind it. By now I didn't care if I slept with the cows. I needed to rest.

Perhaps it was the fatigue that clouded my situational aware-ness, or my single-minded desire to sleep. I didn't see them until they surrounded me.

"What have we here, boys? Looks like a migrant trying to steal something."

There were three of them. They were close enough that I could make a memory of their faces, young, overconfident, looking for trouble.

"*Como esta, chica?*" another one said. "Pretty far from the Mexican border, aren't we?"

A third set of hands grabbed my arms. With no energy left to fight, I couldn't resist.

The first one spoke again. "What did you take, bitch?"

That had to be the leader. The other two were deferential. I had to come up with a story quickly.

"My car broke down a mile back. You can check it if you want. I'm looking for a phone to call Triple-A."

I wasn't expecting the slap. It was hot and wet and stung.

"Answer my question, woman."

The third kid chimed in. "I bet she's with that group that ransacked Genburger's place, Russell. We should search her to see if she has any money on her."

Russell's smile told me that his definition of "search" meant a lot more than just checking my pockets.

"Listen, guys," I said. "Just take me to that house over there. We can make some phone calls and clear this whole thing up."

Then came the gut punch. I should have expected it, but I didn't.

What's happened to your skills, Jessica? Are you totally losing it?

"We'll clear this up right now," Russell growled. "Hold her, Billy. I need boxing practice. And then, we'll see if she's a virgin."

The day's events dulled my reflexes. I should have been able to outmaneuver the punk, but he had me under his control before my body could respond to direction.

The blows came, one after another. I felt teeth rearranging, my cheek bones cracking. I lost all feeling in my face. My eyes swelled shut. At last, God gave me the gift of unconsciousness.

"That's enough, boys!"

The woman stood on the porch of the farmhouse. She wore an oversized T-shirt with "My horse pleases me more than you ever will," stenciled on the front. Sweatpants and purple flip-flops completed her sleeping ensemble. It was the Mossberg shotgun in her grasp that got the thugs' attention.

"Assault on private property again? I thought we talked about this last time."

With a sign from the leader, the accomplice let their victim's body crumple to the ground.

The woman with the gun motioned toward the road. "If you're going to beat people up, do it outside of some bar."

She studied the mass of contusions at Russell's feet.

"And a woman? Three against one with a woman?"

One of Russell's minions came to his defense. "We thought she was one of those migrants who ripped off Genburger, Dr. Sullivan. I swear."

"I know you, Kingsman. And I know your preference for young female flesh."

Dr. Sullivan racked a round into the shotgun.

"Now get the hell off my property. If I see you here again, day or night, you'll get a buckshot butt scope."

Sullivan fired a round into the air to punctuate her point.

The boys ran for the road.

* * *

Paloma Estates Apartments

ALEXANDRA CLARK

I almost missed the turn for the apartment complex. The tableau I knew well looked as if it never existed. Had it not been for the long line of emergency vehicles, I would have driven right past the place.

The look on Captain Batavia's face was new. I didn't think empathy was in his emotional playbook.

"Get hold of yourself, Alexandra."

Alexandra. Another first. Batavia had never spoken my first name.

"It's JRam. She was inside the building when the place went up. The Fire Marshal's preliminary is a gas leak. There was a PNG van in the parking lot at the time of the explosion."

I scanned the foundation that was the sole surviving sign that a building had once stood on this spot.

"Gas?"

"They won't know for sure for a few days. You know the drill."

I felt a hand on my shoulder. The voice was familiar but uncharacteristically soft.

"I'm so sorry, Officer Clark. I'm afraid Jessica is dead."

I turned to face the serious countenance of Chief O'Brien. His words refused to register. "No. It can't be."

The chief gripped my arms as if my body might fly apart. "Michael Wright confirmed it, Alexandra. She's gone. I'm on my way to tell her family and thought you might want to come along."

Batavia could see me process the information. I felt my body vibrate. "Who did this, Chief?"

Batavia came to O'Brien's rescue. "It was likely a gas leak, Officer Clark. Unfortunately, these things can happen. At least twenty other people died in that explosion tonight."

My eyes shot fire in Batavia's direction. "A gas leak? Just like the gas leak that killed Jessica's father?" I nodded in the direction of the embers. "What gas leak vaporizes everything within a two-hundred-yard radius? No, Captain. This was no gas leak."

O'Brien's hands held me in a vice. "Alexandra. You're in shock. We understand the magnitude of this horrible news. Perhaps it's best that you head home to process this. I can call the department counselor and have her meet you there."

I was barely holding it together. "No counselor. And no misogynistic men who took every opportunity to try to break Jessica are knocking on her mother's door. I'll do it."

"Clark," the chief began. "You're in no condition. I order you to..."

I shook loose from O'Brien's grasp, ripping my badge and gun from my belt and thrusting them into his hands.

"I'll handle this. And to hell with your damn orders. You two can't order me to do anything anymore. I quit."

* * *

At the edge of the action, a lone figure in a paramedic's uniform sat inside an ambulance. Two responders lay dead in the back.

The person was close enough to hear the heated conversation, but far enough from the action for the vehicle to blend into the jigsaw puzzle of firetrucks, meat wagons and cop cars.

The paramedic nodded, but not with satisfaction. Getting a pound of flesh would be problematic.

Susan Molinero edged the ambulance out of the maze of emergency vehicles, following Alexandra from a safe distance. She needed to eyeball the location of the Ramirez family's new house. Until she could confirm that Jessica was dead, there was other work to be done.

Chapter Sixteen

Paloma, Illinois

ALEXANDRA CLARK
I made it about a mile before I had to pull over and cry my eyes red. Joni Mitchell's lines repeated on autopilot in my brain.

"Don't it always seem to go that you don't know what you've got till it's gone."

Every intellectual dimension of my cop mind was telling me to accept the evidence. My best friend, the closest person I ever had to a sister, was dead. The authority figures who should know confirmed it.

Jess and I endured the police academy, the incessant hazing, the unfiltered hatred of the majority of male police officers who did whatever they could to make us look bad. It was Jess who reassured me that being who I was had value. Despite my outward bravado, I held the "something's wrong with me" gene deep inside my soul, a product of a conservative Baptist family who still believed dancing was a transgression and loving someone who shared your gender was the ultimate, unforgivable sin.

Jessica lived a parallel life, constantly being told that her self-definition was inconsistent with what a traditional Latina woman should be. The message rode on the edge of a remark, a shattering command from her father, daily negative reinforcement from colleagues who were supposed to have our backs and leadership who should be inspiring, not destructive.

She never gave up. We fought our way out of the worst situations together. We argued about how to do it, but never about the values behind it. Lee may have been my soulmate. Jessica was my sister in every sense of the word.

Get your shit together Alexandra. You need to be the strong one for mama, mamacita and Maria. Grieve later. Do the job Jess would want you to do now.

I pulled away from the shoulder and back on to the nearly deserted road, driving to the Ramirez residence on autopilot, my stunned shock and inconsolable grief overwhelming me.

Until that tiny recalcitrant voice in my head started to yell at me.

It took control of my vocal cords, growing in intensity and anger. Anger at myself for simply accepting what males told me without verification. A Cop 101 fail. "Just the facts, ma'am." What were the facts?

Wait a minute, Alexandra. The people who said Jess was dead are the people you trust least on the planet. Revisit the timeline. Was Jess in that building when the place went up? And where the hell was Michael? Why didn't you ask that question before throwing your shield and gun in O'Brien's face?

I would do what I had to do at Jess' family's place. But I would give them the facts. No body has been found. Nobody is dead until some doctor says so. And the doc I liked and trusted most, Dr. Joey Price wouldn't call it until he saw it.

The EMTs probably took Michael to Paloma General. The

minute I could break free from the screaming Ramirez's, that was my destination.

My car somehow drove itself to their address. Some numb nuts in an ambulance almost cut me off when I turned onto the street.

Situational awareness, Ali. Pay attention to your surroundings. Focus!

The lights were still bright. Jessica's car was still in the driveway. Get in. Be compassionate. Get out.

The paranormal bond I felt with Jess was still rock solid. I felt no disturbance in The Force. No gut level sign my psychic connection to this woman had broken.

Was I planting my feet in denial? Damn right. Until a trustworthy witness could prove otherwise, Jess was still alive.

I was now unemployed, probably not the smartest move I've ever made. But I now had the freedom to accomplish the two objectives stood front and center in my consciousness:

Find Jessica. And destroy whomever tried to kill her.

* * *

The woman called Excalibur could see the big address numbers from the street. She wrote them down and fired up the secure messaging app on her phone.

Need a reliable termination at this address. $5,000 dollars for three souls. Advise.

Chapter Seventeen

Paloma General Hospital

"He keeps asking for you, Dr. Price."

Joey Price frowned at the bruised face looking back at him. "Why the oxygen mask, nurse?"

"He really doesn't need it. Just a precaution. He's had a terrible blow. His fiancée died in that explosion at the Paloma Estates."

Joey Price felt the blow, too. But nobody would ever perceive it.

"Jessica Ramirez?"

The nurse nodded. "You knew her?"

Joey's expression betrayed nothing. "Yes. Is the patient conscious?"

"Sedated, Doctor. But responsive. You can talk with him if you like."

Joey Price showed his medical examiner's shield and gave an order as he entered the private room. "No other visitors of any kind, nurse. That includes his attending physician. This is police business. I'll be closing the curtains. Please stand by the door and ensure we are not disturbed."

The cold forcefulness of Joey's directive had its intended impact. The nurse bowed and left the room. Joey pulled the curtains shut and bent a chair against the door handle to slow anyone who might try to enter.

The M.E. approached Michael Wright's bed. The agent's eyes were closed, but his breathing was normal, as was the telemetry that pulsed away on the data screen above his bed.

Joey bent over so his mouth was next to Michael's ear.

"Agent Wright," he whispered. "It's Doctor Price. Here as ordered."

"Joey." Michael's voice was hoarse. "Can you believe they wanted to intubate me when I got here? I was breathing on my own. Remind me never to get sick in Paloma, Illinois."

Joey pulled up another chair and sat close to the bed. "I've heard about Dr. Engler's distaste for Jessica and Alexandra. Be thankful there wasn't a proctologist in attendance."

The hint of a laugh rumbled deep in Michael's chest. "For a guy with zero personality, you have one wicked sense of humor."

Joey's cheek twitched. Michael respected this guy with brilliance locked in his brain, a man who struggled to contend with a world that could not decode his life language.

The M.E. rested a hand on Michael's wrist, reflexively checking the patient's pulse against the accuracy of the heartbeat on the telemetry screen. "I'm sorry about Detective Ramirez, sir. And I fear my office is about to become a very busy place. How can I help you?"

"I need you to do two things for me, Joey. And this is 'lose your license' stuff, so feel free to tell me to pound sand."

* * *

Michael Wright explained everything in detail. He had no idea what Joey's answer would be until he finished. The Medical Examiner's eyes focused on infinity as he thought about the assignments, before turning to his friend and uttering just two words.

"I will."

The purr of Michael's cell phone vibrated from the plastic bag beneath the bed that held his personal effects.

"Grab my cell, will ya, Joey. That might be the boss."

It was.

"Michael Wright."

"Jesus, Michael, it's great to hear that ugly voice of yours. I thought for sure we had lost you this time."

The effervescent tenor of Associate FBI Director Terry Taylor had so much volume that Michael pulled the cell speaker away from his ear.

He thought carefully about his tone before speaking. "Bad news travels fast. I'm surprised you heard about the explosion at the apartment complex so quickly. Jessica Ramirez is dead."

The silence on the Washington D.C. end of the connection was longer than Michael anticipated. As far as Taylor knew, he had followed orders.

"I did not know about that, Michael. What happened?"

"I'm fairly sure X got to her," Michael lied. "The whole place went up like an atomic blast. The Fire Marshal thinks it was was a gas leak."

Taylor's voice was confused. "It's all over the news networks. I thought you were on the plane to Portland?"

"No, sir. I'm lucky I wasn't caught in the collateral damage. Left the place just before it blew."

Taylor exhaled. "You are one lucky son of a bitch, Michael Wright. That Portland bound aircraft went down tonight just east of the city. Portside engine fire according to the Rolls-Royce people. Everyone on board was killed. I was sure you were playing a harp with them."

The cell phone slipped from Michael's fist. His head fell back against the pillow as the information sank in.

Joey Price processed it too, quietly backing out of the hospital room, his only words an admonition to the nurse to allow no visitors... except one. He pressed Alexandra Clark's number on speed dial.

Michael Wright's worst fears had come to pass. The love of his life had lost hers after all.

Chapter Eighteen

Paloma General Hospital

ALEXANDRA CLARK

My first act as a civilian was to confront Jessica's fiancé. I expected a fight. What I found was a broken man.

Michael's story spilled out in a waterfall of sobs, how the government decided that the woman he loved was expendable, their narrow escape at Jessica's apartment, substituting Jess for himself on the flight to Portland and the horrific news from Director Taylor about the crash.

Michael told me about The Triumvirate, their involvement with my own brush with death in the skies above Moscow and how Jessica had somehow fallen into the crosshairs of three rich men who believed she was much more than just a detective in a midwestern college town.

Finally, he shared the orders he gave to Joey and the likelihood that the assassin would be nearby until X got a pound of flesh.

When he finished, there was no catharsis. I knew that Michael

Wright would carry this burden for the rest of his life. The toxic mix of grief and anger in my own heart was overcome with empathy for a good man who tried to do the right thing.

The emotion was gone from Michael's voice. "I've just violated about a dozen federal laws and told you Top Secret information that could get me executed for treason, Ali." He looked away in shame. "Right now, death would be a blessing."

I needed this man if I was going to exact my own retribution. And I needed him strong and centered. There was no time to grieve.

"What is wrong with you, Michael?" The vitriol among my words surprised me. "Has Taylor been to the crash site? Where are the bodies? And how could you even accept an order to let your own fiancée die? If I were Jess, I would have dumped you on the spot."

I grabbed Michael's chin. "Now center, Michael Wright. Put your punk-ass emotions into a box and let's get some facts. You're still a federal agent. Get us every bit of data about that flight. Airspeed, altitude, ATC communications, the works."

I picked Michael's cell phone off the floor and shoved it into his fist. "And get it now, before Taylor can alter it. Then get your ass out to Portland. Charter another jet. Get to that crash site tonight. I want to know how many bodies are in the wreckage. Do a search within a ten-mile radius for anything, footprints, clothing... Interview the cows if you have to. Get on the horn to NTSB and make sure your ass is next to that investigator when they find the Black Box."

"And if this X person is still in town, you had better figure out how to find the bitch and terminate. You owe Jessica that much."

I was nose to nose with Michael. I wanted to read what was behind the red eyes.

"Do we understand each other, Agent Wright?"

I could see his expression changing. The empty eyes gave way to a hint of sparkle.

"You think you're a badass, Ali."

"Your worst nightmare."

"What do I tell my boss about the plane crash?"

"Nothing. Taylor will think Jess died at the apartment explosion. That's the lie you told Batavia. That's the news story that is orbiting the world at this very instant. Let him draw his own conclusions for now until you can confirm a few facts. You're a grieving fiancé. Only answer direct questions if he asks them."

"Is this how local law enforcement works? Withholding information?"

"As if you don't do it too, Michael Wright. Do you want me to list all of the things you didn't tell Jessica until after she found them out on her own?"

Michael knew he was busted. "Touché, Alexandra. And what will you be doing while I tend to your orders?"

"Recruiting the rest of our team. You've got the easy job. I'm gonna kill three oligarchs. Now get your pants on and get to work."

* * *

The Sullivan Home - East of Portland, Oregon

"Russell and his minions again?"

Dr. Sandra Sullivan placed a cool washcloth on the battered woman's forehead. She lay on the bed where Sandra's daughter had once slept. A daughter who would have been about this woman's age, had she not died in that horrific auto accident on her way home from work at the factory.

Skilled fingers palpated wounds and checked vital signs. Sandra Sullivan squinted at the pulpy, unconscious face.

"It's been a long time since I worked in an emergency room, young lady, but I still have a few skills."

The doctor produced a medic's bag and dressed the worst of the wounds.

"Trauma victims always look bad when they first present. We'll have to see what your options are after some X-rays and the swelling goes down."

Sandra looked toward the bedroom window and the dresser topped with a set of framed photographs, untouched except by a dust rag since the day her daughter died.

"I don't think you are part of that migrant family that has been involved in all those thefts. I think that Russell and his boys wanted a victim and you were in the wrong place at the wrong time. A good lie about Mexicans is easily believed around here these days.

"Who are you, dear girl? And why were you in my back yard in the middle of the night?"

Sullivan noted the bulge in the breast pocket of the woman's sweat suit. With the attention of a surgeon, she removed an exquisite engagement ring from the soft fleece.

"Somebody out there loves you," she said, placing it in a tiny jewelry box on the dresser at the foot of the bed. Normally, Sandra would have made a memory of the exquisite diamond and the gems that surrounded it. But assessing her patient was at the front of her mind and the ring floated into its deepest recesses. The doctor removed the identification information that might put a name with an unrecognizable face. She pulled reading glasses down from her forehead to clarify the blurred words.

Sandra Sullivan's eyes widened. She held an Oregon driver's license up to the light to confirm its contents. Then she stared at the faded picture of two very similar young women on the dresser with indredulity.

"You're Susie. Lucy's friend from work. Susie Molinero."

Chapter Nineteen

The Vine and Barrel

ALEXANDRA CLARK

"Ali Clark. You look rotten."

Rich Marshall, owner of *The Vine and Barrel*, slid into the corner booth next to me. I was in my usual position, at the back of the booth with a wide view of the room in case there was trouble. Once a cop. Always a cop.

I didn't know how else to say it. So, I just said it. "Jessica Ramirez is dead."

Security camera footage of the explosion at The Paloma Arms was all over the flat screens in his establishment. Cops were regulars and he heard of a betting pool that sold calendar dates on which Jess would inevitably be put out of action.

"I'm sorry, Ali. Want to tell me about it?"

I shook my head and swallowed the rest of my third double scotch.

"I still can't believe it. Some really bad people tried to take Jess out at her apartment. Karma was with her and she escaped that inferno."

Rich nodded toward the screens. "That explosion earlier tonight?" Rich heard it. Everyone in town heard it.

"That's the one. Her boyfriend put her on a plane to Portland and it supposedly went down. No survivors."

Rich Marshall knew how my mind worked. I was already planning retribution.

"Do you need a designated driver to get you home after your first night as an alcoholic?"

I had to respect the dude. He wasn't letting me wallow. I resolved to make him work harder at it, waving my empty glass at a server.

"I need an accomplice, Rich. Someone with experience in the darkest corners of this hellacious existence who isn't afraid to point a gun at someone and pull the trigger."

"Any prospects?"

"Most definitely. But he's on the other side of the Atlantic and takes his orders from someone else."

Hailey appeared with another double scotch. I realized I knew this girl since she was an infant. How old did that make me?

Her eyes asked the boss if he was joining his customer in a drink. Rich shook his head. I was glad for that. I needed someone who was sober tonight.

* * *

Bar owners knew when to keep their mouths shut. My eyes darted around the room, the wireframes of revenge forming in my mind.

An hour later, I had a plan. I always felt better with a plan. And a voice still whispered in my heart that Jessica might be alive. I had no reason to have faith in that voice. But it kept me focused and alert despite a high blood alcohol content. It was time to go put things into motion.

Rich Marshall walked close enough to catch me if I fell, but far enough not to tip his hand to the other patrons. Not all men are assholes.

"So you really quit tonight?" he asked.

"Yeah. Shoved my shield and gun in O'Brien's face."

"How did it go with Jess's family?"

"Horror, screams, anger and resignation. The Kuebler-Ross continuum in one long wail. It's as if they knew it would ultimately happen."

Rich shook his head in disgust. "I'm afraid we all did, Ali. But that doesn't make it any easier to accept. So don't. Just because someone with perceived power creates a narrative does not necessarily make it true."

I squinted at the guy. "When did you become a philosopher?"

"I run a bar. If every story I heard came true we would have cured cancer and Garth Brooks would be president."

Rich guided me into the alley next to his establishment and toward Boyd Street, where the Ubers were more likely to be found.

I recognized the voice in the darkness.

"Well, what have we here?"

Antonio Rojas. *"El Asaltante,"* Spanish for "The Assailant," stood in front of six fellow gang members in the alley. I knew instantly why they were there.

"Hey, Tony. It's not like you to join your boys when there's dirty work to be done. Did your handler demand that you actually participate for a change?"

Rojas chuckled. "We're big time now, Gates. After tonight, *El Asaltante* will be revered by every Latino gang member in the country."

"How does killing one girl get a small-time loser a rep, Tony?"

"Four girls, puta. When we finish with you, we have an appointment with Jessie's family."

Rojas snapped his fingers. Weapons of all shapes and sizes appeared in his associates' hands, aimed at the sky for effect.

In my peripheral vision, I saw Rich's hand slide toward the pistol I knew he kept beneath his sweatshirt. That I no longer carried a gun was an annoyance.

"Jess is dead, *pendejo*. Your contract is canceled."

"You're wrong, Gates. We wipe Paloma clean of Jessie's associates. That's the deal." Antonio turned to Rich Marshall. "Hands away from your pants, *gringo*. You picked the wrong girl on the wrong night. Your bar is about to get a new owner. Any last words?"

From behind the duo a deep voice barked, "Drop the weapons, boys."

"Kill them all," Rojas commanded.

The gang bangers should have trained their guns on the targets from the outset. In the half second it took to lower them into firing position, a hail of bullets sliced through dancing bodies.

When the smoke cleared, only Antonio Rojas remained standing, frozen in the crosshairs of Rich Marshall's semi-auto.

I turned to see Michael Wright holding a red-hot Heckler & Koch MP5 submachine gun.

"Evening, Ali. I thought I'd find you here."

Michael circled the barrel of the Heckler at Rojas. "Tell your boss X is next on the list. Now beat it."

Whatever loyalty Tony may have felt for his soldiers in life evaporated with their deaths. He turned and ran.

Michael popped the mag out of the Heckler and showed it to us. "Two rounds left. Glad nobody fired back."

I grinned. "Dang, Michael, someone found his mojo. How do we explain this to the cops?"

"We don't. I'll be long gone and nobody is going to care about some dead gangbangers. Beat it before they get here. I've got a plane to catch."

Rich and I exchanged glances before I vanished into the night as sirens sang in the distance.

Chapter Twenty

University Hospital - Portland - The Next Morning

"I promise you, the woman I took into my home carried Susan Molinero's identification. Why won't you investigate?"

Sandra Sullivan's caustic tone had no effect on the detective on the other end of the phone connection.

"The case is closed, Dr. Sullivan. I saw the body myself. As far as the city, county and state are concerned Susan Molinero is dead. The apartment manager identified her. Her brother claimed the remains. She's off our radar screen."

"So, what about my patient? Is there any way she might be identified?"

The cop sighed. "The DNA you sent us came back without information. That's not unusual if the individual has no reason to provide a sample."

Sandra knew her subject. "Conclusive results can take longer, sometimes months, Detective. Investigators talk to families with relatives who have disappeared and get samples."

The cop's patience was running thin. "That requires time and money, neither of which we have in the budget. Why is this so important, Doctor? Fix her face and let the shrinks sort out her memories."

"Fix her face? As what? She had Susan's identification on her person. And what am I supposed to call this Jane Doe in the meantime?"

"Call her whatever you want. I predict someone will come looking for her, or she will get her brains back and tell you who she is."

"I'm about to mold her appearance to match a dead woman, Detective. If I get it wrong, I'll make sure your superiors know it. I hope the city has good legal counsel."

The Detective lost his cool. "I know what this is about, Dr. Sullivan. You're grieving the loss of a loved one and see an opportunity to diminish the pain by saving someone else. Your daughter and Susan Molinero were friends. I saw their pictures together; they could be twins. But they share only one thing in common now. They are both dead."

With those words, the cop hung up, leaving Dr. Sandra Sullivan fighting mad with nobody to absorb her anger.

* * *

JESSICA RAMIREZ

The sign over the dry erase board says Portland Research Hospital Hospital. Even before I awoke from the long nightmare, I could smell the cocktail of industrial cleansers, plastic, and flowers. Unfamiliar names were scrawled next to Doctor and Nurse. At the top of the board, someone wrote, "Good morning, Susan," with three exclamation marks.

An IV in my left arm connected to a couple of bags filled with clear liquid. The words on the bags were too small to read. I recognized the morphine injector and the button within my reach.

The haze in my head told me someone recently pressed that button.

Everything hurt. My face pulsated with each heartbeat, the elastic holding an oxygen mask over my mouth felt like razor wire. Every muscle screamed at me.

I tried, without success, to organize the puzzle pieces into a nonexistent larger picture. It felt like the present moment was encased in some steel box in my brain. The river of memories that made up my identity, my experiences, my life flowed around the box. I could feel it. But I couldn't touch it or see it.

The morphine did its work and I drifted in and out for about an hour. A day? A week? Time was another thing I couldn't process. I concentrated on the clock above the door. The snapshots I took dissolved in my head almost as soon as I tried to file them.

After an interval a nurse appeared. She was smiling, but I could tell she was worried.

"Do you know where you are?"

I shook my head and instantly regretted it. The pain was off the charts.

"Can you tell me your name?"

It was out there, but out of focus. I grabbed for it but couldn't grasp it.

"That's ok, kiddo," the nurse said. "You've had a bit of an adventure. I will alert Dr. Sullivan that you are conscious. She will be here soon."

The nurse put a hand on my arm, glanced at a screen that was pinging away with my vitals. When she looked at my face again, she couldn't disguise the wince.

The nurse punched the morphine button.

"Rest now, Susan. Heal."

Something was wrong. Very wrong.

* * *

More time passed. I drifted in and out of sleep. The whoosh of the door awakened me. The woman in the white lab coat had a name. Sandra K. Sullivan. It was embroidered over a pocket with a pen and her cell phone in it. A stethoscope hung around her neck.

Sullivan. The person the nurse mentioned. I remembered! Progress!

"Where am I, doc?" My voice sounded strange. Deep and sandpaper rough. What should it sound like?

"Good morning, young lady. How is the face?"

"A bubble of searing gelatin. What happened?"

"Three punks. You were in my back yard when it happened." She held up three mug shots of a trio I seared into what little memory remained. "Remember how you got there?"

I tried. I tried hard. Nothing. Dr. Sullivan's knowing smile didn't make me feel any better.

"You have what's called 'Dissociative Amnesia.' It can happen as the result of trauma. And you had more than your share of trauma last night."

My gravelly voice suddenly sounded small and vulnerable. I hated it. "What's my name, doc? All I can remember is waking up. And even that is foggy."

"You are Susan Molinero. At least that's what your driver's license, passport and social security card say. You used to work in a factory with my daughter. They called you two "the twins" because you looked so much alike. Karma put you in my back yard when the boys ganged up on you."

I had zero memory of any girl named Sullivan. "Did your daughter remember me?"

Dr. Sullivan's expression darkened. "Lucy died right before you dropped off the map."

"Dropped off the map?"

"That's something we'll work on after I put you back together."

"Put me back together?"

The doctor turned serious. "Your face has been badly damaged, Susan. You're not going to like what you see in the mirror. But I have pictures of you and Lucy." She bent her fingernails over a palm and blew on them to reassure me. "And I have the skills. We'll make you as good as new, maybe even better."

I struggled to keep the conversation flow in my mind. "You said I dropped off the map. What does that mean?"

"There was a story in the paper about three weeks ago, three days after Lucy died. You were found in your apartment. The apartment manager identified you."

Sandra Sullivan took a deep breath.

"You are supposed to be dead."

* * *

NTSB Crash Site - 10 Miles West of Portland

Savvy Schmidt flipped a strand of blonde hair back over her shoulder. "This was one hell of a marshmallow roast."

Michael Wright thought she looked younger than her years. The Nirvana hoodie, the aged blue jeans and fire-engine-red Nikes seemed more appropriate for a high school kid. The NTSB Chief Inspector made a note in her iPad.

"Looks like a fuel leak in the left wing tank took out the port engine."

To Michael Wright, what was left of the aircraft and the smoldering remains of the Portland Fuel Depot looked like a dozen puddles of mercury. He shielded himself from the heat that still radiated from the moon crater carved out of a farmer's field.

"You deduced those details from that mess? The fire turned everything into soup."

"Happens sometimes," Savvy answered. "All depends on how the plane augers in. This one decided to drill a bullseye at the center of five hundred thousand gallons of gasoline. Auto fuel and Kerosine don't play well together."

"Bodies?" Michael bit off the word he didn't want to say.

"There might be some DNA in there somewhere. Have fun trying to find it."

"You can't tell me how many souls were on board when it crashed?"

Inspector Schmidt regarded Michael like a confused puppy. "Just what was on the manifest. That says 'three.' Whoever was in that aircraft when it crashed met their maker last night."

"And the Black Box?"

"ICAO Type 1A. That's it over there."

One of Savvy's associates held an orange and black device in gloved hands near where the tail section of the Citation once was.

"Still warm, Eric?"

"Red hot. I don't know, Savvy. This guy was in the oven for longer than his rating. Structurally sound, but I'm not sure what we'll find inside."

Savvy waved toward a van parked in between a pair of state cop cars. "We'll take it to the lab. Ask the Mounties to keep the site cordoned off until our full crew arrives."

The inspector pulled a folded piece of paper from the back pocket of her jeans. "The transcript you requested, Agent Wright. ATC communications from take-off until the jet dropped off the scope."

It was a foreign language to Michael. He tried to sound like he understood it. "Anything unusual?"

Savvy pointed to the last line of the printout. "There. That last transponder ident."

Michael's cluelessness must have given him away. "Seventy-Seven Hundred is the Mayday setting," Savvy explained. "Someone set this one to five-five-three-seven."

"I'm sorry, Inspector Schmidt. That's Greek to me."

"ATC tells pilots what numbers to use. That's how they know which plane is which in the system."

Savvy circled the numbers with a finger. "Nobody was talking to this guy when he changed the setting. Either he was trying to reset to the Mayday numbers when things went south, or someone up there was trying to tell us something."

She fixed Michael with an interrogator's gaze; emotionless, intense, in search of a clue wrapped in a lie. "Any idea what that something might be?"

Michael returned the intensity. Inspector Schmidt was a badass. He liked her.

"Not a clue. But I know someone who might be able to enlighten us."

Savvy Schmidt turned toward the NTSB van. "There are a hundred factors which could have contributed to this crash, Agent Wright. The answers lie in the anomalies. Those transponder numbers are neon warning signs. Decode them for me and we'll both have what we need to get closer to an answer."

* * *

Paloma University Computer Lab

ALEXANDRA CLARK

Andy Milluzzi tapped in the final commands. The virtual private network sprang to life and with it the ultra-secure video application on the computer lab's Mac Mini.

I pulled my chair close to the desk to get a good view of the screen. Seconds later a familiar face materialized on the other end of the line.

"Alexandra Clark, you old hacker. What are you doing pinging me on Andy's computer?"

"Commander Tom Anastos of MI6 in the digital flesh. You look like you've completely recovered from your experience as a guinea pig for Russian poison."

"You always open with the most seductive lines, Ali. Where's Jessica?"

The nuance in Anastos' voice told me he knew. I swallowed the emotion Jessica's name brought up. "I think you know, Tom. According to her boyfriend, her body is burned to a crisp in some fuel dump in Oregon. The work of our trio of old friends."

Anastos' expression betrayed nothing. "I'm sorry, Ali. We all loved her."

"She's not dead until I say she is, Thomas. Either way, I'm not letting these bozos get away with it."

I studied the MI6 Commander's face for nuance. There was none. "Listen to me, Ali. You're talking about going after three of the most highly protected human beings on the planet. And that protection includes my Prime Minister. We need stability as we work through the fallout from the Pandemic, the war in Ukraine, inflation. Taking out The Triumvirate shakes the foundation of what keeps the earth spinning."

"Is that MI6's view?"

"MI6's view is irrelevant, Alexandra. We do the government's bidding."

I pressed. "What does Gerhardt say?"

I saw a flash of annoyance on the other end of the line. Anastos put a palm behind his ear. "That and everything else on this subject is Top Secret, Officer Clark. If you go after The Triumvirate, you'll be fighting the same people who helped you and Jess neutralize The Captain."

I felt the adrenaline course through my body.

"You're gonna help us, aren't you, Tom." It was a statement, not a question.

Anastos made a fist dipping it up and down. "Not this time, Ali. You're on your own. And I must sign-off. Got a dinner date with an old friend of yours. Please pass my condolences on to Jessica's family."

The connection broke. I turned to face Andy. "Know American Sign Language, Andrew?"

Andy grinned. "Beyond giving someone the finger; a little, here and there."

I repeated Anastos hand motion, rocking my fist. "This means 'Yes.' We've just recruited one more member to the team."

Andy Milluzzi mimicked my hand movement. "Make that two more members, Officer Clark."

"Good. Your first assignment is to build me a tracker that nobody... and I mean nobody can detect."

"Done," Andy answered. "It may take a couple of weeks to do it right."

I slapped my favorite nerd on the back. "You got it, cowboy. Oh yeah. It needs to be waterproof."

I felt my cell phone vibrate. Only three people outside of work knew the number. A flash of hope that it might be Jessica increased my heart rate.

The caller ID said it was Michael Wright, checking in from Portland.

Michael Wright
"No survivors found... so far. Got any idea what a 5537 transponder reading means?"

Chapter Twenty-One

Our Lady of Guadalupe Catholic Church - Two Weeks Later

Obituary: Jessica Mary Ramirez-Duarte - 1984-2022

Jessica Mary Ramirez-Duarte passed away on May 16. She was born December 9, 1994, to Luis and Rosa Ramirez. Jessica attended Paloma High School where she set state records as a competitive swimmer. She earned bachelors and master's degrees in criminal justice at Paloma University and served as a police officer in Paloma for eleven years, rising to the rank of detective.

She is survived by her mother, Rosa Ramirez-Duarte, one sister, Maria Louisa, her maternal grandmother, Elena Ramirez-Hernandez. She was preceded in death by her father, her maternal grandparents and paternal grandfather.

A funeral mass will be held on Saturday at 9am at Our Lady of Guadalupe Parish with graveside services to follow at Paloma Glen Cemetery.

Memorial contributions may be made to the Paloma Police Widows and Orphans Fund.

* * *

ALEXANDRA CLARK

"How do you distill a human life into less than one column inch?" That was Father Diego's opener at the mass. "The Jessica we knew was so much more."

The sanctuary at Our Lady of Guadalupe Catholic Church was packed. A flag-draped coffin rested on a mahogany bier at the altar. In the front pew, the immediate family, Rosa, Maria and Mamacita Elena were flanked by Michael Wright, Danny and Christina Lopez and a host of relatives I only recognized by resemblance.

I sat in the second row, Tom Anastos on my right represented MI6, with Michael's FBI boss Terry Taylor next to him. A phalanx of the Paloma cops of color and gender with careers made possible thanks to Jessica's tenacity and sacrifice filled the rest of the pew. I thought it appropriate that the rabid dogs who prayed for the opportunity to rip out her throat were relegated to the rows behind.

Sgt. Sokolove made sure of that. "For over ten years, you bastards were all betting Detective Ramirez wouldn't survive as a cop. Well, you got your wish." Sok eyed each hang dog in turn with the intensity and disdain of a cynical police officer who caught a dead-guilty perp, knowing they would be roaming the streets within the hour.

"But I'll tell you all this: she'll be remembered long after the rest of you are dead, gone and forgotten."

"Jessica Ramirez had Olympic dreams," Father Diego continued.

Here it comes.

"She set statewide high school records that still stand. Jessie had the goods and was approached by her childhood hero to try out for the US Olympic Team. But her father, as fathers often do, guided her in a different direction. And we became the beneficiaries."

Father Diego eyed Anastos and Taylor. "Jessica's most storied exploits will likely hide behind the veil of national security. Her character and humility would never seek the spotlight. And yet, she was unafraid to stand up for what she thought was right, even when it was not popular. She was fearless, unafraid to neutralize deadly force." The pastor pressed an upturned palm in Rosa's direction. "And yet, Jessie was a loving daughter, granddaughter and sister, compassionate with both the predators and prey in her profession, understanding the deep pain that is often at the root of wrongdoing. Family and community will be her everlasting legacy. Our city is diminished by her death. But we are better for Jessica having walked among us."

After expressing condolences to the, Father Diego motioned to Chief O'Brien.

I muttered an obscenity. "Of all people, they are letting O'Brien eulogize her?"

The chief was decked out in his dress uniform, a quartet of gold stars reflecting the colors of the church's stained-glass windows on each epaulette. As TV cameras from as far away as Chicago rolled, he walked solemnly to the chancel.

O'Brien's sober gaze scanned the crowd. "Taking attendance," I muttered. "And looking for the press."

I felt Anastos' hand on my knee. "Temper, Alexandra," he whispered. "Keep it in check."

He took a slow, deep breath. It seemed to me like O'Brien was sucking all of the air out of the sanctuary.

"Detective Jessica Ramirez exhibited the best qualities of a police officer. Honesty, tenacity, respect and humility. She was a trailblazer for women in law enforcement at the close of an era where men in blue were still the paradigm. She served with honor and was an exemplary officer in every regard. We shall miss her." O'Brien swept a hand across the row of young officers, both female and of color. "But her presence will be felt in the hearts and minds of every new generation in our profession forever."

I heard a grunt from Sgt. Sokolove. It was meant to catch the chief's attention. O'Brien acknowledged it with discomfort, his eyes straying from his prepared remarks.

"By acclamation of her peers, the central meeting place for all police officers in Paloma shall hence forth be known as the Jessica Ramirez squad room."

I didn't suppress a tiny cough that covered my second favorite expletive. The place was already being called "The Ram Room," under muffled breaths.

O'Brien put a hand into his pocket, producing something silver that I couldn't make out.

"I have this day conferred with the mayor and city aldermen and they have approved my recommendation that Jessica Mary Ramirez be posthumously promoted to Captain, in recognition of an extraordinary life of selfless service to law enforcement and to our community."

O'Brien stepped down from the podium and approached Jessica's mother. "Please accept these bars as a token of our gratitude for your daughter's dedication from a grateful city."

Rosa Ramirez cupped her palms as the chief's white-gloved hand placed the shiny object in the center. He bowed. She bowed. Cameras flashed. I knew what tomorrow's headlines would be.

"After a private interment," Father Diego intoned, "the family will receive visitors at the Ramirez residence, the address noted on your bulletin."

From somewhere behind me, a single voice began to sing in the choir loft. It was quiet and angelic, the antitheses of the lyrics and melody.

What you want, you know I got it.

What you need, you know I got it.

All I want, is a little respect when I come home.

The magnificent church organ swelled. An electric bass picked up the bottom end. High hat cymbals tapped a beat that grew into the bluesy rhythm everyone in the congregation knew by heart.

The rest of the choir provided a harmonic wail as the lead singer morphed from a tiny cherub into a flame-throwing Arcangel, belting Aretha's rendition of the Otis Redding composition.

I felt a rock in my gut. I swallowed the emotion but could not stem the tears, nor the smile. There would be no doubt in the minds of every male cop who ever stood in Jessica's way that the community knew her real story.

But who arranged this perfect final tribute? My attention was drawn to Jessica's mother. Her hand gripped the sharp cornered captain's bars with such force that sharp edges sliced her palm. Blood dripped from her shaking fist. She nodded, a stoic gaze locked on the casket that all knew contained only a few remnants of what might or might not be Jessica's body.

Crimson droplets stained the chief's white cuffs as the mother of the deceased's iron glare bored into what remnants of a soul might still exist in O'Brien's icy heart.

I put a hand on Rosa Ramirez's shoulder. "Well done, Mama," I whispered. "Well done."

* * *

Michael Wright felt his phone vibrate in tandem with Ali's. He stole a glance at the screen.

"Package retrieved as expected. J.P."

His eyes met Ali's as a second text, this one from Andy Milluzzi populated both screens.

"Tracker Initiated. We have a location."

Michael could see the flames in Alexandra Clark's eyes.

"Someone seems to have broken into Dr. Price's storage facility at the morgue," he said.

"Excalibur," she growled. "I shall look forward to killing you myself."

Chapter Twenty-Two

Portland Research Hospital - One Month Later

JESSICA RAMIREZ

I was liking Sandra Sullivan. I guessed her age to be nearly sixty, but I wasn't sure how I came to that conclusion. Perhaps it was how she paid for my every medical need out of her own pocket. One thing I did remember – a private room and a plastic surgeon were not cheap. Whenever I asked about the bills, everyone around me simply said they were "being taken care of."

My memory for events since my encounter with the boys seemed to be working but everything before was still a whirling blur.

It took me a week to convince Sandra to let me borrow a laptop so I could check out the news stories about my supposed death in some apartment that was nowhere in my memory banks.

I was drawn to Lucy's accident. For reasons that were still unclear, my gut was telling me something wasn't right about the whole investigation. The car was consumed in fire and the body was un-identifiable. Lucy's records had gone missing from her dentist's office. It was her mother who had to identify personal effects amid the charred remains so the funeral home could get on with a cremation that began in a conflagration of smoke and fire on the night of the accident.

Fire. That was a constant in my nightmares. Images of fire consuming buildings and a series of orange mushrooms I couldn't place. They felt connected. But my brain couldn't tie the threads together.

This morning, Dr. Sullivan was all smiles.

"Well, Susan. Your face is starting to look almost human. Still hurt?"

I rolled my eyes. "You know it does, Doc. When do I get to stop the narcotics? My plumbing is plugged up worse than a kitchen sink with a sock in the drain."

"You'll be glad you have them nearby when I've given you today's update."

Dr. Sullivan touched my arm. It felt familiar, as if someone else I knew well but couldn't describe was touching me.

"I've got the go-ahead from the surgical team to schedule your reconstruction. Tomorrow, we give you your face back." She held up my driver's license. "And when I'm done with you, you'll look more like Lucy's old friend than this ugly driver's license photo."

My stomach lurched. Somewhere in the back of my brain a voice was screaming something. I struggled to understand it.

Dr. Sullivan could read my expression despite the damage to my face. "I wouldn't blame you for being nervous. We women are sensitive about our looks. But I can promise you, everyone who has ever met you will recognize you as Susan Molinero when the swelling from my artistry goes down."

The scream started to make sense. It was the word "No!" repeated over and over again.

"I wish I knew my life story, Doc. I would feel a lot better about your slicing and dicing if I did."

I studied the curtains that covered the rectangular observation window that provided a view from my room to the hallway. "Why have you kept me in this room since the incident? And why are those curtains always closed?"

Dr. Sullivan didn't look where I was looking. That told me the curtains were closed on her orders. "If you could see yourself right now, Susie, you would see a face you probably would wish you could forget."

"That bad, eh?"

"That bad. You'll frighten women and children."

"And the dirt bags that did this to me?"

Dr. Sullivan's disgust was evident. "Arrested the next morning. Out on bail. How anyone can be a police officer these days is beyond my comprehension."

Her words echoed through torn canyons of memory. When they came back the timbre was different. There was a dinner table and faces still out of focus. I heard a voice just like mine respond. "He keeps secrets, even when they might be important for someone he cares about to know."

Then the vision blurred into darkness. I wrestled my consciousness back to the moment. It was time to get back in the game, even if I had no idea where the game might lead.

"Ok, Doc. I'm in. Let's get me fixed so you and I can start working on what really happened to Lucy."

* * *

Paloma University Computer Lab

"It's been four tricking weeks. Why aren't we closing in on that tracker and grabbing whoever has the damn thing?"

The annoyance in Ali's voice tugged at Michael Wright's heart. *Just like Jessica.*

"We have a dozen people watching from a safe distance, Ali. The package keeps changing hands. Excalibur expects us to make an arrest. Our perp won't show up to claim the prize until she's sure it doesn't have followers."

"How long do we wait?"

"As long as it takes."

"And what if Andy's little invention suddenly stops transmitting?"

Michael shrugged. "We descend on its last known location and arrest everyone we find."

Chapter Twenty-Three

Portland Research Hospital - The Next Evening

Dr. Sandra Sullivan watched her patient's gentle breaths register on the telemetry screen in post-op. The face, too shocking for the battered woman to see, was wrapped in white gauze, covering the careful artistry that required nearly twelve hours on the operating table. Tiny slits provided openings for the patient to see and a pathway for the nasal cannula to supplement the oxygen while she slept.

"I did my best work, Susie," Sandra Sullivan whispered. "In another week you'll begin to see what perfection looks like. In a month you'll never know anybody touched the beautiful face of Susan Molinero."

Chapter Twenty-Four

Three Weeks Later

JESSICA RAMIREZ

Tomorrow I would see my face for the first time. Sleep was elusive and when it finally arrived, a vision came with it.

To my throbbing, confused mind, the dream made no sense. I had no body. Just a presence. Nothingness surrounded me... except for a mirror that should have framed my face. Clouds boiled within its rectangular oak frame. At intervals familiar faces appeared. But I couldn't put names or context with them. None looked at all like the pictures Dr. Sullivan was using to restore my damaged features. But they felt spiritually close, as if we had some special connection.

The last image was a woman about my age. She radiated a tough exterior. And yet, I could sense shaky self-confidence beneath her outer shell.

She looked tired. Her eyes were red as if she had been crying. Behind her was some sort of bulletin board with pictures and notes on it. Her lips moved as if she was trying to say something to me.

But of course I heard nothing. I saw her eyes focus on one of the scraps of paper on the board behind her. Some casual brush of a shoulder might have turned it upside down. Even at a distance I could make out a number on it. 5537. The girl squinted at it. It felt important. Those numbers meant something. She would know what that was. I began to yell the numbers to the woman. I felt my vocal cords vibrate. But there was no sound.

I screamed them at her over and over. Her eyes narrowed, recognition dawning. The woman grabbed the scrap off of the board and ran from the room as the vision disappeared.

The darkness returned. I felt satisfaction, but did not know why.

Alexandra Clark's Apartment - Paloma

ALEXANDRA CLARK

I considered the face in the bathroom mirror. It looked older than my years. The zoom visit with Lee in London had not gone well. I was impatient and grumpy. My love was growing tired of my obsession with finding the woman everyone believed was ultimately responsible for Jessica Ramirez's death. Lee wanted me to take the MI6 gig, to move on with a life that included my UK soulmate at the center.

And I was tiring of the dozens of hand-offs Joey Price's package took on its supposed trek to Excalibur. Andy Milluzzi was beginning to worry that the battery in his tracker might die before it led them to their target.

"This is aging you." I spoke to my love's words in the mirror's reflection. "Thanks Lee! Just what I needed to hear tonight. Thanks for the affirmation."

I couldn't blame her. This thing was a compulsion. "I'm sorry Lee," I said to the mirror. "You didn't deserve my anger. I'll send you flowers tomorrow. And maybe life in London wouldn't be such a bad thing."

I rubbed my eyes and looked at the reflected image of the cork board on the opposite bathroom wall. A carefully arranged array of photographs, post-it notes and screen shots from my computer filled it to the edges. Images of Lee and me populated almost a dozen selfies from my trips to London. But there were an equal number of shots with Jess, interspersed with notes and scans from the two months of fruitless effort and near zero progress.

I concentrated on a picture of the two of us from our first day as cops in the field. Jess bagged a murderer that day and the adventures that culminated in me finding love and Lee began.

"Will I ever be able to let you go, Jessica? I refused to believe you were mortal. But each day that goes by I find myself losing touch with your spirit."

I zoomed in on the reflection. "Give me a sign, partner. The world is telling me you are dead, but I can't say goodbye."

My eye caught a tiny scrap of paper below the photograph. It was a scan of Michael's text from the crash site. An errant elbow, or perhaps a burst of wind as I came and went had flipped it upside down. How, I wondered, could my obsessive compulsiveness not have noticed it.

Michael Wright
"No survivors found... so far. Got any idea what a 5537 transponder reading means?"

My brain spun the visual Rubik's Cube in every possible direction. I finally flipped the Seven horizontally. The image hit me like a thunderbolt.

JESS

It was a stretch. Jessica would have had only seconds to think the puzzle through, the presence of mind to interpret the dials on a transponder and program it properly.

Could it be true? Or was I grabbing at straws?

From the not-so-distant past, I heard Jessica's voice as clearly as if my best friend was standing beside me.

"I depend on straws, Ali. They always deliver the tastiest cocktails!"

I ran to the kitchen table where my laptop was still warm. I pinged Lee in London, praying she was still awake and not too angry to answer the call. A sleepy face materialized on the screen. I let go of a thousand different emotions crammed into an overflowing mental wheelbarrow since the day I was told my best friend was gone forever.

"It's Jess, Lee. It's Jess. She sent me a message. She's alive!"

Chapter Twenty-Five

ortland Research Hospital - The Next Morning
JESSICA RAMIREZ

Perhaps it was the bandages. In the preceding weeks, Dr. Sullivan let me escape the hospital room that had been my prison since the attack.

The first place I went to was to the fitness center. I attacked the weight machines and treadmills with a vengeance, as if an elevated heart rate might knock some sense back into my confused gray cells.

Dr. Sullivan was pleased at the speed with which I regained my strength.

Time was still hard to process. Days ran into weeks without comprehension when you existed in the same surroundings.

Walks with the nurses around the hospital grounds gave me a welcome new set of visuals to process. I was able to make memories again, but the Iron Curtain between present and past was as thick as ever. I could still hear muffled words on the other side and suffered through nightly excursions into defocused imagery of things that made no sense.

Fear of the present was there, too. What if the operation was a failure? What if I never regained my sense of identity? Were there people out there who were worried about me? Did I have a family? Friends? Some sort of career?

The strange dream that manifested the night before stayed with me. Who was the woman in the mirror? What did the numbers mean?

I spent hours and hours trying to find my past on the web. But aside from the brief news cycle where Susan Molinero's body was discovered, I was an Internet non-entity.

What I wanted most was to be free of my hospital prison. If I never spent another day in its confines, that would be a good starting place for an uncertain future.

* * *

"Good morning, young lady!" Sandra Sullivan's eternal optimism could wear on a person. "I brought you a couple of presents."

The door to my room opened and a second woman entered with a thin, rectangular box under her arm.

"This is my friend, Assunta Sebastian. She has a mental health practice associated with the hospital."

"Need some backup as you reveal your handiwork?" I asked.

Backup. Another word that resonated. I heard a familiar voice in my head. It was sarcastic and appealing, if those two opposing descriptions can go together. *"Someone has to hang around to pull your chestnuts out of the fire."*

Assunta laughed. Her speech had a European accent I couldn't place but found pleasing. "Exactly, Susan. I never let Sandra unveil without a wing woman."

Dr. Sebastian radiated a calm confidence. I was certain she was one of the best at what she did, with fees to match. I could see the hospital tab growing faster than unchecked ragweed in a strawberry patch.

Dr. Sullivan sensed my concern. "Assunta is a friend. We've never had a case like yours here and she's fascinated."

Dr. Sebastian's smile revealed a patchwork of wrinkles surrounding two appealing dimples, aqueducts of wisdom I imagined were earned over years of patient experience and study.

"I spend a month each summer working in Pigalle," she said. "The red-light district in Paris. Pro bono is one of my favorite Latin phrases."

I accepted it. "What's in the box, Dr. Sebastian? Chocolates for the occasion?"

Assunta patted her package. "Better than chocolate, Susan. It's this marvelous invention called, 'a mirror.'"

I felt my heart skip a beat. A combination of excitement and uncertainty churned away in my stomach. Would seeing my reflection break the Iron Curtain?

Dr. Sullivan read my mind. "Understand that there will be places where I nipped and tucked that will need time to relax before you're one-hundred percent Susan again. But you are about to get a good gander at what you looked like before three boys danced on your beautiful face."

I darkened. "They are still walking around free, Doc. What kind of justice system allows that?"

"You're the important link in that chain, Susan. Their arraignment and trial have had to wait until the star witness can identify them. But let's focus on prettier things."

Dr. Sullivan pointed to the foam and plastic piece of furniture that accounted for a comfortable chair in my hospital room. "Have a seat. Let me show off my brilliance to Assunta and get the patient's reaction."

I hopped off the bed and sat. Dr. Sebastian kept the mirror in its case. I assumed they didn't let the Frankenstein monster see its face until they were sure the visuals wouldn't terrify.

Dr. Sullivan produced a pair of surgical scissors and began to cut the bandages. She found the key strand and began to unwind its long tail.

I looked at the framed photographs of me and the late Lucy Sullivan that had been constant companions since the night I arrived. There was something strange about the smiles. Susan's felt forced. Lucy's bordered on desperation.

Assunta's expression was more telling. I guessed she was a shrink, there to intervene if my brain chose this moment to explode.

I watched Dr. Sullivan's face. With each spin of the gauze her own features brightened. She was pleased.

The last of the long bandage slipped free and the two women stood side by side inspecting her handiwork.

"The mirror, Assunta," my surgeon / savior murmured, snagging the largest of the photos of her daughter from the dresser.

Dr. Sebastian had it out of the box in an instant. She held it face down as Dr. Sullivan positioned the picture in my field of view and nodded to her colleague.

The mirror rose, revealing a face identical to the photo in almost every detail. Dr. Sullivan was right. There were still places where her magical micro sutures would need to relax. But the resemblance was near perfect.

"What do you think, Susan?" Assunta's voice was soft and strong at the same time. Typical shrink, I thought. "Does seeing this image release any memories?"

My mind was spinning all right. The past was still beyond my grasp. But I knew one thing for certain. I had seen that face somewhere else. The perfect reflection of Susan Molinero in the mirror was not me.

Chapter Twenty-Six

Paloma University Computer Lab

"Dammit!"

Andy Milluzzi had been anticipating the moment. Its arrival was not a time for celebration. He fired up the secure text group on his Signal app that pinged Ali and Michael and sent a text.

Andy

Bad news guys. The battery on our pound of flesh tracker just died.

* * *

FBI Headquarters - Washington

Michael Wright engaged the secure video messenger app that served as a meeting place when Ali and Andy needed his attention. The faces that greeted him each betrayed their unique frustration.

Michael

OK, guys, before we melt down, let's look at the data. Andy, what was the last location report?

Andy

Portland, Oregon, Agent Wright. I started losing the regular pings an hour ago. Coordinates just outside of the city was the package's last stop before the Portland report.

Michael

Bring up the map for me, will ya?

Ali

Boys! I have news.

Andy

Looks like it's the executive terminal at Portland International is on the dance card. Our courier has access to some high-class transportation.

Michael

OK. I'll alert the Portland office to get some assets out there, but it won't do much good if we don't have something to follow.

Ali

Michael! Andy! Will you both shut up and listen? I decoded the transponder numbers. Give me screen-share privileges, Andy.

Michael's mind was still thinking about how to find a needle that had just disappeared into a very big haystack. It took a second to process Ali's news. Andy worked his magic and a screenshot of the mirror image of the transponder settings filled monitors.

Ali

Jess signed her name for us. She was in that cockpit before the plane crashed. I think she found a way to get out of that thing alive.

Michael felt a shot of adrenaline flow through him. He fought its effects.

Michael

Let's not get too hopeful just yet, Ali. Jess would have had to take control of the aircraft, bring it to safe altitude, find a parachute, open the door and jump clean. There were two crew members flying that jet who were somehow incapacitated. And the time frame between the transponder reading and the crash was less than five minutes.

The FBI agent could see Ali fume.

Ali

That's exactly what the flight data says, Michael. Descend from 36,000 yo 24,000 feet. Level flight for about two minutes before the corkscrew descent into that gasoline inferno. And we're talking about Jessica. We all know her capabilities. All along my gut has been telling me she got out of that plane alive. She's in the same town with your pound of flesh.

Andy

I'm sharing Agent Wright's skepticism, Ali. If she survived, why haven't we heard from her? It's been almost four months.

Ali

I can give you a half dozen reasons why. She could have been seriously hurt and is in some hospital with a tube down her throat. Someone on the ground could have grabbed her and locked her in a basement. Mr. Wonderful here took her cell and her ID so the only identifying documents she's carrying belong to Silent Susan. Nobody's going to confuse her with our killer so she could very well be in some dumbass sheriff's lock up still waiting for her one phone call.

Michael

I want to believe that your little puzzle solution is real, Ali. But my mission is still to find and neutralize Excalibur.

Ali

What is it with you, Michael? Two months ago, you risked your life to save Jessica. Now, there's a chance she might still be alive and you're not even going to give it a modicum of credence?

Michael

I'll be on the phone to the Portland office the moment we sign off, Alexandra.

Ali

Using my whole name to assert your male authority, Mikey? You'll do more than that, cowboy. You'll get your ass on an airplane back to Portland today and personally take charge of the investigation.

Michael

You know my situation, Ali. There are political dimensions I have to deal with.

Ali

BS, Michael. If you still love Jessica, you'll be in Portland before sunset. And I'll tell you something else. I'll beat your lazy ass there.

Michael should have expected this development. He did his best to freestyle a response.

Michael

Listen to me, Ali. You have no law enforcement credentials anymore and even if you did, Portland would be way out of your jurisdiction. Let us handle this.

Ali

You disappoint me, Agent Wrightl. If the roles were reversed, Jessica would go to the ends of the earth to save you. See you in Portland.

With that terse goodbye, Ali signed off. Michael stared at the buddha-like expression on Andy Milluzzi's face.

Michael

I guess I'm headed to Portland, Andy. Any chance we'll get another ping before your little invention totally goes silent?

Andy

Perhaps. The power draw is super low and I put a zener diode in the line to shunt the circuit if the voltage fell below minimums. There's some invisible gallium arsenide on the package but it's probably been too dark for it to do much.

Michael

I have no idea what you just said, my friend.

Andy

Batteries often get a second wind. If ours does, you'll get some more data before it gives up the ghost. And I added one more thing that could help if conditions are right.

Michael
You enjoy pouring stomach acid on my ulcers, Andy. Out with it.

Andy
Gallium arsenide, Agent Wright. It's an invisible solar cell. If Excalibur puts the package anywhere near a light source, it will recharge the battery in less than an hour and we'll be back in the game.

* * *

The Office of Dr. Assunta Sebastian - Portland
JESSICA RAMIREZ

"For all I can't remember, lying on a psychiatrist's couch feels like a first-time experience."

Assunta sat in an overstuffed chair across from me in the overstuffed office. Books and search engine printouts lay in piles that had no discernible organization. Behind me, her desk area consisted of a simple Ikea outfit, a huge wraparound monitor and a MacBook, tethered to a power holster. Earth tone curtains obscured a window, above which a procession of lifelike all-encompassing rubber faces covered a shelf of plastic busts. I could see why she kept them out of her patients' line of view. Some were terrifying.

"Why the masks?" I asked. "Is that a magician's trick to frighten patients into continuing therapy?"

Assunta considered the lineup as if they were old friends. "A previous life, Susan. I've always loved the stories faces tell us. I was a sculptor and did some special effects work in Hollywood. Mostly monster masks and aliens for Lucasfilm. I call these my 'Wall of Failure.' These are all rejects. 'Too human,' the effects supervisor said."

"Is that how you met Dr. Sullivan?"

"Very good, Susan! Yes. I create a complete life mask in latex based on photographs. Sandra keeps it handy in the operating room along with a huge bulletin board filled with pictures from every stage of her patient's life. You were a challenge because all we had was a driver's license and a passport pic. Sandra reconstructed you from memory."

"So, you have a mask of my face someplace? Like those scary rubber things kids wear at Halloween?"

"You do remember things from your past. This is progress. Can you think of anything about Halloween when you were growing up?"

I strained to reach for something. But the harder I tried, the more the past recoiled from my grasp.

"I'm not sure where that one came from, Dr. Sebastian. When I try to pull something from memory, it's like I'm the positive end of a magnet and the memory is a negative, it's repelled."

Assunta wrote something on her iPad. I felt annoyance, not sure where it was coming from.

"When you make notes, that means I said something important. What was it?"

The shrink showed me her screen. "I wrote 'trauma,' Susan. We compartmentalize trauma, and dissociative amnesia is exacerbated by trauma. You likely have experienced a lot of bad stuff. Remember any of it?"

I chuckled, "No, thank goodness. What's the treatment for dissociative amnesia?"

Dr. Sebastian tapped a few characters into her iPad and showed me the screen. "This infographic details the three types of memory, Susan. Episodic or event memory, Semantic; knowledge about the world and Procedural; things like motor skills and reflexive things you've repeated over and over. I'm trying to assess the extent of your memory loss in each of these areas before we agree on a treatment protocol."

I was feeling restless. I wanted to get away from the hospital that had been my prison for the past three months.

"I'll tell you one treatment protocol that I'd love, Dr. Sebastian.

An escape for awhile. Can you sign us out and take me somewhere we can both relax?"

Assunta slipped her iPad into its charger. "I know just the place."

Chapter Twenty-Seven

Alaska Airlines flight 669 - Airborne between Chicago O'Hare and Portland International Airport

ALEXANDRA CLARK
I was headed to an unfamiliar city with no friends, no intel, and no plan.

The mission to find and take out The Triumvirate had met with universal condemnation from my tiny team of co-conspirators. That confirmed that I was on the right track. Trusting my gut and engaging my brains always delivered the goods.

This situation felt different. A vast, unfamiliar town. No side-kicks. No badge. And no positive proof that Jessica was even there.

Think like a cop, Alexandra. Start with the hospitals.

I signaled the flight attendant for a vodka. At this late date, only first-class seats were available on my flight. Might as well enjoy the perks.

It would take Michael at least an hour to pull the political levers in Washington. I was a step ahead of him. Now that a game plan had formed, the energy filled me with hope.

Jess was alive. I knew it. And I was determined to be the one to find her.

* * *

ABV Public House - Rock Creek, Oregon
JESSICA RAMIREZ

Dr. Sebastian sat across from me at a bar called the ABV Public House. It wasn't the place she wanted to be. For a shrink to enable an amnesia patient to go to a bar, let alone consume alcohol bordered on malpractice. But I wasn't in the mood for the local steakhouse across the street. And in my previous existence, I must have been pretty good at arguing my point.

The rays of the evening sun illuminated invisible dust diamonds, casting an almost spiritual glow into the establishment. The wonderful aroma of bar food and beer felt good. I placed myself at a table where I could take in all the goings on around me.

When the server asked for my order, my brain delivered a margarita and nachos.

"That's a combination of episodic and semantic memory, Susan," Assunta said. "You have memories of enjoying Mexican food and your knowledge of the world delivered the menu items you ordered."

"I wish I could tell you more, Dr. Sebastian," I said after a swallow of a poorly constructed fishbowl-sized cocktail. The sharp mixture felt good going down, even if they were using cheap tequila. "There is still this huge wall between the moment I woke up in that hospital and everything that happened before."

Dr. Sebastian nodded, unsurprised by my answer. "Please call me Assunta if you feel comfortable doing so. Your experience is common. But usually by now a patient starts to get some whispers of recollections that ultimately fill in the blanks."

I took another pull off the margarita.

"Does the drink bring back any flashes?" Assunta asked.

"Only how lousy the house liquor is." I chomped on a nacho. "This recipe is nowhere near authentic."

Assunta put a forkful of some innocuous, healthy salad into her mouth. "How would you know about authentic Latin cuisine? Your surname sounds Italian."

"Maybe I'm a mutt," I said. "And an affinity for cultural cuisine isn't limited to natives."

"True," Assunta said, washing down her salad with sparkling water. "I'm French and I hate crepes."

Without understanding why, I recited a strange stream of consciousness. "You're a woman of the world, Assunta. Your MD degree is from Harvard. You did your residency in Mexico City. You still have a place in Paris but since you lost your husband, you've avoided home, immersing yourself in the troubles of others to mask your own grief."

My sudden Sherlockian assessment stunned us both. Assunta looked pleased. "Where did that come from, Susan?"

I found myself laughing. "We stopped by your office on the way out and I saw the degrees on the wall. There's a photo of you outside the Museo Nacional de Antropología in Mexico City on your desk, along with two photos of a man. One at the Eiffel Tower with the two of you, and a more somber portrait off in its own corner of your credenza that reflects social distance. It's either divorce or death. I rolled the dice on that last one."

Assunta put her fork on the edge of her half-eaten salad plate. "You're correct on every point, Susan. That is a window into your past life. That level of observation may have been born into your genes, but it's been perfected through practice."

I still had nothing. Whatever barfed out that assessment was a synapse that had zero connection to anything else I could remember. I resumed my radar scan of our surroundings, assessing every face as if one might hold some secret that only I could discern.

"And another thing, Susan." Assunta leaned forward to make

141

sure I was looking at her instead of scanning the rest of the bar. "Your Spanish is perfect. Where did you learn that?"

* * *

I saw them. They sidled into a booth about twenty yards behind Dr. Sebastian. Assunta noticed the change in my expression. "What is it, Susan?"

"The dirt bags who jumped me. They just walked in."

My assigned shrink raised a palm. "This is not the time or the place, Susan. You're still recovering. Now that you're healthy enough for a court appearance, the district attorney can pursue assault charges."

"They'll walk, Assunta." The forcefulness of my voice surprised us both. "It happens all the time. They'll find some public defender who will challenge my mental competency. I'll have to admit my memories are foggy. It won't matter that I recognize every freckle on their faces. No judge will remand them."

How in the hell did I know so much about the judicial system? I would have to ponder that later. Right now, I would mete out my own form of justice.

Assunta looked desperate. I felt a tingle of joy seeing her expression. "Don't do this, Susan," she said. "There is a quarter million dollars of plastic surgery still healing on that beautiful face. One clear punch and Sandra might not be able to fix things next time."

I stood. "Order me another drink. And tell them to use top shelf stuff this time. Patrón and not that watered down *gringo* knock-off."

Before she could stop me, I was headed towards the table where my assailants were about to know Karma's sting.

Chapter Twenty-Eight

MI6 Headquarters - London, UK

Assistant Director Mo Gerhardt regarded his agent across the special desk, built to accommodate his wheelchair.

"The Prime Minister's position has not changed, Commander. The government wants The Triumvirate to remain untouched."

Tom Anastos tried hard not to betray emotion. His boss was trained in nuances and could sense Anastos didn't like it.

Gerhardt gave the joystick that controlled his movements a tiny press, squaring his view. "I hear that Andy's tracker died."

Anastos nodded. "He says we may get another ping or two before it quits for good. And there's a countermeasure he described that gives Agent Wright some reason for optimism."

Gerhardt moved the electric chair closer to the desk. "You must tell your American friends that the British Secret Service will not be a party to any activity that could disrupt the delicate balance that keeps our world centered."

The commander stood. He knew when an audience was at an end. "Yes, sir," he said, turning to the door.

"Tom."

Gerhardt never used Commander Anastos' first name. Something was up.

"I see unused vacation in your payroll profile. Have you considered taking some personal time? You've been working non-stop since your Moscow assignment."

Anastos studied the face of his supervisor. It was an impassive enigma.

"I've built up two months, sir," Anastos said. "With so much going on, is it appropriate to be away from the job for that long?"

Gerhardt's attention returned to paperwork on his desk.

"We'll cover for you, Commander. Enjoy your leave. And try to stay out of too much trouble."

* * *

ABV Public House - Rock Creek, Oregon
JESSICA RAMIREZ

The bastards didn't recognize me. Was it the darkness of that night they took away my identity? Or was it something else?

I studied their photographs on the web. I knew their names, their faces and every bit of their sordid pasts by heart. Russell had a rap sheet a mile long from petty crime to armed robbery. He always found some way to get off. Kingsman was suspected in a dozen sexual assaults. His victims all seemed to lose their nerve hours before their court dates. Carlson was small time, a follower who kept enough distance to populate police reports solely as a "person of interest" and never a suspect.

"Hello, boys," I said. "Attacked any defenseless women lately?"

Russell spoke first. The alphas always do.

"What in the hell are you talking about, woman?"

"Do you feel powerful when you call a person, 'woman?'"

Kingsman chimed in. "They are hiring a lower class of waitresses here, Russell. Shut up, bitch, and go get us some beers."

My eyes stayed locked on the leader. I rubbed my new face with a palm. "You owe me a quarter million in medical costs, *Gringo.* I'm about to take it out of your face. Do you want to pay that debt outside where the EMTs can get to you easier or in here where more of your friends will witness me beating you into sobbing submission?"

Russell finally made the connection. It must have been the voice. "It's the Mexican from Sullivan's place. Almost didn't recognize her in this light."

Mexican? A tiny synapse connected. *Maybe that's how I know my tequila.*

Customers around us started to fidget. I guessed someone was dialing 911. "Inside or outside, punk? Time is wasting."

Russell laughed. He motioned to Kingsman and the third kid I knew as Carlson. "Outside, guys," he said. "It's three against one so be gentlemen. Hang back while I rearrange her face again."

We filed out the front door. Darkness had fallen. They circled me in the parking lot, their bodies silhouetted in the glow of the mercury vapor streetlights.

"Let's get to it," I barked. "In about two minutes there will be a half dozen cops here, and I don't want to embarrass you in front of grownups."

"Listen to this one," Russell said. "Sounds like she's initiating felonious assault. You two are witnesses."

Kingsman rubbed his crotch. "I'm getting excited just hearing her talk, Russell. Make it quick and let's take her someplace where nobody will hear her scream when I have my way with her."

Russell made his move. The old-school jab was easy to block. My kick to his groin sent him reeling.

"Want to take your shot at my honor, Kingsman?" I growled. "Idiots like you shouldn't be allowed to reproduce."

The dirt bag knew some martial arts and tried a back-spin kick.

I ducked under it and slammed an elbow against his carotid artery. He crumpled to the pavement.

Russell's anger must have been hotter than the pain in his nether regions. He charged me. The guy was bigger and stronger. But he was stupid. Never assume a shorter woman can't defend herself. A sidestep and a push and Russell's face slammed into the right-rear quarter panel of a pickup truck.

Carlson must have had some sense. He kept his distance. Kingsman wasn't as perceptive. He came at me with a knife.

"Attempted murder?" I said. "Time for a visit to the vasectomy clinic."

I caught his wrist when he thrust the razor-sharp steel at my chest, twisting the bones until they broke. A down stroke drove the blade between his legs. He screamed.

Vitriol materialized out of the fog that permeated my amnesiac brain. "Your lover boy days are over, Romeo."

The trio's leader had more resilience than I expected. He also had a gun. "You're a dead woman, bitch."

Out of an unremembered past, muscle memory took over. With speed and dexterity that surprised me, I relieved him of his weapon and began to pistol whip his face, alternating the blue steel butt of the gun with an opposing fist. Russell teetered backward against the pickup truck bed. His knees locked, keeping him upright throughout the beating. The blood vessels near the surface of his skin burst, splattering my shirt and fist with crimson. I didn't care. I channeled my fury toward my abuser until Russell's face was an unrecognizable mass of Raspberry Jam.

With every blow, I felt a tiny onionskin layer of post-traumatic stress peel away. Why had I not cleared this poison out of my body before? What trauma in my past compartmentalized so much rage?

It felt good. Too good. Who was I? A positive force? Or was I just like my attackers, a ball of repressed anger, looking for someone weaker to suffer the brunt?

The familiar wail of sirens in the distance brought me back into the moment. Kingsman was on the ground holding what remained of his balls, his blood coursing across the asphalt. He was one rapist who would never again harm another woman. Russell lay unconscious on the pavement. It would take more skill than Sandra Sullivan had to put his face back together. Only Carlson remained.

"Well?" I said, beckoning him.

The kid turned and ran.

* * *

I felt great. The pain in my face was under control for the first time in weeks. Somewhere in my past, I had skills, reflexive skills that didn't require thought or memory. I had power, determination, and attitude. If Susan Molinero had those qualities before the beating, she was my kind of badass.

Assunta cringed when I returned. "Everything OK?" She asked. My shrink waved a paid receipt for our meal in one hand, studying the blood on my fist as she stood. "Are you aright?"

"Let's talk about it in the car," I said, reaching over the bar to the controls of a security camera system that was strangely familiar. Pressing the Erase / Format button, I took my psychiatrist by the arm and out the back door to her vehicle. No sense in forcing her to feel the need to administer first aid to two bloody bad guys. The security system whistled a reset beep in the distance. The cops would not get a look at a beautiful new face pounding a pair of punks into the pavement from that device.

We pulled into traffic just as a line of police cars screamed into the parking lot.

* * *

Dulles International Airport - Washington D.C.

Michael Wright cinched his seatbelt ahead of the flight attendant's expected admonition. He felt good about getting both permission and a flight in such short order. Delta would have him in Portland before midnight.

As the crew instructed passengers to set their phones to airplane mode, Michael felt the vibration.

A message from Director Taylor.

X has been seen at a bar in Rock Creek. She dismembered two small-time hoods in the parking lot.

There was a clear shot of a woman throwing an elbow against the neck of some thug almost twice her size. While much of the photo was a blur of motion, the face was crystal clear.

Excalibur had allowed herself to be seen and photographed. She was slipping.

Michael patted the comforting bulk of the Beretta pressed against his chest in an old school leather shoulder holster. His FBI status allowed him to carry on this flight.

If Karma was on his side, Michael Wright would soon put a bullet between those pretty eyes.

Chapter Twenty-Nine

3519 NE 15th Avenue, Portland, Oregon

Fremont Place was perfect for the hand-off. The go-between confirmed he was not followed and left the package in the personal care of the manager of the UPS store at Fremont and NE 15th Avenue just as instructed.

He chose a booth at the nearby Starbucks with a good view of the parking lot. His hand wrapped around an untouched latte. Perhaps he might actually see Excalibur. An identification was worth money, more than his puny payday for delivering some silly brown package.

* * *

The K1 Covid mask obscured her face. It was against policy to hand over a package without ID, but the customer had tipped the manager well to do just that.

Even the voice was hard to judge. Its husk was affected, and the extra-large hoodie gave no indication of a reliable body type. Except for the height, 5'7", this one was a mystery.

"A gentleman left me a parcel. Square, brown paper, 'Will Call' written in red ink."

The manager handed the box over as instructed.

"Anything else we can do for you today, ma'am?"

"There is one thing. Did you happen to see where the gentleman went? I hoped to link up if he had time before his next meeting."

The manager was usually too busy to observe his customers. But the customer in question came in at a rare moment when the store was almost empty. His exceptional height and the simian gate with which he walked caused the manager to take notice.

"I think he may have stopped at the coffee shop next door, ma'am."

"Thank you very much," A gloved hand pressed a fifty-dollar bill across the counter. "For your trouble."

The woman in the black hoodie turned and left.

* * *

The manager studied the bill with the practiced eye of someone who has spotted more than a few forgeries. He rubbed it with his palms, pressing an edge against his nose, inhaling the bouquet of parchment and printer's ink. The paper was genuine. It had the aroma of authenticity, and the bill was almost brand new.

He pocketed the tip. No sense in letting his young co-worker know about this.

* * *

That's when the convulsions began. The part-timer watched it all, even as she dialed 911. The vibrating body, the vomiting, the constricted pupils, the gasping for breath. And then, inert silence.

Her boss entered the hereafter splayed on the tile floor, eyes focused on infinity, mouth open, the skin on his face slowly turning blue.

* * *

The fire trucks caught the go-between's attention. An ambulance followed. When the police cruiser arrived, he decided it was time to forget about identifying Excalibur and to get as far away from the drop location as possible.

He was about to walk out the door when a masked woman in a black hoodie touched his shoulder.

"You forgot your latte."

The go-between took the cup without comment. He would need the caffeine for the long drive to his extrication point.

He took a drink as he started up the stolen rental car. The go-between noticed the woman with the black hoodie leaning against the coffee shop's brick exterior, arms crossed, waiting.

The latte tasted like burnt almonds. Only then did he realize he had met Excalibur.

Seconds later the cyanide did its work. The man slumped against the steering wheel, a white froth dripping from his mouth.

* * *

Rotherhithe - London, UK

"Possible kidnapping in progress Little Pips, Rotherhithe."

Detective inspector Liyanna Evans always kept her hand held in whisper mode when off-duty. The preschool was a few doors away from her restaurant date. She acknowledged dispatch and thought about how much she disliked domestic calls.

* * *

Ronnie drew a Webley revolver from his pocket. "Seth is coming with me."

The intern on the front steps of the preschool felt the four-year-old's hand tighten around her own. The woman she recognized as the boy's mom, screamed at her ex. "The court says he's mine, Ronnie."

Ronnie wasn't having it. "My pistol says he's mine."

* * *

"What's all this now?" Ronnie instinctively swung the Webley toward the authoritative feminine voice. A dark-skinned fist chopped his wrist. The weapon fell to the pavement.

A woman's leg slipped behind his as a hand gripped his throat. Off balance, Ronnie found himself on his back, staring at a rare cloudless UK sky. A second later, the woman flipped him on his stomach, a pair of strong zip tie handcuffs binding his wrists. "Are you going to cooperate, or do I need to tie your shoelaces together?"

Ronnie roared in frustration, arching his back in an attempt to roll over and kick his assailant.

"We are not following directions, young man. Adding 'assaulting a detective inspector' to the charge of possessing a handgun without proper license won't be very good for you in the dock."

With the speed and precision of an American rodeo cowboy at a bull roping competition, Liyanna Evans zip-tied Ronnie's ankles and held him face down with a foot pressed on the center of his back.

She shot a grin at the astonished child. "Seth, do you know which one is your mum?"

The boy nodded vigorously, still in awe of the beautiful black woman who neutralized the threat. A short blonde ran to the boy, hugging him with an intensity that made her son cringe. She focused on Lee, a confluence of gratitude and tears in her eyes.

"Thank you, whoever you are. We've had a rough go with the divorce and my ex just lost custody rights. He can get belligerent when he doesn't get his way."

A pair of beefy school security guards appeared on the doorstep.

Lee grinned. "Is that so?" She looked down on the prostrate figure. "You have to learn to respect authority, sir, or you won't be allowed to play with grownups for a long, long time."

Lee nodded to the security men. "Can you two gentlemen keep this one from flailing until my associates arrive?" She winked at Seth. "Flailing is a word adults use to impress one another. It means wiggling when you are mad."

She made eye contact with several other mothers waiting to pick up their children. "I assume you ladies can recount the proceedings for my brother and sister coppers. Unfortunately, I have a previous engagement, or I would be honored to visit with all of you."

"We've got this," one of the security men said, placing a huge boot next to Lee's sandal-clad foot on Ronnie's back. "Enjoy your evening, DI Evans."

"Harold!" Lee was elated. "I'm so proud of how you've reinvented yourself."

The security officer, who's name turned out to be Harold, blushed. "I'm grateful to you, DI Evans. You gave a bad boy a second shot and I intend to make the most of it."

"Truth be told," Lee said, a twinkle in her eye. "I have a dinner date. Thanks for covering for me."

"Anytime, anywhere, Ms. Evans. You changed the course of my life."

The detective inspector waved to the crowd. "I'm so glad I happened to be in the neighborhood." She bent over and ruffled Ronnie's hair. "And be kind to this gentleman. Many of us know the bond between father and son. This poor bugger just let it get out of hand and got a taste of the bitter side of the Karma cookie."

* * *

The Mayflower was Liyanna Evans favorite pub. Four centuries of clientele consumed fermented beverages here. Tom Anastos must have known Lee appreciated the menu and the privacy of crowded conversation.

Since the publicity surrounding Moscow, Lee found privacy increasingly problematic. Perhaps that was why Maddox kept her in research. "There's the lass who kicked a Russian spy in the stones," was a common recognition. Offers of everything from free drinks to matrimony usually followed.

Liyanna Evans didn't join the MET to work at a desk. She would have accepted the dinner offer when it came across her encrypted messenger wherever Anastos proposed.

"You look bored, Lee. Miss being beat up and shot at?"

"Let's just say I prefer anonymity to fame."

"How's it going with Officer Clark?"

"You mean 'Citizen Clark?' Since she quit, she's been insufferable. Our video chats all end up as arguments."

Anastos circled a finger in the direction of a server. "True love is a cocktail of fire and ice."

"We both need a different kind of fire, Commander. Is that what you came here to talk about? My romantic issues?"

Anastos laughed. Lee perceived the irony.

"What's funny, Commander?"

"I'm sorry, Lee. I'm looking at this exquisite African beauty, if you'll pardon the objectifying language, and hearing the voice of a Scottish bagpiper."

"Ahh. It happens often, Commander. Mum was a Zulu from Johannesburg. Dad was a foreign service official from Glasgow. I got her looks and his accent."

Pints arrived. "The combination is wonderful, DI, Evans. Bravo to your parents. Actually, I'm bribing you with good food because I have a vacation proposition for you. Got leave time to spare?"

Lee regarded the scrunch of Anastos' eyes and the way he sniffed the bouquet of his Guinness. "Plenty," she said cautiously. "As long as it doesn't give me any additional fame. I don't know how our Royals stand it."

A moment later a basket of Panko Chicken arrived. Someone had spoken with Ali recently about Lee's food preferences. Her shields popped up. Nobody treated you this well without strings attached.

"OK, Commander. What's up?"

Anastos took a pull from his pint. "How do you feel about cold-blooded murder?"

"I arrest murderers."

"Are you capable of killing someone who you knew was responsible for the deaths of many others if that person was evading justice?"

The Panko Chicken suddenly looked unappetizing.

"Am I neutralizing a direct and eminent threat to my life in this scenario?"

Anastos nodded. "Yours, Citizen Clark's, Detective Ramirez, probably your former partner and your boss."

Lee pushed the food away and drilled a hole in the commander's eyes with her own. "Stop mucking about, Commander. What exactly are you proposing?"

* * *

Paydirt NE Pacific Street, Portland - 10pm

ALEXANDRA CLARK

I liked Paydirt immediately. It was a distinctly local bar with a delightful mix of class and kitsch. And it was small enough for conversation but big enough for the ambient sounds to keep it private.

The stolen Smokey Bear head logo with the bar's name on the hat was a nice touch.

It felt a bit odd that Diana La Pierre was so quick to respond to my invitation with enthusiasm and a location. I wondered how she would react to what I had to tell her.

"Ali?"

She was tall, my height, skinny but firm. Shoulder-length hair that deserved a better colorist was piled under a Portland Trailblazers baseball cap. What was behind Diana's yoga top could have benefited from a sports bra. A matching skirt covered her ass but not much more. A pair of bamboo-colored sandals and a Swatch completed her ensemble. She wore no other jewelry but carried a butt-pack sized purse that could easily have held a 380 handgun along with the usual female accoutrements. Diana didn't look like the type who carried heat.

"I must radiate cop," I said. "You found me pretty quickly."

Her laugh was bubbly to the point of annoyance. "Not many women sit alone in a booth at a bar."

I offered some Naugahyde. "We had better fix that. Have a seat and tell me what I should be drinking."

"Black Saddle 12 if you're a bourbon girl. The Gold Rush is a nice cocktail for Jim Beam Black Label fans. I'm partial to the House Boulevardier."

"Spoken like a regular."

Diana glanced toward the parking area as if she had forgotten where she left her car. "Susan and I used to come here after her trips. She could put away her liquor and it felt like she needed to refuel before going back to the factory grind."

"Jess told me all you talked about was work and travel. Did Susan ever say where she went?"

A server appeared. Diana ordered the Boulevardier. I did, too. When in Rome...

"She never shared specifics. But sometimes she brought me something that gave clues."

Diana unzipped her butt pack. No gun. She placed a small, greenish buddha on the table in front of me.

"It's real jade. I had it appraised one time when I was short on rent money. Worth over a thousand. Thailand."

I studied the trinket. "Who gave you the number?"

"Susan sent me to someone she knew. The guy said she brought stuff to him all the time. 'Hang on to this,' he said, 'and don't show it to anyone until you want to fund your kid's college education.'"

"Any chance these were working vacations, Diana?"

Susan's friend gave me her best confused look. It wasn't convincing. "If they were, I don't know what she would have been doing. She's held production line jobs since high school. Told me she liked the routine."

"And you?" I asked. "What do you do when you're not putting circuit boards together?"

The cocktails arrived. We both took equal pulls.

"Yoga," Diana said it sheepishly. "I know that sounds like a stay-at-home mom thing. It keeps me limber, especially after eight hours of feeding green plastic squares into soldering ovens and waiting for disc drive controllers to come out of the other side."

I stole a glance at her left hand. No recent evidence of a ring on the appropriate finger. "Not married."

Diana's laugh felt a bit more genuine. "No, ma'am. Look at the merchandise. What dreamboat would be interested in this?"

Actually, I thought, a lot of guys would. Especially men who held down boring production line jobs in semi-conductor plants. But I let her have her moment.

"Was it the same with Susan? In the boyfriend department, I mean."

Diana concentrated as if she was trying to pull a memory out of her mind. "I never remember Susan ever mentioning anyone special, male or female. I guess she led a pretty boring private life."

I lifted my drink, glad for another swallow. Diana did, too, copying my moves right down to the amount left in the glass. Identical.

"Actually, Diana, that's why I'm here. Your friend Susan was a lot more interesting than you may have thought. We believe she's an internationally known assassin, who goes by the code name Excalibur. The times she's traveled? She wasn't sight-seeing."

Diana leaned back against the red rubber padding against the wall of the booth and whistled. It was a pretty good whistle. "Are you certain? That's not the woman I roomed with."

"Yes, it was, Diana. And we have reason to believe she faked her own death when the FBI started to get close to her."

Susan's co-worker pressed her palms toward me as if she was pushing what I had just described back toward me.

"That can't be. Susan was nice, but she was the most one-dimensional, private person I ever met."

There was that glance again.

"Are there a lot of car thefts in Portland?" I asked. I had to be sure.

"We have our share. More than Pittsburg. Less than Las Vegas."

"Paloma is off the charts. Thieves love to steal the new Lexuses mom and daddy send with their kids to college. It's easy to get out of town and onto a freeway. By the time we know about the theft, the thing has been repainted with new license plates and VIN numbers to match."

I looked around us. "Where's the girls' room in this place?"

Diana pointed. "To the right of the bar."

I picked up my drink. "One more swallow before I go make some room."

Diana raised hers and clinked it against mine. We drank like we were synchronized swimmers, again leaving equal levels in our glasses.

I released a satisfied "Ahhh," and meant it. "That's good stuff. I'll definitely order another after we finish these."

I grounded the edge of my glass against the top of the tiny napkin coaster and stood. "Hope I don't sneeze or I'll wet my pants."

Diana La Pierre's laugh was genuine this time. I hoped my plan of action would be worth the risk.

The first thing I did when I slipped into the stall was to text Michael Wright.

Alexandra

Michael. If you've landed in Portland, get your ass to the Paydirt bar on NE Pacific St NOW. And unholster that cannon you carry. I may have the delivery you're looking for.

* * *

The Mayflower Rotherhithe - London, UK

"The men behind Jessica Ramirez's death are the most closely guarded people on the planet. The financial resources they control gives them virtually unlimited personal and political power. World leaders tolerate them and seek their favor. No significant event on the planet takes place without their knowledge and approval."

Anastos paused to fortify himself with another dose of Guinness.

"They are known and feared as 'The Triumvirate.' The two most recent initiatives they attempted would have had a detrimental effect on the balance of world power."

Lee parsed the words. "Attempted does not mean achieved."

Anastos agreed. "They failed. These were huge, world-changing incidents. And the common denominator in both situations was your late friend Detective Ramirez. We are certain that The Triumvirate is responsible for her death."

Lee raised a hand. "Hold on, Commander. Go easy with this 'we' conversation. I don't know anything. This sounds like firing-squad stuff for a small fish like me."

Anastos ignored her. "Want to stop the three men who killed Jessica? The same chaps who ordered those thugs to jump you and Zoey just outside of this lovely establishment? The scum who would destroy the lives of millions of innocents without a single regret?"

Lee felt the need for medication. She took a long drink from her pint. "We both enforce the law, Commander. And we both know that when you take out one rabble-rouser, there are ten more who are happy to replace him. We're not extinguishing evil. Who knows? We may be enabling someone much worse."

Anastos wiggled a finger. "Ahh, but we create fear, uncertainty and doubt, the weapons of autocrats... and their worst fear when pointed in their direction."

Anastos leaned forward to emphasize his point. "Movements begin with a single act, perpetrated by one person. What if three men the world believes to be invulnerable turn out to be as mortal as the people The Triumvirate so carelessly dispatches? Paradigms change. The many follow the one. New world orders emerge."

"Ghandi, Kennedy, King." Lee said each name slowly to make sure Anastos knew she understood his point. "They are all dead and the world is still on the edge of oblivion."

Anastos leaned back in his chair and drained the last of his pint. "Ever shot anyone, Liyanna?"

The DI nodded. "Right after I got certified to carry a weapon, I get a call about a shooter at a primary school. We have no second amendment here so American-style mass murder is rare. It was some anarchist from a former Iron Curtain country who wanted to make a political point. He had the headmaster in a choke hold with an AK pointed at the man's skull. I happened to be closest and arrived first. The lunatic turned the AK at me, spouting some dogma gibberish. I double tapped him. One in the chest, one square between the eyes."

The commander frowned. "And how did you feel, DI Evans?"

"Slept like a baby that night. Declined a visit to the department head shrinker. I'd do it again."

Anastos pressed his fingers together in a triangle, staring over the peak at his colleague. "You killed a psycho who might have taken dozens of lives. I'm offering you a mission to take out three men who would kill millions without a second thought."

Lee pondered the notion for a long moment. If she failed, her own death was assured. Even if she succeeded, the victim's associates would come for her if they discovered her identity. This was crazy, just the sort of idea her beloved Alexandra might think up.

Alexandra.

Lee circled her chin with an index finger. "This is Ali's game plan, isn't it?"

The suppressed edge of a smile worked its way up the right side of Tom Anastos' face. "Chapter and verse."

Liyanna Evans pulled the Panko Chicken platter back in front of her and stabbed a significant bite.

"Is she in?"

Anastos nodded.

"So am I. Where and when?"

Chapter Thirty

Paydirt

ALEXANDRA CLARK
"What can you tell me about Susan's features?" I asked, my hands still a little damp from the ineffectiveness of the sanitary hand blower in the restroom.

I pointed to a clump of women seated about twenty feet away and behind her. "Does she look like any of those girls?"

Diana gave the group a cursory glance before shaking her head and turning her attention back to me. It was enough time. "She had darker features. Brown eyes, about three inches shorter than you are. Thinner lips. And never wore make-up."

I nodded in approval. "No make-up. Just my kind of low maintenance morning ritual. I'll drink to that."

I guzzled the rest of the cocktail in the glass before me and waved for our server. "Hey, Diana, you're falling behind. Finish that so we can get another round."

Diana's smile had an edge to it that I didn't like. "Are all cops as smart as you are, Ali?"

She drank. Her eyes never left mine.

"I'm not a cop anymore, Diana. Quit the moment I heard Jessica was dead."

When the server answered my signal, I waved her away. "Sorry, babe. Suddenly, I don't feel so good."

Diana's face paled a bit. She fought it. I continued.

"I think I need to use the restroom again, Diana, but I feel a little unsteady from that beer. Would you help me get there without falling on my face?"

Diana nodded with a slow confidence that was further confirmation of my hypothesis. "Absolutely."

It was perhaps twenty-five feet from our booth to the ladies' room. By the time we got there, Diana La Pierre was barely conscious. I locked the door to the handicapped stall and sat her on the commode. "OK, babe," I said to an unconscious audience. "We're gonna do a little cosplay act. I'm gonna be you and you're gonna be me. Let's see how long it takes for us to switch outfits.

* * *

We weren't twins by any stretch of the imagination. But I hoped the darkness and the baseball cap would buy me something. Our waitress did a double take as I helped Diana out of the restroom and handed her a twenty.

"Sorry to leave so soon. My friend just can't hold her alcohol."

"One drink?" she said. "You're kidding me!"

I guided Diana toward the exit. "Actually, I think it was the peanuts. I'd have them checked before giving them to any other customers."

* * *

We made it to my car without incident. Apparently, these situations were as common in Portland as they are in Paloma. I balanced Diana against the side of the rental, parked at the end of a far row of patrons, away from any human traffic.

"You really need some wardrobe advice, woman," I said to her unseeing eyes. "And if you're going to put something in a cop's drink, remember where she put the glass on the napkin."

I slipped my hand under her chin to steady her head. I had to admit her silhouette and her body in clothing in the moonlight looked damn attractive. I could see what attracted Liyanna Evans to a sexy same-sex-oriented cop during my London escapades.

From somewhere behind me, I heard the distinctive cough of a suppressor, probably ten to fifteen yards away. Diana's neck snapped backwards. An exit wound the size of a golf ball splattered the contents of her skull on my roof.

I ducked below the row of car roofs, looking over my shoulder to see if the shooter was visible. The darkness that saved my life also protected the assailant. I let Diana's body slide to the pavement, said a silent prayer of thanks for the fake ID and credit card I used to reserve the vehicle, and began to search the parking lot with another piece of this ever-expanding puzzle in my grasp.

The Sullivan Home
JESSICA RAMIREZ

Dr. Sebastian laid me out on Lucy's bed. Now that I knew Susan Molinero's connection to Sandra Sullivan's dead daughter, I didn't like the chill that ran down my spine as I thought of a life and death I couldn't remember. On top of my little violent outburst at the bar, it had been quite a day.

Drs. Sullivan and Sebastian sat in a couple of dining-room-style chairs on either side of the bed. The aroma of Assunta's tea was starting to bug me. I wanted another margarita.

"How are you doing, Susan?"

"I feel great. Beating the crap out of those thugs was exhilarating. It was like I was shedding layers of snakeskin. There's definitely a lot more bad juju crammed inside my head, but I feel... lighter? Is that the right way to put it?"

Assunta assented. "Any more memories to report? You seemed to know what to do to erase all the surveillance videos at the bar."

"Yeah. Where the heck did that come from?"

Assunta's voice was calm, almost hypnotic. "There is still a lot we don't know about the brain, Susan. But there is a theory that layers of memory exist in different parts of our heads. Some of it plays back like a video or an audio recording. Some of it is the result of repetition and reflex."

"Am I some kind of martial artist?"

Dr. Sullivan stifled a laugh. "Not that I remember, Susie. You were only here for dinner a couple of times with Lucy. You talked about your wanderlust and how you counted the number of circuit boards you had to process to earn another escape."

I might not know my past, but there were questions my present mind wanted answered. "How did I meet Lucy?"

"You recruited her to work at the factory. You saw her schlepping food at a restaurant and told her she could make better money in the technology sector."

I turned to Assunta. "That's something a good person would do, right, Doc?"

Assunta nodded. "I don't think you're a bad person, my dear."

I avoided digging deeper with Dr. Sebastian. Lucy's mother had my attention. "How long was it between the time we met and the day she died? If it's not too hard for you to talk about."

"If it helps us find out what really happened to my daughter, I'll do anything. It was about six months. Lucy hung out with you almost every night after work. She admired you and tried to act like you. Toward the end, you both morphed into these twin-like daughters of different mothers."

"Did I ever talk about my mother?"

"Not a word. Lucy told me..." Sandra Sullivan swallowed an emotion. "She told me you looked up to me as a mother figure."

I took Sandra's hand and held it as tenderly as I could. It felt strange and unnatural, but I somehow knew how to sell it. "Over the last few months, you've done more than any mother ever could, Dr. Sullivan. I can't thank you enough for saving my life and for giving me a pretty face again."

I stopped short of saying, "giving me MY face again," and didn't know why.

Dr. Sullivan gripped my hand so tightly that my knuckles began to hurt. "I feel as if God gave me a part of Lucy back when you showed up in my life that night." She turned to Assunta. "Is that transference, Assunta?"

Dr. Sebastian smiled. "Textbook. But you are both under psychiatric care at the moment so run with it."

Dr. Sullivan's eyes grew wet. "I can't ask you to call me 'mom.' That wouldn't be fair to whomever your own mother may be. But it would honor me if you called me Sandra."

"Sandra." I returned the strong grasp as I said the word. "Works for me. I'm afraid I must ask you about the events surrounding Lucy's death and my own disappearance. How closely were they linked?"

Sandra pondered that one. "You stopped showing up at work about a week before the accident, Susan. Diana, another of Lucy's friends at the factory thought you had just decided to travel again. She said you had done that a lot before you and Lucy became friends."

I pressed her. "But something was different."

"Yes. Diana said that Susan always gave her supervisor notice when she was going to take a leave of absence. She wanted to remain on good terms so she could get her job back when she came home."

The seed of an idea was forming in a part of my brain that still worked. It made me nauseous. "Do you remember the last conversation you had with your daughter before the accident, Sandra?"

"She was excited about something. She called from the factory to tell me that she had a surprise for me. But she wouldn't elaborate."

Sandra closed her eyes, as if pressing a traumatic memory away from her consciousness. "The next call was from the police. Her car rammed the back of a gasoline truck. Both exploded. The truck driver survived the accident. Lucy didn't."

An image of a fuel tanker, a rental car and a cornfield flashed in my head. My insides felt like a snowball rolling down a steep hill, gaining velocity every second. "And what did the truck driver tell the police?"

"Very little. He said he was at a stop sign about a mile from here and Lucy's car ran into the back of his rig at a very high speed."

"What else did he tell the police, Sandra?"

"That's another strange piece of the story. The poor guy died of a heart attack the next day. He was an independent operator. They found him dead in a motel where transients stay."

I looked at Dr. Sebastian. She wore a strange sort of knowing smile. I recognized the look. She was making her own deductions.

"What do you think about all of this, Assunta?"

"You first," she said.

It was all there, a timeline as clear as a roadmap with the route highlighted in bright red. The thought of my involvement in this trip terrified me.

"Sandra, I think your daughter was picked out of the crowd because of the resemblance. She was groomed to become a look-alike. The police found Lucy's corpse in that apartment. If you can exhume the body, my guess is that you will find your daughter."

The chain of events I described left Sandra Sullivan open mouthed, a look of horror I knew well from some other time and place. Had I just confessed to killing her daughter? It took a moment for her to stutter the next question.

"Then who was in Lucy's car when it burned?"

"We'll never know, Sandra. But I'd bet my life that the person who killed your daughter put someone else in that vehicle and arranged a scenario where there would be no way to identify the body."

Sandra Sullivan looked like the piercing figure in Edvard Munch's classic painting. *Hey! I was remembering stuff! I hated that stupid painting.* We both turned to Dr. Sebastian.

"Your turn," I said. "Am I a cold-blooded killer?"

"I've come to two conclusions, young lady," Assunta said, her arms crossed and confidence radiating from her being. "Number one: I think events happened exactly as you described them." She gave Sandra an empathetic look. "I'm sorry, Sandra. I believe your Lucy was murdered."

"And number two?" I said.

"You're not Susan Molinero, dear. That's certain. And whoever you are... you're a cop."

Chapter Thirty-One

Paydirt

The fresh Covid mask was black, plucked from a bamboo bowl in a church narthex nearby. When combined with the hoodie, the figure looked monastic, one with the shadows accentuated by the flickering lights in the parking lot.

Excalibur stood parallel to the tree which protected her from discovery yet gave her a perfect view of the two females exiting Paydirt. The evening breeze that often materialized as the cool of the air interacted with the warmth of the earth caused the leaves to undulate in a gentle wave.

Standing her target up against the vehicle, carefully parked out of the view of the security cameras was a nice touch. Totally Diana.

Her friend had earned entry into Excalibur's inner circle after she disposed of the turncoat with heat and flame in Lucy's car.

And yet, the assassin was still cautious. Another crack in her anonymity emerged. An enemy somehow followed her here and had to be dispatched.

She waited until she was certain her movements would remain

unseen, allowing the breeze to embrace the small postage stamp of skin that was not covered in black. She paced the twenty steps to the white vehicle, its roof splattered with a parabola of brain matter.

The body lay face down. A pool of blood slowly expanded, filled by tributaries in the folds of the leather jacket, emanating from an ugly hole in the back of the woman's skull.

Too bad about the jacket, Excalibur thought. She liked the woman's sense of style.

The assassin retrieved a serrated hunting knife from the pocket of her hoodie. A gloved hand grabbed a lifeless arm to flip the body on its back. Perhaps a pound of flesh from a breast would be appropriate to send to the cop's chief back in Illinois. She heard he was partial to submissive women.

Something was wrong with the face.

Excalibur placed the Covert SRS-A2 sniper rifle on the pavement and retrieved a tiny LED flashlight to illuminate the face.

It was Diana La Pierre.

"Losing your touch, Susan?"

Excalibur spun around, extending the knife toward what her ears told her might be the person's neck. A powerful heel knocked the wind out of her, pressing her back against the white car, parallel to Diana's lifeless corpse.

"This is for Jessica."

The back spin kick caught Excalibur squarely on the right temple. But she anticipated the move and relaxed so she could absorb the G-forces. She let her body cartwheel, retrieving a pistol with one hand as the other executed the gymnastics.

Her attacker dived behind the car ahead of the line of mushrooming lead slugs that followed.

Excalibur calmly side stepped in pursuit. She wasn't worried about stealth or silence. Survival was the singular goal. She fired at anything that moved.

* * *

The Sullivan Home

JESSICA RAMIREZ

So, I was a cop. That explained a lot. I wished I could remember who had taught me the martial arts stuff. I wanted to kiss them.

Horror remained plastered on Sandra Sullivan's face.

"Sandra?" Assunta's expression morphed from confidence to concern. "Sandra? Are you all right?"

Sandra Sullivan began to shake. She stood, leaning back against the dresser, the vibrations convulsing its contents like an earthquake. Her friend, the psychiatrist moved quickly to her side, her hands guiding the surgeon's face to look her in the eye.

"Oh my God, Assunta," Sandra gasped. "What have I done?"

She seemed to look through and beyond her friend. Assunta shook Sandra's face repeating her name. "Sandra. Sandra, look at me. What is it? What have you done?"

Sandra pointed an unsteady finger at me, grabbing one of the pictures of Susan and Lucy from the top of the dresser, knocking the contents of a small jewelry box to the floor. She shook the frame at her colleague. "I gave this innocent woman the face of a killer."

* * *

Paydirt

ALEXANDRA CLARK

I counted thirteen shots before the mag feeding bullets into Excalibur's pistol emptied. I heard the slide lock in anticipation of fresh ammunition. This bitch seemed to have everything in the belly pocket of that hoodie. But it would take her at least three seconds to reload or pick a new toy.

I ran at her, tackling X mid-torso to control her arms. We landed on something cool and damp. The aroma said grass.

171

The veins in her neck bulged. That's when I saw the tiny mark on the left side. The laceration was familiar. My imagination painted her hair black and poured her body into some leather.

"Katrerina Reid."

"Bravo, Alexandra,"Excalibur snarled. "I thought DeSalvo's psychosis was higher functioning. And I have a voyeur's taste for watching my victims die, even when the work is contracted to others. Engaging him was a rare mistake."

I replayed the scene on Dennis street in my head. The CPR. The defibrillator. The ride to the hospital. Behind the black makeup, this woman was the gothic cosplay."

"I saved your life."

"At least you won't have to live to regret it," Excalibur hissed, thrusting a shoulder to try for a wrestling reversal. She was messing with a high school girls' state champ.

"Time takes its toll, Susan. Everyone eventually makes one mistake too many. Your three bosses will soon find that out."

Excalibur struggled under me. I wasn't about to let her go. "Murder becomes a mindless job after a while Clark. But killing you will be something I will savor."

I head-butted her to calm her down. "You had better pray that Jessica is still alive out there, Susan, or this ex-cop will make you wish you had never considered the profession."

I could feel her anger building. "I was planning an exit before our encounter, Clark. But now I think I'll hang around until I can watch you bleed to death while I rip your eyes out."

Excalibur turned out to be stronger than I expected. She snaked an arm from my grip and shot an uppercut that caught me square under the jaw.

That hurts.

I heard a single gunshot and a voice I knew well shout, "Everybody freeze."

X's punch got the job done. Involuntary reflex loosened my bear hug enough for Susan to execute the reversal. But instead of pressing her advantage on top of me, she kept rolling away on the grass. She pulled her knees to her chest and pitched her legs upward in a Gene Kelly move from the beginning of Singin' in the Rain. X was on her feet a second later sprinting into the shadows.

I shook the sting out of my jaw and tried to sit up. I got as far as my elbows when I felt the hot muzzle of a pistol against my forehead.

A cell phone flashlight blinded me, and the voice said, "I thought you had her, Gates."

I deflected the glare enough to make out the face. "Where were you five minutes ago, Michael? And why didn't you shoot the bitch?"

Michael Wright ignored my questions, holstered his weapon, killed the light, and nodded toward my rental car.

"Diana La Pierre?"

"One of Susan's minions. X thought she was me and put one between the eyes."

Michael scanned the yoga suit that was a tad too small for me.

"Nobody would think a woman in that thing you have on was Alexandra Clark."

"Yeah, I'm pretty smart. But not smart enough to kill Excalibur when I had her in my arms."

Michael held out a hand and pulled me to my feet. "Get a good look at her?"

"Burned into my brain, Agent Wright. Next time I'll shoot first, like you should have."

I felt a little unsteady from the punch. It must have showed. Michael snaked an arm around my waist, guiding me toward his vehicle. I didn't normally appreciate the male intimacy. But tonight, the proximity of strength renewed my own.

Michael gave the late Diana La Pierre's body a quick inspection.

"Wow. Nice shot. You could draw a perfect triangle from her

eyes up to her forehead. Is that the murder weapon on the pavement next to the body?"

"Yes, Michael. It's a Covert SRS-A2. Let's not inspect the crime scene. I want to get outta here before the Gendarmes arrive and start asking uncomfortable questions."

I was regaining my sea legs. Michael felt it and released his hold on me.

"Sorry about the public display of affection, Gates. I was afraid if you crossed swords with X, I would be putting you in a body bag. Still think Jess is alive?"

False bravado is my favorite defense mechanism. I needed Michael to believe the fear I felt wasn't a thing. I thumped his bicep. "Jess is probably standing by your car waiting to slap you for taking liberties with a lesbian."

"Oooh." Michael skipped a step like a kid who just found a Playboy magazine in his brother's sock drawer. "Liberties with a lesbian sounds like fun."

I shook my head and sighed. "We gotta find your woman, Michael. Celibacy is adversely affecting your judgment."

Our favorite FBI agent held open the passenger door of an SUV the size of Kansas for me. "I love it when you use big words, Gates. Vocabulary is the new sexy."

I buckled up. "Since when is 'celibacy' a big word? I'm so glad I'm not in love with a man."

He patted the spot behind his sport coat where the Beretta lay, probably still warm from its exercise. "Do you think we've seen the last of Excalibur for a while?"

"Not a chance. She wants to rip out my eyes and watch me bleed to death. Clichés like that are so yesterday."

"Watch your back, Alexandra. She's very dangerous when cornered."

"So am I. Can we please leave now?"

Michael Wright put his hands at the ten and two positions on the steering wheel, just like drivers ed class. "Yes, ma'am. Hospitals first?"

"I have a list in my GPS app. Are you a male who is capable of following directions?"

Jess's fiancé revved the engine and dropped the tranny into drive. "You say where, and we're halfway there. But can we do this in the morning? We'll both be better for eight hours of sleep."

He was right. With the adrenaline leaving my body, I suddenly felt exhausted. If Jess was out there, she deserved me at my best.

"Know a good hotel?"

Michael held up a reservation slip. "The best. Two queens in my room. Want one of em?"

"Think about what you just said, hetero-boy. And I'll pay for my own room, thank you very much."

"Why spend the money, Gates? I promise to keep my distance. I'm harmless."

"Not according to Jessica. She says you fart in your sleep."

Chapter Thirty-Two

The Sullivan Home

JESSICA RAMIREZ

I was suddenly invisible; a move I realized was Assunta's doing. She needed to get Sandra away from me. The two friends retreated to the back porch. I listened to the hushed intensity in the shadow of the screen door for a few minutes before deciding to return to Lucy's bedroom to focus these deductive cop skills I supposedly had on my own predicament.

The framed picture of Lucy and Susan lay askew on the bed. At the edge of the dresser, Lucy's jewelry box balanced on end, a yawning rectangular cedar enclosure with the words, Seattle – Space Needle, wood-burned into the top.

The contents vomited down the side of the dresser, a fairytale pathway of carnival trinkets left as clues for rescuers to follow in search of children lured to some witch's gingerbread house.

I sat on the hardwood floor trying to imagine the meaning of each tiny item in the life story of a young woman, seduced into becoming a substitute corpse for a killer.

A cheap compass you might find in a popcorn box spun around in the center of my palm, ultimately pointing its accusatory black positive pole directly at me. Several plastic cowboys of varying colors seemed to sync with the western vibe of Sandra's place and the horse barn I knew held equine transportation behind the farmhouse. A single baseball card, featuring a team photo of the Chicago Cubs' 2016 World Championship team lay face down, the statistical side autographed with the words, "We are the Champions... To LS from SM." It didn't take much police sense to deduce that it was a gift from Susan to Lucy.

I would have missed it, if not for the moon. I was about to give up the search when the Earth's only satellite peeked around the edge of the windowsill.

Full moons bothered me every month since my Portland incarnation and I didn't know why. Assunta said it might have to do with bad memories of things that happened during full moons in my unremembered past. Voices I couldn't identify kept whispering, "It's going to be a long night," and "The crazies are on the loose," whenever the white ball was in its most perfect circle.

Tonight, a synchronous celestial laser beam reflected off something on the floor. It lay below a door hinge with loose screws that could benefit from a Phillips screwdriver. The bright rays painted the back of my hand as I lifted a palm to shield my eyes for a better view.

I crawled toward it on all fours, like an infant mesmerized by some glitter that glowed in the dark. It took a fingernail and some perseverance to free the thing from the bottom of the door.

My body blacked out the light, but I could tell I had found a ring. Closing my fist around it, I stood and walked to the chair Sandra had set on the right side of the bed near the window. The full moon radiated shafts of light powerful enough to give me a solid view.

The ring was beautiful. Two smaller diamonds shouldered against one huge rock, held in place by four sturdy gold claws. The piece was thicker than the anorexic engagement bands I was somehow aware of. Wide enough for an inscription on the inside. I strained to read the cursive.

"Yours Always," was inscribed with a pair of two letter combinations pressed so close together as to be almost illegible. The fishhook of the letter "J" was topped by the half circle and outward leg of an "R" followed by a plus sign and then the letters "M" and W" as one logo-esque combination.

JR + MW.

I found myself sliding the beautiful thing onto my left ring finger. The fit was perfect.

From somewhere in a dream, I perceived the hum of jet engines, could smell the sweetness of white wine, and heard a deep male voice. "How about it, Jess? Got the *cujones* to risk it all for love?"

I felt my lips mouth the words in response, my voice strong, seductive, and almost sassy. "I'm still a little uncertain, Michael. You've got seven hours and forty-seven minutes to convince me."

Then I saw the apartment explode. The assassin's gun pointing at my forehead in a private jet bound for Portland, Oregon, my elbow move that pressed the weapon toward the opposite window as he fired, massive depressurization that followed and the view of flames licking the engine cowlings. I saw my own hands set an aircraft transponder to 5537 before jumping into the darkness missing the orange eruptions of instant death on the wing by less than a foot. The image dissolved and I felt leather straps restraining me while a man with a Russian accent exhaled an unpleasant spicy breath inches from my face. Another whisp and I saw the man turn into flames in a dark tunnel. Then the waters of a gargantuan river enveloped me as two powerful female fists tried to choke me to death. I felt my own hands smashing her head against a rock, the sound of a high-powered rifle's report above me and a body falling from some high place in the darkness of a deep canyon. The Grand Canyon. All these things came at once, in a single tornadic whirlwind, fading away almost as quickly as they appeared, leaving the sound of a cellphone message repeating in my ear.

My father's last words.

"I hope in your heart you know how proud I am of you and how much I love you. And I hope that someday you can forgive me for my sins."

Tears suppressed in a hundred moments of trauma began to flow. I no longer wanted to stop them.

I tried to stand, suddenly feeling trapped inside a strange body that was slowly, excruciatingly revealing itself to me. Dizzy and nauseous, I fell to the bed weeping. My voice was that of a little girl speaking a language I suddenly knew by heart.

"Papi! Papi! Te echo de menos. Te quiero. Te necesito. Te amo."

I didn't bother to dry the tears. Compartmentalization was bad. It could explode at the wrong moments. That was the lesson I learned when I lost control with three thugs at the bar. Assunta turned to me when she and Sandra heard the squeak of the screen door. She saw the wetness of my face and the redness of my eyes accentuated by the full moon.

"What is it, dear? What has happened?"

The command voice I heard was familiar, dramatically different from the partial person who inhabited my body for the past excruciating months. "My name is Detective Jessica Ramirez, Dr. Sebastian. I live and work in Paloma, Illinois and I know how we can capture the woman who killed Dr. Sullivan's daughter."

Sandra Sullivan caught her breath. "Jessica Ramirez. Thank God!" She stood to embrace me, but I stopped her.

"I need to make a phone call."

I felt Assunta's hand on my shoulder. "Give your mind a rest,

Jessica. You've had one very busy day. Let's bring you back to life in the morning."

"There are people out there who must think I'm dead, Assunta. How am I supposed to sleep?"

The shrink produced a pill from her pocket. "Trust me, Detective. You'll be better equipped to shake up the world tomorrow."

Chapter Thirty-Three

Saint Serenity Hospital - Portland - The Next Afternoon

ALEXANDRA CLARK
Michael's immense SUV rolled to a stop in the hospital parking lot.

"My turn," he said, jumping out the door and jogging toward the ER entrance. "Let me know if I miss anything while I'm gone."

I held up my phone. "I'm just about to become a 'three-star-island' on *Animal Crossing*. If you get back fast enough, you might meet KK Slider."

"I don't know what you just said, Ali. One more hospital after this?"

"Portland Research Hospital," I answered. "And my turn."

He disappeared between the Star Trek swish of the emergency room doors.

I felt the vibration. I didn't recognize the number. But the text took my breath away.

5537 - Call me back.

* * *

The Sullivan Home - Portland
JESSICA RAMIREZ

"This is Detective Jessica Ramirez."

Hearing myself say that when I connected to the phone number I knew best felt great. The world was still a hellish catastrophe. My life was more complicated than ever. And with the face of a killer, both my friends and enemies would shoot first and likely never ask questions.

The voice I prayed I would hear again spoke. "5537."

"5537," I repeated. "Pretty damn smart for someone trying to jump out of a burning airplane before it turned everything in it into unrecognizable charcoal."

Her voice had the same sarcastic lilt. But there was something else hidden in its timbre. Alexandra Clark was damn glad to hear me. "Jessica Ramirez, where in God's holy name have you been? We buried you. Your family is devastated. Hell, I was devastated."

I turned to the mirror that now hung over Lucy Sullivan's dresser and stuck out my tongue at Susan Molinero's reflection. "You're not gonna like what you see, partner. Three dirt bags got the jump on me and took away my memory and my face. A kind surgeon got a little confused when she put me back together again."

I could hear Ali's excitement growing. "You spoke to me in the bathroom mirror, Jess. You pointed me to the transponder code to tell me you were alive. Nobody believed me. Everyone in the world thinks you are dead."

I laughed. It was a laugh I remembered and liked. "The bathroom mirror? I hope you were decent."

"I looked like crap. Liyanna and I had a huge fight. I was a broken-hearted, tearstained wimp."

"Did you two break up?"

"No, thank God. That woman has the patience of Job. And you

know what I think about religion. I'm in Portland. Where are you and how do I get to you?"

"I'm at a farmhouse about ten miles west of town, Ali. Michael didn't know X had a ringer in the cockpit of the jet. The boy did his best to put me out of my misery, killed the pilot and damn near killed me. But I got out. I knew the world would think I was cremated in the crash and was trying to think of an advantage when three punks got the better of me."

Ali wasn't having any of this cell convo stuff. "Not on the phone, Jess. Where can we meet? I want to... I need to see you."

"That's the worst of it, girlfriend. You won't like what you see. Pick a place and I'll meet you. Come alone. And promise me... Please promise me you won't kill anybody, and I mean anybody you see walk through that door."

The silence was longer than it should have been. "OK, Jess. There's a bar near here. I'll text the address to you and be in some corner booth where I can see all the patrons."

"Once a cop, always a cop," I said.

Ali's voice shook. That was a new experience. "That's my news, partner. I quit. And there's more... Excalibur is in Portland. We shared an intimate moment at a bar last night and I found out how dangerous your middle school friend truly is. Michael and I were checking out the hospitals for dead people who looked like you when you pinged me."

"Michael Wright?"

"You'll be glad to hear Mr. Wonderful has not jumped into bed with anybody since you died. I guess that's a good sign."

That one grabbed me. I reflexively touched the ring on my finger. "I can't see him yet, Ali. Wave him off for now. It has to be just us. Send me a text and I'll be there in thirty minutes. And I repeat. Don't shoot anybody, no matter who you think they are."

* * *

Saint Serenity Hospital
ALEXANDRA CLARK

Michael rolled his eyes when he emerged from the trauma center. "Nobody wants to take responsibility for anything anymore. And my shield didn't buy me any help. We have to wait twenty minutes for the hospital CEO to return from a late lunch."

I tried not to let my excitement show. "So, what do we do? Just hang here?"

Michael pointed to an empty parking space with a tow-away zone sign in front of it. "That's the dude's spot. Best to do the stake-out thing and catch him when he gets out of his vehicle. These guys like to hide from people like me."

I tried scorn. "So, I just sit on my ass in this SUV while you sweat a couple of bureaucrats? It's past lunchtime and I'm getting hungry."

Michael thought for a moment. Men can be so slow to figure out solutions. "I guess you could slip into the cafeteria and grab something."

"Hospital food? Are you nuts? I'd rather grab an Uber. Tell you what. Text me when you're done, and you can pick me up then." I switched from livid to smart-ass. "We wouldn't want to miss nabbing our person of interest before he hides behind an admin."

Michael frowned. "Excalibur is out there, Ali. And she's not very happy with you."

I hugged the lug, lifting the Beretta from its shoulder holster without drawing his attention.

"Excalibur is not going to expect me to take an Uber to some Denny's. Relax Agent Wright." I popped the door open. "Text me when you've finished your interrogation."

* * *

At the far end of the lot, Susan Molinero sat behind the wheel of a stolen Mazda Miata, carefully parked in one of the few spots the security cameras didn't cover. She watched her prey bound from the SUV. The woman skipped toward the emergency entrance like a teenager on the last day of class.

The two were partnering, probably looking for information on Detective Ramirez.

Alexandra Clark would get hers in time. The woman called Excalibur decided to wait and watch.

She thought about how much she shared with Ramirez and Clark. A honed ability to seek out her targets. The rigors of staying sharp, physically, and mentally. Skill with weapons. And a sense for things that were out of place.

The blue Crown Vic Police Interceptor with fresh "Security" decals on the front doors didn't fit the fleet of pristine Chevrolet SUVs branded with the hospital's name. The aging Ford also didn't sweep the parking lot the way the other security vehicles did.

The driver pulled in front of the Miata, blocking Susan's exit. She sized the enormous man up as he sauntered toward her, popping open the trunk as he circled his vehicle.

He was dressed in jeans with a light blue uniform shirt a size too small for his wrestler's body. The badge over his left breast pocket tilted on an angle, devoid of any markings. The only thing brand new on his person was the Sig Sauer P365 XL that tilted forward in a Kydex holster on his waist.

Susan stepped out of the claustrophobic interior of the tiny vehicle to face him, centered behind his ride so she could inspect the trunk. The tie wraps and duct tape inside might come in handy later, she thought.

"Everything OK, ma'am?" The voice had an Albanian accent. Susan prided herself on parsing that type of detail and began to flip through her mental card catalog of clients and victims, looking for a match.

"You're new here, aren't you?" she said. "I'm Sally McAuliffe from accounting. I eat my lunch in this spot every day. What's your name, my friend?"

The man fumbled for an answer. "Darrel. Just started this week. Still waiting for them to order my vehicle." He pointed to the Crown Vic. "So I have to work with this thing until then."

"Nice to meet you, Darrel. Recently arrived from Tirana or is your family from a suburb?"

She saw the right hand rest on the Sig, the back fingers wrapping around the gun butt as he spoke. "Prush. Just east of Tirana. How do you know Albania?"

The man made his move. But Susan was ahead of him. Her suppressed semi-auto put a single slug into his forehead. As Darrel started to go down, she guided his body toward the trunk. The big man's torso crumpled inside. Susan shoved his legs in after it and shut the lid.

As she hopped into the driver's seat to move the car to another secluded space, she noticed the print-out on the passenger seat.

A familiar face was attached to a lithe body in the process of beating some unlucky man senseless. Below the pristine phone camera photo, was her name. At the top, a long list of email addresses.

Susan Molinero folded the paper and slid it into a pants pocket. Her mental card catalogue dispensed a name and a place. Prush, Albania, one year earlier. The politician she whacked must have had some powerful friends.

How many more killers were headed her way?

Chapter Thirty-Four

Bantam Tavern - 922 NW 21st Ave, Portland

JESSICA RAMIREZ

Cops can tell a lot about a person based on the car they drive. The shabbier the vehicle, the more likely the driver has a record. I know that's the kind of generalization that make people judge police officers in a negative light. But ride with me for a shift and I'll prove it's true.

The exterior of Assunta's Toyota Corolla carried tiny battle scars from a dozen encounters with carelessly opened doors in tight parking spaces. Otherwise, the vehicle was in excellent condition. Colorful peacenik memes, politically slanted in the direction of 1960s idealism covered every inch of the back bumper. The interior oozed the aroma of the cinnamon scent squares they hand out at car washes. The back seat held two eighty-pound bags of mulch, a plastic bottle of liquid tomato fertilizer and a new shovel. My shrink obviously de-stressed in the garden.

With Sandra's cell phone in my pocket and Michael's ring on my finger, I pulled into the lot at *The Bantam*, a tavern at 922 NW

21st Avenue where Ali would see my face for the first time in months. Even though my former partner was no longer a sworn officer, I knew she would be armed. I prayed Ali listened to my admonitions and would ask first and shoot later.

* * *

My appearance in the doorway triggered her. She was exactly where she said she would be; a corner booth with a good view of the lay of the land. She gripped the edge of the linoleum like a vice when she recognized the face. I could see her right hand vibrating as she willed it not to go for her weapon.

I scrunched my lips into a kiss and itched my nose with the middle finger of my left hand, mouthing the words, "fuck you," our universal greeting in public places.

For an uncomfortable moment, I thought she might not be buying it. I kept my mitts where she could see them and drifted to the table. Ali edged out of the booth to give herself room to move. She studied every centimeter of my new look as she faced me down.

"5537," I said. "Where's Mr. Wonderful?"

"What's your favorite song?" Ali asked.

"Don't Let Me Be Misunderstood. Santa Esmerelda."

"When was Maria born?"

"March 24, 1990. But you don't know that."

"Who was my first and only boyfriend?"

"Jimmy L'Etoile. Third grade. Can we sit down, Alexandra? You're drawing attention."

"What's my favorite beer?"

I rubbed the cheek that didn't look a bit like my own. "Pilsner Urquell. Why are you drinking Labatts?"

"Canada's closer here than it is in Paloma." My partner brushed my right carotid artery with a pair of fingers. "X has a scar there."

"And I don't. Can we sit?"

Ali's heart pumped blood to the capillaries in her face. She was as red as a July sunburn.

"I buried you, Jessica. Michael, Commander Anastos, Tio Danny, Joey Price, Maria and I were your pallbearers. I threw the first dirt on your casket and vowed to kill Excalibur with my bare hands."

"And you still haven't? What happened, partner? I'm dead for a few months and you lose your edge?"

There was another uncomfortable moment of silence as we both processed the reality of existence. Cops don't do that very well. When we let emotion erupt it's usually not pretty.

Ali threw her arms around me and buried her face in my neck. I could feel her chest heaving with the sobs. "God dammit, Jessica. I thought I had lost you."

In every stressful situation, one person must keep it together. The old Jess could have done it. The new Jess failed.

My own tears flowed. I hugged her back, still finding it hard to believe she was real. "I'm so sorry, Ali. I've been lost in a maze without a past, without a name, trying to figure out who I was and what the hell happened."

I wrapped my left arm around her neck so she could see the ring. "Michael's damn diamond brought it all back. This guy is supposed to be my soul mate, the love of my life. And the only person I wanted to talk to was you."

Ali pulled back so our tearstained eyes could focus . "If you die on me again, douche bag, I'm gonna spit on your grave."

"If I die again, it's gonna be because you screwed something up. Did you order me a margarita?"

Ali's eyes narrowed. "Excalibur is walking dead. And I'm gonna kill those three zillionaires, too."

I nodded to the table. "I admire a woman with goals. Can we please sit down? This isn't a gay bar and we'll be explaining things to some good ole boys if we don't quell the drama."

A switch flipped and the Ali I knew came roaring back into the moment. She punched me in the shoulder and slid back into the booth. "Jimmy L'Etoile. How did you remember that name?"

I laughed. "A name like that gets you beat up in the school yard. Did he survive puberty?"

"He's a Chicago cop. Badass as they come. All American offensive lineman in college. My hetero girlfriends up in The Windy say he's a dreamboat. Half Mexican, too. Were you aware of that?"

I whistled. "I was not. Maybe I'm engaged to the wrong guy."

Ali dropped Jimmy like a stone and was back in the present. "Speaking of, we've only got about twenty minutes max until your Mr. Wonderful shows up and I have a lot to tell you."

* * *

Saint Serenity Hospital

Henry Morris, CEO of Legacy Health rose from the front seat of his Jaguar to face the imposing figure of Agent Michael Wright, Federal Bureau of Investigation.

"May I invite you to my office, Agent Wright? I'm sure my staff can assist me in answering any questions you may have, assuming you have the proper warrants."

Michael felt the anger radiate down his neck, pumping blood to his vital organs to prepare for a confrontation. He fought the urge, presenting as friendly a smile as an FBI agent could summon. "This isn't official business, Mr. Morris. Just a missing person investigation. A cold case from a few months back. I was hoping someone on your medical staff might remember a Latina police officer from Illinois, presenting with injuries."

Morris squinted. "We handle a lot of traumas here, Agent Wright. I would have to look at the admitting logs. Do you have a name for me?"

"Jessica Mary Ramirez. Five-foot-seven, one-twenty-five, dark features, brown hair, and brown eyes. But she might have arrived without identification."

Michael could see Morris's memory grab something. "There was a woman. I remember the incident because she was a Jane Doe. Unresponsive and badly beaten. They say she had amnesia and needed facial reconstruction."

Jessica's fiancé fought to keep his reaction professional. "That could be the one. She's been missing from her home jurisdiction and the last information we had was that she might be in Portland."

Michael saw Morris relax. This had nothing to do with whatever he was really trying to hide. "She wasn't brought to our shop; I can confirm that with confidence. She was admitted to OUHS by the surgeon who found her. Pretty darn lucky. I hear it was Dr. Sandra Sullivan. If someone had destroyed my face, she's the one I would want to fix it."

The information hit Michael like a body blow. "Her face?"

"No next of kin but she had plenty of ID," Morris said, shutting the car door and consulting his watch. "Sandra put her back together. But I hear she's still under a psychiatrist's care."

"What for?" Michael asked, the answer already gelling in his mind.

"Dissociative Amnesia," Henry Morris said, turning away from Michael and walking toward the building. "She can't remember who she is or anything about her past. They hope it's not permanent."

* * *

Bantam Tavern

JESSICA RAMIREZ

Ali briefed me with her usual machine-gun efficiency. About the aftermath of the plane crash, her argument with Chief O'Brien, her encounter with Susan and the plan she had formulated to exact retribution against the three people responsible for my assumed demise.

"Michael doesn't know it, but I'm headed to London. Lee and Commander Anastos will meet me there and 'Operation Triple-Header' will commence."

"And you are going to singlehandedly dispatch the three most protected men on the planet?"

Alexandra's eyes narrowed. The dangerous grin I knew well pressed her cheeks into dimples.

"Look, partner. The FBI may know what Excalibur looks like, but I'm betting the rest of the world doesn't. I'm going to have Anastos circulate my picture to Interpol just before I meet these three little pigs, with Susan's name right below it. If their security is as good as it should be, they will have all the gun toting macho men on their boat memorize every zit on my face."

"Every cop and killer on the planet will be looking for you Alexandra."

"Yeah." Ali said the word as if I had just offered up her favorite dessert. "For twenty-four hours, I'll be more popular than a Kardashian. Just long enough to get on that boat, get paid and take out The Triumvirate."

I flicked her nose with a finger. "Do you have any idea what the odds are that you'll be killed before you even get near that damn boat?"

"As long as there is a one at the end of that last number, I'm on board. Motive and opportunity will be the easy part. Commander Anastos' job is to furnish a method."

"You can't let it go, can you, Ali. I've been alive in your mind for less than an hour and you're risking your own on the micro chance you can get some revenge."

"When have the odds ever stopped us, Jessica? And anyway... If I get blown up in the process, it will make one hell of a movie script. Do me a favor and get Spielberg to direct it."

"All these false identities, and a single-combat attack on a well defended boat without backup. This has to be the most ill conceived and ridiculous plan you have ever created, Alexandra Clark."

Ali's grin deepened. "You're in, aren't you, Jess!"

"Yeah, I'm in" I grabbed a piece of my cheek. "While you're killing three boys, I'm going to take down the bitch who gave me this ugly mug. Can't have you upstaging me or the books they will write about us will have your name above mine."

Ali took my defiled face in her hands and kissed me. It was long and tender and drew the uncomfortable attention of every conservative in the bar who feared their daughters might grow up to be bisexual.

When she broke the kiss, she whispered, "That thing you said at your house about marrying me if you weren't head over heels for boys? I would say yes."

"We'd be divorced in two months. I'm a bitch to live with."

Ali nodded in acquiescence. "That makes two of us. I don't know how Liyanna could ever do it if we got that far."

Ali slipped me her cell phone and Michael's Beretta under the table. "Take these, partner. Andy gave me a burner phone for overseas and if Excalibur has figured out how to track my GPS, she might as well be following you instead of deciding whether or not to chase me across the pond. I've already ordered an Uber. We should pay our tab and split."

It all seemed so fast. Our reunion, and now another parting. I longed for my Tahoe squad car, my partner and something less stressful... like a bank robbery... with hostages.

Ali looked at her iWatch. "OK, Jess. I'm gonna use tonight's airline tickets and get outta here. You'll have to deal with your boyfriend alone. Can you handle it?"

I wasn't sure if I could. "We'll find out in about ten minutes, partner."

Ali dropped cash on the table, and we moved toward the exit.

We opened the door. A tall man in a trench coat, out of place in the warmth of the evening, slammed against my shoulder as he entered the establishment. Ali was too focused for her radar to catch it. But mine did.

"Dammit," I muttered.

Ali frowned. "What is it?"

"Something's about to go down in there."

"And we are two civilians trying to bag an assassin and three of the world's most dangerous men. Let it go, Jessica."

The Ford Explorer with an Uber light on the dash chose that moment to arrive. Ali jumped into the back without so much as a final handshake. "Take care of Michael, Jess. This whole thing has been hard on him."

I watched the red taillights recede down Washington Avenue in the afternoon sun and heard a shotgun blast inside the bar.

Every fiber of my being wanted to engage. "Discipline, Detective Ramirez, "I said, tapping an address a block away from the bar into Ali's cell phone. I signed off with:

I'm ready. Michael. Come rescue me.

I fingered the Beretta, fighting the urge to go back inside where the action was. An idea popped into my head. It wasn't nearly as elegant or detailed as the extermination plan Alexandra outlined. But it was fair to good and didn't involve discharging a firearm.

There is always a getaway car. This one was just like what I described earlier; beat up and in need of some serious maintenance. I grabbed the tomato fertilizer and shovel from the back seat of Assunta's vehicle, slipped behind the rider's side of the idling vehicle and poured 36 ounces of liquid morganite into the dirt bag's gas tank.

Then I stood by the entrance to The Bantam and waited in a batter's stance with the shovel, anticipating a fast ball across the center of home plate. I gave it my best Harry Carey voice.

"It's a beautiful afternoon for baseball here at Chicago's storied Wrigley Field and an historic moment as Jessica Ramirez becomes the first ever female to face a major league pitcher in a Cubs'

uniform. Ramirez is a true Cinderella story. No minor league experience, just youth baseball. And now the Latina police officer from Paloma, Illinois is going up against one of the dirtiest hurlers in the National League... Ramirez's stance is picture perfect. The lefty holds the bat high and wide. I'm not sure this piece of pine is quite a regulation model, friends. Looks more like a shovel bought at some hardware store... But I'm told she can hit a tennis ball over the roof of the Mitchell's house with a whiffle bat, so either way, we're in for one heck of a show... She awaits the pitch with a concentration I've rarely seen in all my years of calling the game... Single combat between two motivated adversaries with one thing on their minds... defeating the enemy."

When the perp in the trench coat exited, I swung for the fence. The numb nuts never knew what hit him.

"Holy Cow! She's done it. Ladies and gentlemen, Elvis has left the building."

I retrieved the perp's shotgun, pointing it at his chauffeur.

"Beat it, scum bucket. The cops are on their way."

It felt so good to watch the car gag to a stop less than a block from the scene of the crime and see the low life behind the wheel bail and run.

When I heard Mr. Trench Coat moan, I whacked him in the melon with the butt of the shotgun to put him back to sleep until the good guys arrived. I wiped my prints off the weapon, sliding it through the door and across the tile floor of *The Bantam.*

I skipped away from the scene and happily in the direction of scaring the pants off of my boyfriend.

Chapter Thirty-Five

Corner of NW Northrup and 21ˢᵗ Avenue – Portland

JESSICA RAMIREZ

It is said that men size their motorized toys in inverse proportion to the extent of their reproductive parts. I can attest that in Michael Wright's case this is not true.

The massive SUV pulled up to the corner of NW Northrup and 21st Avenue, slid into a loading zone and waited. I swatted a wandering hand away from my thigh as I stood among the homeless at the entrance to Jerry's Domicile, Portland's downtown homeless shelter. The afternoon was getting on and the patrons were gathering to swap stories ahead of a final few hours of panhandling before the place closed its doors for the evening.

People avert their gazes from the homeless. It's not right but it's the way of the world. I could hide in plain sight in their midst. No sense giving myself away until I had prepared Michael for the shock.

I palmed Ali's cell and sent him a text.

What's one thing only you and Jess would know? Tell me in a single word.

"Necklace" came back.

Please don't shoot the woman who approaches you. Just say the word. Listen to her answer and then decide what to do.

"Quit the games, Alexandra. I have news."

It was time.

* * *

He couldn't see my head until I had jumped in the passenger seat and shut the door.

"You have a word for me, cowboy," I said, fully exposing my face to a pair of sexy, stunned eyes.

"Necklace."

"Juliette," I answered, producing the name of Michael's sister, in whose honor the beautiful star-shaped Down syndrome necklace with that damn GPS tracker was created. It saved my life in Moscow, but I was still angry with Michael for not telling me about it until well after the fact. I imagined my mother and sister fighting over who got to wear it now that I was dead.

"Dr. Sullivan did one hell of a job," he said, slowly, sadly shaking his head. "I sure hope you have enough flabby skin left so she can fix it."

Why do men always say the wrong things? "Flabby skin? When have I ever had flabby skin?"

"Your neck," he said, tweaking the erogenous zone above the edge of my collar bone that he knew sent me into the coital stratosphere. "And Excalibur, aka Susan Molinero, aka Katrina Reid, victim of the late great Tony DeSalvo has a nice little scar right about there. You don't. The good Dr. didn't address that."

The dude was an ice man. Once again, he was ahead of me. "You're way too calm and cool about this, Michael. How did you find out?"

"A hospital guy gave me the puzzle pieces and I put them together. I'm going to have our local guys check him out. I think he's hiding something."

He was playing with me. I hated it when Michael did that. "I come back from the dead after four months and all you're thinking about is some white-collar criminal?"

Michael Wright grabbed the face that wasn't mine and pulled me toward him.

"I've always wanted to make love to an assassin."

Then I was on top of him like an animal in heat, grateful for legroom in the front seat of the SUV and for the bulge I could feel below his belt line that spoke the words his bravado tried to hide.

"Show me how much you missed me, cowboy. And don't waste time. I need to get a borrowed car back to my shrink in time for therapy."

* * *

Michael Wright may have been able to conceal his surprise, but Excalibur could not. She nearly fainted when she saw her perfect double emerge from a cluster of homeless men. Through the front window of her tiny car, she witnessed the entire reunion, her mind sorting out the sequence of events and their meaning. Her own GPS tracker told her that the woman in Michael's vehicle had Alexandra Clark's cell phone.

But the ex-cop they called "Gates" didn't matter anymore. Excalibur's primary target was alive. The killer surely deduced Jessica's identity and the opportunities it presented. She knew the pound of flesh sitting in the refrigerator in her hotel room was a trap. She would soon be able to retrieve the genuine article and earn her pay.

Excalibur fingered the secure messenger application on her phone. "Ramirez alive... for now. Clark likely to attempt assassinations. Beware! X."

Susan Molinero hit the send button. She rolled down the rider's side window and motioned to one of the homeless men. He was younger than the rest. He had dark hair, recently cut and was clean shaven. Mirrored sunglasses concealed his eyes. The man registered surprise when he recognized her face. "One minute, you're hanging with us, the next you have a sports car."

She decided to take the risk, handed him a tiny, magnetized disk and a one-hundred-dollar bill. "Stick this where it won't be seen on that big black SUV and the hundred is yours. If they see you do it or you try to run away with my money, you'll be dead before you take three steps."

The man saw the intensity in her eyes but seemed unfazed by her threat. "A simple task, sweetheart. Need any other work done? I'm good with computers and could use a job."

Susan produced a handgun, pointing the weapon at the man's face. "Go, before I change my mind."

The couple in the SUV regained control over their emotions. The woman who had been devouring the driver slipped back into the passenger seat just as a drunken personage in reflective sunglasses stumbled, pushing his shaky body away from the vehicle before regaining his footing.

Nobody noticed. The SUV pulled away from the loading zone and into the afternoon traffic. The woman in the tiny Mazda waited a suitable period before following suit.

The homeless man returned to his tribe. "What was that all about, Andy?" a compatriot asked.

Andy Milluzzi pulled his sat phone from a ragged pocket and studied the data stream feeding geo location information from

Excalibur's encrypted cellular device into a server back in Illinois. With a satisfied smile, he folded the C-Note and pressed it into his friend's pocket. "Thanks for loaning me the outfit, Bill. Gotta make a phone call."

* * *

The Office of Dr. Assunta Sebastian - Portland
JESSICA RAMIREZ

"How are things with Michael?" my shrink asked.

Why do psychiatrists vector right to the edge of your comfort zone? "Do you guys always start with the sex questions when there's a man involved?"

"That's your word, not mine, Jessica. Anything you want to share?"

"It was the first time we didn't make both love and war at the same time."

"How did you feel afterwards?"

"It was a quickie in his SUV. I felt like I was in high school again. Don't you want to hear about our first time in Arizona or fist-fight sex in London?"

Assunta said nothing. She had asked her question and was waiting for an answer.

"It felt empty. It always feels empty. Michael is the most protective, kindhearted, funny, smart ass, selfless person I've ever met, Assunta. He should be the man of my dreams. Why isn't he?"

She wrote nothing on her pad. Either she knew exactly where this was going, or she was still fishing.

"Now tell me about the fist-fight sex in London."

"He's always trying to protect me. He wants to stop me from doing what I think should be done so I don't get hurt. He hides information that I need to know because he thinks I'll use it to put myself in harm's way. He wants to preserve my life. I want to live it."

That smile that annoyed me appeared again on her face. She nodded. "What does that tell you?"

"That he better understand the rules of engagement if we are going to be a team."

Assunta nodded again. "And so do you." She knew where this was going and was just waiting for me to catch up.

"What annoys you most about the other male officers you work with?"

"That they still don't believe a woman is good enough to be a cop. They try to cut us off at the knees at every turn. And they put obstacles in our way to try to stop us from being successful, getting promoted and being better police officers."

"Because..."

"Because they see us only as sex objects. Blowup dolls for their pleasure. Ziplock bags for their babies. Bartenders who mix their drinks after work and reassure them that they are Gods in the bedroom."

Assunta finally wrote a note on her iPad. "How do they really treat their spouses?"

"It depends on the relationship."

"But if you had to generalize?"

"They fawn over them at events where the wives are included. Their women are their trophies, something they won and don't want to ever lose. Yeah, cops sometimes stray and cheat. But divorces usually happen because the wife can't deal with the lifestyle. I know guys who still pine for the ex-wives. And God help any male who tries to take advantage of a cop's woman."

"Let's overlay that thought with London. Similarities?"

I had to process that one. After a moment I gave it a try. "You're saying that Michael is a cop protecting his wife?"

"It's a natural male thing," Assunta said, pleased with my ability to make the connection. "Wired into their dinosaur brains since they were cavemen. Protect the female so the species can survive. Somewhere along the line the concept of love came into it, but love is far down the Maslow Hierarchy of Needs. Back then there were so many daily dangers. There wasn't time to pull the iceberg out of the deep water far enough to see it."

I wasn't getting her point. "Are you saying that Michael's behavior is reflexive?"

"It's hard for men to fight evolutionary programming. I'm not excusing harassment or bad behavior. Just pointing to the origins. If you want any relationship to work, you're going to have to understand the underlying experience that created the person you're seeing and meet them halfway."

There it was. The thing behind every twist and turn in my life story. Daddy dashed my aquatic dreams. I responded by choosing a profession that scared the hell out of him. When my colleagues harassed me, I fought back on principle without thinking about the forces that molded their attitudes. Even when you are right, it's possible for things to turn out horribly wrong if you don't take the other person's experience into consideration. I knew that. The reason I was so good with the people I had to arrest was because I felt their pain and could build a trust relationship where they spilled their guts because they believed I had their best interests at heart, even when that best interest might mean incarceration.

I knew what to do. I let my singular focus on what I thought was right blind me to everything else.

"What fascinated me about your altercation with those three poor guys at the bar was how you were totally focused on retribution, without any compassion for their own suffering."

Another outburst. "Jesus H. Christ, Assunta! They took my memory, my face, my identity. I'm supposed to let them get away with that?"

"I'm not judging what you did. The bastards probably deserved it. And your assessment of the weaknesses in our judicial system were right on the money. Did you think about what caused their behavior before you acted? And if you did, would you have acted differently?"

I gave my shrink the benefit of a few brain cycles before responding. "From the clarity of hindsight, I would probably have understood that they might have been abused children, fallen in with the wrong crowd, or just were unlucky and made a series of bad choices. But I would still have done what I did."

The smile came back. I wanted to slap her. "So, using that same thought process with Michael, what should you do about the relationship?"

"We both need to understand boundaries and agree on how we will interact with one another. And then decide if the rules of engagement are workable over the long term."

Dr. Sebastian stood; a quick nod of affirmation told me that today's lesson was concluded.

"Good. That's your homework. Go forth and do what you need to do with the full awareness of what motivates the behaviors of others... and," she added, "what motivates you."

I thanked her, realizing that we were just scratching the tip of a very deep iceberg.

"Do you think we're gonna make it, Assunta?"

"You and Michael?"

"Yes."

That damn Cheshire Cat grin again. "Time will tell."

Chapter Thirty-Six

The White House Situation Room – Washington, DC

Terry Taylor's interpersonal charm and his ability to get things done under the radar gave the Assistant Director of the Federal Bureau of Investigation job security in the mercurial, ever-shifting tides of political opinion.

It was rare that he was ever called into the spotlight. The Director got the glory. Taylor did the dirty work.

So, a summons to the White House that evening made Terry Taylor nervous. He sat next to his boss at the long table in the Situation Room. Both were impeccably dressed in Ralph Lauren suits, buttoned-down, white shirts and matching ties, appropriate to the color of the party in power. When Taylor saw the personalized briefing folders placed in designated spots around the table, it became clear why he was there.

On the other side sat the more well-known faces. The Secretary of State, the newly named head of the Central Intelligence Agency, the director of the National Security Agency and the head of the military's Joint Chiefs of Staff.

Dawn Elick, the president's Chief of Staff entered the room with the alchemy of poise and confidence that made her a natural choice for the second most important job in the nation. She took her place at the head of the conference table, in her boss's seat, the de-facto leader of the meeting.

"Thanks to everyone for coming on such short notice," she said. "Associate Director Taylor is with us to answer questions about this rogue operation." She emphasized "rogue," causing a shot of stomach acid to boil in Taylor's gut.

Elick turned her attention to the CIA Director. "Ron, what do we know about this?"

Since Ali's plans would execute outside of the confines of the 50 states, they were naturally in the prevue of Central Intelligence not the FBI where every adventure seemed to begin.

Another swipe at the Bureau, Taylor thought. This was not beginning well.

"A small group of current and former law enforcement officers and a commander from MI6 have devised a plan to liquidate The Triumvirate. It involves assassinations at a yet unspecified time. The group has intelligence about the whereabouts of The Triumvirate and intends to deal with each in turn."

"We don't know the when, the where or the how?" Elick pressed.

"Our contacts have purposely not inquired about specifics, Dr. Elick. Plausible deniability."

"More likely plausible cowardice," the NSA director muttered.

Elick nodded in his direction. "Something to add, Dr. Wolthuis?"

"Any boss that purposely doesn't know what his or her team is up to just to protect his own ass is derelict."

Elick remained cool. "And do you have intelligence with which you can enlighten us doctor?"

"There are three of them we know about so far," Wolthuis said. "Possibly a fourth. An agent in Director Gerhardt's MI6 operation is the lead. He's recruited a MET cop who was involved in the Prokofiev Affair last year. This Detective Inspector is in a relationship with a law enforcement officer who just quit her job with an Illinois municipal police force. The ex-cop is the one formulating the plan. There is also a possible connection to the director of the Paloma University Computer Lab."

The CIA Director interrupted. "Prokofiev is the common denominator. All were involved in that incident, along with one of Associate Director Taylor's agents and a dead colleague to whom the man was engaged."

Elick smirked. "A family affair."

"The dead cop is the common denominator, Dr. Elick," Wolthuis continued, contradicting his colleague. "Our office believes these are revenge killings."

"How so?" Elick probed.

"The Triumvirate hired Excalibur to kill the FBI agent's fiancée. The dead woman also happened to be the ex-cop's partner. The late detective ran afoul of The Triumvirate's plans on two occasions. They ordered her murder."

Elick was impressed. "Excalibur? Why engage a rock star like that to kill a street cop?"

Secretary of State Sutro raised a hand. Taylor was a fan of the fast-rising head of the State Department. She came from a long line of police officers and had an unmatched gift for diplomacy. "Optics, Dr. Elick. This woman was simply in the wrong places at the wrong times and happened to trigger a chain of events that ended up foiling two pretty serious situations."

"Serious is an understatement, Secretary Sutro." The deep voice of Army General Morrison ratcheted up the tension in the room. "Destruction of the nation's financial infrastructure and castrating our nuclear deterrent are DEFCON 1 level threats."

Secretary Sutro ignored the general. "It was bad luck for the detective, Dawn. There are political factions in every organization, and some saw this woman as an opportunity to emphasize The Triumvirate's weakness." Sutro regarded the three men on her side of the table. "The trio in charge want to maintain their hold on power. Killing Detective Ramirez was seen as a necessary show of force to warn would-be competitors to stand down."

Taylor was aware of the friendship that had developed between the Chief of Staff and the Secretary. Few called Dr. Elick by her first name.

"How do our allies feel about all of this, Emma?" Elick asked.

Secretary Sutro referred to her notes. "Opinions have changed over the last few days. Number Ten is now in favor of The Triumvirate's elimination. The Prime Minister has his own political troubles, and the public relations spin would be a welcome distraction. The Indian government has always been in favor of eliminating the oligarch associated with their country. They see him as an embarrassment and potentially escalating tensions with Pakistan."

Dr. Elick shot Taylor and his boss a glance. Terry couldn't read judgment or emotion connected with it, nor an invitation to weigh in. She looked at each of the cabinet members in turn. "So, what is the consensus? Do we intervene to stop this operation, or do we let it proceed?"

"Stop it." The CIA Director was emphatic. "We have strong intelligence links into The Triumvirate's organization now. Recent actions to the contrary, they are ultimately a stabilizing influence?"

General Morrison exploded. "A stabilizing influence? Anyone who tries to open our nation to nuclear annihilation is a clear and present threat to national security. We need to tell the world that attempts to destroy us will not go unanswered."

Wolthuis and Sutro remained silent. The Chief of Staff poked the NSA Director first. "What about it, Mike? Your vote?"

"I'm with Ron on this one, Dr. Elick. Their communications leak like a bad roof. We intercept every conversation. If there's a change, we're back to square one, in the dark. And that's not a place where I like to be."

"Emma?"

"Why does there even need to be a Triumvirate?" Sutro asked. "They answer to no political entity. They are, in essence, businessmen who want to further enrich themselves. And they have shown that they have no qualms about killing millions of innocents to achieve their ends. Their elimination might open the door to a new level of diplomacy that could be a unifying force. We never know for sure how these things play out, Dawn, but I'm uncomfortable in any situation where three men control the destiny of the entire world."

Taylor saw the Secret Service agent guarding the Situation Room door touch his earpiece. He stepped back as the door opened. The President of the United States entered the room.

Everyone stood.

The president held out his palms in the self-deprecating manner that helped get him elected. "Please, folks. Have a seat. Sorry to eavesdrop on this most interesting conversation, but sometimes having the boss in the room stifles debate." He singled Taylor out, shaking the Associate Director's hand with a grin.

"Terry Taylor. You are one hell of a troublemaker. Do you have a holiday greeting card list at home with eccentrics you call when my team gets their feet stuck in the mud?"

The president lingered behind each of his cabinet members. "General," he said, gripping the Joint Chiefs Chairman's shoulders. "You are absolutely right. If somebody throws a stick of dynamite in my house, you can be damn sure, I'll toss it right back through their front window to give 'em religion." The president gave his NSA and CIA chiefs gentle shoulder punches. "And my two Intel guys have a good point. Always stay close to the nosey neighbor who can't keep her mouth shut." He grimaced as he looked at his Chief of Staff. "Apologies, Dawn. We had one in our neighborhood when

I was a kid, and she was a tenacious investigative reporter. I'll try to think of a more ecumenical analogy."

The president walked to the other side of the table standing behind Taylor and his boss so he could focus on his Secretary of State. "And God bless you, Emma. Too often, we get stuck in old paradigms and think of how things are, when we should be dreaming about how they could be. Yes, ladies and gentlemen, the unknown zone is not a fun place. But it's the only place where meaningful change happens."

The leader of the free world leaned against the wall, crossing his arms. "I made a few calls after Emma briefed me on the shifting sands. Our friends in Mumbai and London have come around to the notion of negotiating our own destinies without three rich bullies pushing chess pieces around the board." The president put a hand on Taylor's shoulder. "And Terry here has given us the perfect way to throw dynamite through their windows. This Triumvirate knows Terry's kids are coming. And they know we haven't condoned their actions. Without national will behind them, they will be perceived as a small group of free stylers, driven by laudable emotions in the direction of righteous revenge. Perhaps that lowers shields just enough where the team could succeed. And if they don't, they have bought us the time to agree with our friends on a common strategy... have fun with that one, Emma... and a set of talking points to sell it to the voters."

The President of the United States motioned to his Chief of Staff. She stood, backing toward the wall to give him room to pass. He stopped at the head of the table to address the entire group. "Terry, your rogue warriors have my support. Get 'em whatever they need. But if you breathe a word to anybody about it, I'll deny this meeting ever took place."

With that, the president and Dr. Elick left the room.

"Good luck finding work in the private sector, boys," General Morrison muttered.

"Godspeed, Terry," Secretary Sutro said. "May your rogue warriors be the change they hope for in this troubled world."

* * *

East of Puyallup Ridge Lookout, Eatonville, Washington

Susan Molinero sat in the lotus pose on a rug at the center of the small cabin. Leaving her cell in Portland was a necessary inconvenience. She needed time to think, and she didn't know if the counter measures her techno geek friends installed on the device truly rendered it untraceable.

Her richest payday ever was now at risk. Michael Wright had Detective Ramirez under his protective wing. Ex-Officer Clark was closing in on her benefactors. And the only way she would earn her bones was to personally deliver a pound of Jessica's flesh to three men who might well kill her when they perceived her usefulness to be at an end.

She had no guarantees that she would be paid, let alone walk out of the meeting alive. Such was the mercurial mindset of the men who hired the best of the best.

Susan needed an exit strategy. Money never motivated her. Susan's need for affirmation perverted into the sheer joy of watching other people die. Being well paid was a nice perk. But her gut told her this might be her last kill unless she could find a way to hide in plain sight.

She could find Detective Ramirez with ease. As long as she carried Clark's cell phone, the woman called Excalibur had her in the cross hairs. Even under Michael's protection, enough of Susan's enemies had likely seen pictures of her face. Ramirez might be mistaken for the famed assassin and be killed instead.

Susan pressed her hands together in the prayer pose, asking for the Devil's guidance. That surgeon, Dr. Sullivan was the only person who could give Jessica back her Latina good looks to again become the physical embodiment of all that Susan despised.

Whether good or bad, "Ask and ye shall receive," delivers an answer. The idea that came to Susan Molinero was so horrifically perfect in its simplicity and elegance that whatever stresses she felt about The Triumvirate, her enemies or her future vanished.

She knew exactly what she was going to do. The only question that remained was when.

Chapter Thirty-Seven

The Sentinel - 614 SW 11th Ave, Portland

JESSICA RAMIREZ

"That's the one."

Gina Manson's confidence reminded me of my younger self. Andy Milluzzi's colleague defied convention and chased a dream, becoming exactly the woman she wanted to be in the process.

The digital nerd from the Paloma University Computer Lab pointed to Room 316 of the historic Sentinel Hotel.

Comprised of two buildings, both of which are listed on the National Register of Historic Places, The Sentinel reflected the six-million-dollar renovation its current owners invested to transform the property into an icon attracting movie people from Gus Van Zant to Madonna.

Apparently, it also attracted Excalibur.

Gina was about to swipe the housekeeper's key when Michael stopped her. "Any traps or security devices we have to worry about?"

Gina punched up a screen on her iPad. It revealed the layout of the hotel room with hot spots depicting each power outlet, a WIFI access point and the MAC address of a single cell phone on what looked like a desk.

"No motion detectors. No magnetic switches. No explosives. Nothing generating RF of any kind beyond the WIFI and that cell phone. Oh, and there's something very cold in the refrigerator."

Michael wasn't convinced. "That's a smart cell phone. Are you sure?"

Gina produced a device from her backpack. "Not as smart as this is. It's an exact copy of the hardware, with a few of Andy's enhancements."

I ignored Michael's concerned expression. "You can tell us later how you pulled that one off, Gina. What's the plan?"

"A simple swap," Gina said. "Your friend X won't know the difference and we'll have the device The Triumvirate thinks she's using for our own creative purposes."

Michael relented. "Do your voodoo, Gina. I hope you're as good as Andy says you are."

Gina gave me a knowing smile. "I'm better."

* * *

The moment we were inside, Gina Manson went to work. She pulled a double charging holster from her backpack and dropped X's phone and its twin into the slots.

"Andy got a good look at Excalibur's hardware when he was playing homeless. We found the identical model. I'm cloning ours with her data and we'll leave the copy here."

She patted the clone. "This little baby has a few minor mods that will be useful. Should X decide to text your bad boys, the message will come to Agent Wright's cell instead."

I was impressed. "And what will you do with the original device?"

"Andy suggests sending it to your partner in London, Detective Ramirez. It may be of use with whatever plan she and her friends are cooking up."

Michael inspected the cold spot in the fridge. It was Joey's package with the pound of flesh. "Looks like someone finally delivered the goods to our ultimate recipient."

Gina turned her attention away from the cell phones, reaching into her backpack. Seconds later she handed Michael an identical parcel.

"With love from Andy and Dr. Price. They thought you might want a duplicate."

That's when everything fell into place. I'm not much for the paranormal, but in that moment, I could feel the connection with Alexandra. She needed a way to get close to The Triumvirate without detection. We had her pound of flesh and her cell phone. I slipped a hand around Michael's waist and nibbled his earlobe.

"Do you think Director Taylor could get a priority FedEx box to London in record time?"

* * *

The Nines – 525 SW Morrison, Portland – 1700 Hours
JESSICA RAMIREZ

"Dear Senator. Are you aware that FBI agents are staying in 5-Star hotels? While I am grateful to have personally benefitted from one such experience at The Nines in Portland, Oregon, I feel it's my duty as a citizen to alert you to this blatant waste of taxpayer money. Please investigate. Sincerely, Jessica Ramirez, Concerned Taxpayer, Paloma, Illinois."

Michael ordered us another round of cocktails at the hotel's rooftop restaurant as I dictated my diatribe aloud. He rested his chin on his fists and stared at me with those same hungry eyes that devoured me in Flagstaff, Washington, London, and at 35,000 feet.

"Do you want to hand-write that one on hotel stationery or send it as an email?"

"You're looking at Susan Molinero's face with the same drooling lust you slobbered all over me in DC. What is wrong with you?"

"Some things you can't change, Jess. That golden spot among the brown in your right eye. The way your teeth glow when you smile."

"I floss," I interrupted.

"Let me finish. While you and X have similar body types, yours is more..."

"Pick your next word carefully, cowboy."

"More athletic."

"As in the athletics you intend to pursue after you get me drunk?"

Michael glared at me. "I thought the love of my life was dead, Jessica. I thought I had sent you to that death on an aircraft that was supposed to be my last ride. Even after all this time, I haven't been able to imagine my world without you. You're back. You're sitting across from me. And yes, even that killer's face is beautiful when I know your heart is behind it. And of course, I'm horny. Let a guy adjust to a miracle, will ya?"

The umbrella drinks Michael kept coming at me were doing their work. I felt as warm and relaxed as a traumatized person emerging from amnesia with the face of an assassin could be. With each round I consumed, Michael's faults seemed less severe and my brain started feeding me memories of our unclad bodies dancing the nasty. To hell with my troubles. I wanted his hopeless love to engulf me. I wanted to forget that the last few months had ever happened. The man who could work that magic was sitting across from me ready to pounce the moment I put on anything close to a mating display.

"I'm sorry, Michael. It's going to take me awhile to process all this stuff. You're a good egg to carry the torch for me even after you thought I was gone. But all those things I said back at my mother's dinner table are still true. I need to go my own way and I'm not sure it's the path you want me to take. Hell, I don't even know what path I want to take."

Michael signaled for the check. "I get it, Jess. That's where we are different. I've seen so much death that I have to live in the moment. In this moment, my purpose is enforcing the law, accepting the fact that any day could be my last and making the most of every moment I have with you in this second life we've been given."

The server appeared and Michael scribbled his room number and a signature at the bottom.

"Don't forget to tip the guy," I said. "He looks like a college kid, probably with student loans up the ying-yang."

Trying to gain my favor, Michael put an obscenely generous number under the total. He tossed the pen onto the plastic tray that held the bill, put on his most serious face, and took a deep breath.

"Right now, you and I are between catastrophes, Jessica. The universe has given us a huge bed with a beautiful view of a great city and a few hours without somebody trying to kill us. We are both carrying more stress than any sane person should have to compartmentalize. We are reasonably compatible when you're not trying to save the world. And sex with you is the closest I've ever been to heaven. All things considered, I'm sure your psychiatrist, your mother and your pastor would approve of ten to twelve hours of non-stop, jungle boogie. Let's give each other that gift and see how well insulated the walls between the suites are against screaming ecstasy."

He was good. "Jungle boogie? Wow. Is that improv or something you memorized?"

He placed both hands over his chest. "It's from the bottom of my heart and a place under my belt that will embarrass us both when I stand up."

I flicked Michael's nose with an index finger. "OK, cowboy. I think we've earned it. I promise not to argue with you and I'm not a screamer, so you don't have to worry about annoying the neighbors."

I saw the source of his embarrassment as we both stood. I slid in front of him to hide it from onlookers as we exited the restaurant.

We barely made it into the room before diving into the jungle. We made love with the frenetic abandon of star-crossed Shakespearian protagonists who both knew that the next few hours of passion might be our last.

* * *

Heathrow Airport International Arrivals – UK – 2200 hours local time

ALEXANDRA CLARK

Why in the name of Mother Mary and her all-girl orchestra did I ever leave London? As the British Airways Boeing 777 turned on final for runway 27R the exquisite expanse of the one-time center of an empire gave me chills.

Memories of my extended vacation with Lee flooded back. Seeing Big Ben and the London Eye in the distance brought back the smell of her cologne and the taste of the strawberry Chapstick she wore on those delectable lips.

This time, there were no armed gunmen waiting for me at passport control and I did not contain my joy at seeing my love on the other side of security.

I'm certain we drew stares during a prolonged and totally inappropriate reunion smooch. She still wore the same Chapstick.

"Still stuck in Research, babe?" I asked when our temperatures cooled enough for conversation.

"Right, you gorgeous hunk of American flesh. And it has its benefits."

"I hear that James Bond has news."

Lee frowned at the distraction. "Patience, my love. Patience. Tomorrow, we go to Tottenham to plot world domination."

"And tonight?"

Lee tickled the edges of my ear with her tongue. "Tonight, we make up for lost time."

Liyanna grabbed my backpack, wrapped an arm around my waist and we danced our way to the car park.

Chapter Thirty-Eight

The Nines – Portland - The Next Morning

JESSICA RAMIREZ

I couldn't decide whether the feeling of Michael's arm wrapped around me in the huge bed we destroyed the night before gave me a sense of security or claustrophobia.

In my pre-Portland life, cops rarely sought psychiatric care. We all knew there were lifesaving benefits. But if word got around, it was another sign of weakness; a question in your partner's mind as you faced down a domestic that paralleled your own upbringing; or the instant you had to make a life-and-death trigger decision without a nano-second of doubt.

We portrayed pillars of strength and confidence on the outside, even though we shared every other human frailty on the inside.

Michael stirred, remembered where he was and pulled me closer. The low purr of his voice gave me tingles in places still warm from last night. "Good morning, beautiful."

I responded in kind. "Morning, handsome. Although I can't

imagine how you could feel concupiscence for a woman with this ugly face."

"I love it when you use four syllable words, Jess. It's the new sexy."

"Everything is the new sexy with you, Michael."

"If it's connected to you, my sweet, it's the new sexy. Is 'my sweet' approved language in the Jessica Ramirez Relationship Lexicon?"

"It passes muster," I said. "We should talk about our game plan. She's still out there and she probably knows where we are and what I look like by now."

Michael yawned and tossed his cell phone on the mattress in front of me. "She does."

Andy Milluzzi's text stream was as succinct as usual.

X behind you at the Shelter. She saw everything. Grabbed her phone deets and MAC address so your app will render her location. Thanks for the Portland adventure. Off to visit some old friends in London. AM

I rolled over to face his stubbled smile. "Andy was here?"

"I thought a little backup might be helpful. Hit the blue app icon if you want a little entertainment."

I did. Our location centered on the screen as a green circle. About two miles away a red skull blinked with the word "Stationary" below it.

Michael's finger illustrated his brief lecture. "The green dot is us. The skull her. She's smart, so I imagine she's seeing something similar on her screen. X probably hacked Ali's phone. The one she gave you at the bar. We'll get alerts if she moves, and alarms will ring if she gets closer than two hundred yards."

I sniffed. "I hate technology. It was much more fun when we had to find our perps the old-fashioned way. What's the plan for our day?"

"I need to report. DC still doesn't know about your new superpower."

I pinched the skin on my cheek. "I wouldn't call this ugly thing a superpower. And you actually prioritized us over instantly phoning home yesterday?"

Michael nuzzled my nose. Or was it Susan's nose? "I needed to know what your mental state was and if you were up to a little undercover work before we send you to Dr. Sullivan to get your face back."

"And your diagnosis is?"

Michael sighed. His satiated smile replayed a long night of... what are the appropriate PG 13 words? "Romantic Escapades?"

"My diagnosis is that behind that face is the same badass Latina cop I fell in love with. Dr. Sebastian will have to weigh in, but I think you're ready to help me take Excalibur out of the game, permanently."

* * *

26 Togginham St. - London, UK

ALEXANDRA CLARK

Commander Tom Anastos' two-bedroom London flat was nothing like the Broccoli James Bond version. Its Spartan accoutrements were almost bland by comparison.

"Forgive the heterosexual stereotype reference, Commander," I said after he gave us the tour. "But this place could use a woman's touch."

He rubbed the top of a five-by-seven photograph that was the only accessory on the tiny desk in his guest bedroom. The woman's face was warm, playful. Her shoulders told me she was a fitness freak. The commander studied it as if it were a Rembrandt. "Soon, if I'm lucky, Ali."

"Who is she?"

He wasn't ready to give up a name. "We've known one another since primary school. Gotta get around to popping the question."

I was incredulous. "And that beauty has waited this long for you to get your act together?"

Anastos winked. "I'm worth the wait. Ready to kill some people?"

* * *

The Nines – Portland

JESSICA RAMIREZ

After breakfast, Michael got confirmation that our package was out for delivery in London. We returned to our room to find Gina ensconced at a desk, pouring over a data stream that slid upward on her laptop screen.

"This Excalibur has been following Officer Clark since she landed in Portland. Now that you have her cell, Detective Ramirez, she knows exactly where you are."

I knew it. Michael knew it. I didn't like it. "Time to ditch the phone and get Gina to make me something a little more secure?"

Michael thought about it. "There is some benefit to our mutual location awareness. And there are two of us watching your back. Maybe we keep Ali's phone lit up just a bit longer."

Nervous energy was consuming me. The enlightenment from my time with Assunta was sinking in. Michael's shift from protector to using me as bait had a familiar Moscow ring that soured the breakfast digesting in my stomach. I needed to run off some stress.

"Am I ok to head down to the fitness facility for some treadmill time, Agent Wright? Without Ali's cell?"

Michael chuckled. "Of course. Gina and I have to dig through X's movements and cell usage. Wherever X is, she'll likely retrieve her cell before she does anything important. Leave Ali's device here and enjoy some focused exercise."

* * *

26 Togginham St. - London, UK

ALEXANDRA CLARK

We circled our laptops around a table in the Commander's combination kitchen and dining area. Lee started the proceedings.

"It turns out that our Triumvirate is stuck on a super yacht in Bodrum, Turkey."

She flipped her laptop around so Commander Anastos and I could see it. A satellite photo filled the screen. The dog-faced peninsula at the southwestern edge of the country looked to be about the same latitude as North Carolina, mild winters, and unbearably hot summers. It was August. Not fun.

Lee zoomed in on a huge vessel, moored off the north end of a circular inlet perfectly designed for both privacy and shelter from the unpredictable Aegean Sea.

"There she is, *The Triarchy*. Three hundred forty-eight feet long. Two hundred eighty-six million pounds of ostentatiousness. The inlet is popular with rich folks because it's close to Bodrum Castle and the Mausoleum at Halicarnassus. Halicarnassus is one of the Seven Wonders of the Ancient World, completed in the 4th century B.C., and Turkey's casual attitude toward the rich and famous brings lots of big boats to town."

Lee zoomed out, revealing a huge, gray cockroach floating within sight of the inlet.

"This is the USS Bainbridge, DGG dash ninety-six. She's an Arleigh Burke-class guided missile destroyer, famous in Hollywood as one of three boats that shadowed the Maersk Alabama, boarded by Somali Pirates in 2009. Remember 'Captain Phillips'? I may be gay, but I would totally jump into bed with Tom Hanks."

That thought had crossed my mind, too.

"The Bainbridge waits in international waters with orders to board any vessel exiting the inlet connected with Russia's elite. A gift from Director Taylor, no doubt."

Commander Anastos picked up the narrative. "Turkey isn't the most secure place on earth these days, so our three bad boys and their guard detail are enjoying an extended stay on *The Triarchy*. She'll be sitting there waiting for us when you board her and dispatch your targets to the eternal fires of hell."

I pressed two fingers on the touchpad of Lee's laptop to take a closer look at the boat. It was surrounded by mosquitos that grew into wave-runners as I zoomed in.

"Looks like she's well defended, Commander. You forgot to mention that."

Anastos swallowed hard. "She always has a dozen of those little fish swarming around her. There are also ten cameras, both land and boat mounted. They feed monitors in the vessel's security cabin. Someone's on duty there twenty-four seven and shouts if anything unauthorized gets close."

I split my fingers on the touch pad to focus on the fly bridge. "Looks like a couple of snipers keeping watch up top, too."

"With night vision goggles, Ali," Anastos added. "This won't be a walk in the park."

Lee flipped her laptop shut, as if removing the picture from my view might minimize the threat. "There are a few factors in our favor."

I couldn't imagine any.

"The Triumvirate prefer to sleep in silence, so the wave runners idle in place after lights-out. They won't move unless there's a threat." Lee checked her watch. "And we are importing some talent to give the security guys something benign to watch when you make your move."

A soft tone pinged the commander's cell. He smiled as he looked at the door cam image.

"Right on time."

* * *

Fitness Facility - The Nines - Portland
JESSICA RAMIREZ

Since I had no expectation of spending the night anywhere, I had no workout gear. Just the Nikes that were permanently attached to my feet. I picked out enough Spandex at the welcome desk gift shop to catch the sweat, charged it to Michael's room, and jumped on a treadmill.

The attendant was closing her retail shop during the lull between post-breakfast guilt and afternoon stress reduction. The place was all mine. The televisions were Bluetooth enabled, so the only sound was the whir of the belt and the sixty-hertz hum of the treadmill motor.

What was Susan's next move? She had to know we were backing her into a corner, that Ali was heading to wherever X's bosses were to neutralize them and ruin Susan's payday.

The pictures of my takedown at the bar were in circulation. People could at last put a face with a name. Every victim has friends. Soon some would come looking for Excalibur with the same objective we shared: killing her.

I thought about Lucy and how Susan used her to try and escape. If not for her assignment to kill me, she might well have disappeared. Without a probable payday, would she find a way to disappear again?

I saw Susan's reflection looking back at me in the long glass mirror that made the fitness room seem bigger than it was. I wanted to drop everything, go to Sandra and have her give me back my face and my life. Being a good cop in a college town felt like the ideal existence. I was ready to stop being a superhero and start being a nobody.

A couple of roid boys appeared and went straight for the free weights. They looked a little too buff and had a few too many tattoos for regular Nines clientele. But I still didn't know Portland. Perhaps they were millionaires from Seattle on holiday.

They ignored me, conversing about form, protein powder and

how much they could bench press. My meditative mood broken, I decided it was time to head to the room.

The warmth of the shower felt great. I let the cascades massage my head and neck longer than I would have back home. We were always behind on paperwork and the motivation to catch up kept me on task.

The steam fogged the mirrors as I ruffled my hair with a deliciously thick cotton towel. Maybe slowing down to smell the roses wasn't such a bad thing.

I shook the damp locks off of my face and saw her standing next to me. She was dressed in my street clothes. The two roid boys stood behind her.

"Michael is in room 608," I said. "Twenty bucks says he figures out who you are in less than ten minutes."

I felt a chloroform cloth cover my nose and mouth. Susan told one of the boys to take my shoes. Seconds later my legs buckled and my consciousness began a peaceful descent into darkness.

Chapter Thirty-Nine

26 Togginham St. - London, UK

ALEXANDRA CLARK

Andy Milluzzi's wide grin shot a dose of adrenaline through me. I hugged the nerd and gave him the most delicious kiss he probably ever had.

"You, young man, are a sight for sore eyes. How in the hell did you get here so fast?"

It took Andy a moment to recover. "Your friend, Director Taylor knows some interesting people. Three of them gave me a ride from Portland International Airport to Gatwick in a B1. Did you know that thing can make the trip in less than six hours?"

For an administration to flip from sacrificing a lowly Illinois cop to burning military millions to ferry a civilian to London was a good sign. I hoped Taylor's boys had a solution for my toughest problem.

"How is Jessica, Andy?" I asked. "Did you leave any backup in Portland?"

"She doesn't look like herself, Ali. But I think you know that. When I last saw her, she was glad to have.." He paused, parsing his words for general audiences. "To have *reconnected* with Agent Wright. As for backup, Gina Manson is on site. She's smarter than I am. I think Detective Ramirez is getting the better deal this time."

"Sorry to get right to business, Andy," Anastos said, offering our friend a Coke and guiding him to our Knights of the Roundtable workspace. "Did you have a chance to research the stuff I sent you?"

Andy had his laptop out and functioning in less than a minute. "Yes, Commander. And I think you'll like what I've got for you.

* * *

The Nines - Room 608

"What did I miss?"

Susan Molinero slid the room key into her breast pocket, recognizing Michael's handsome face, but surprised to see a young African American typing away on a laptop.

The girl's smile dimmed a bit when she regarded Susan. She closed the device, swinging her chair around for a closer inspection. "Reporting to Michael's superiors, Detective Ramirez," she said. "We are getting close enough to Excalibur to smell her perfume."

Michael's distracted focus returned to his phone. "How was the workout?"

"Not long enough," Susan lied. "Barely broke a sweat and the place started to fill up. Company makes me nervous."

"See anyone suspicious?" the girl asked.

"Just a bunch of rich women who talk too much about too little."

Michael keyed in some characters and sent a message. "OK, friends. We have a game plan. Want to hear it?"

The girl at the computer threw a fleece over the desk, covering the contents before Susan could finish her inventory.

"After lunch, Agent Wright. I'm famished."

Michael Wright glanced at Susan. "Worked up an appetite yet, Jess?"

Susan gave Michael her best salacious look. "Hungrier with every passing moment."

Michael's smile was quizzical. Susan didn't know how to decode it. "OK, ladies. To the roof restaurant, my treat!"

The girl twirled Susan's hair as she headed for the door. "I'll be right with you. Need to swing by my room and freshen up." She winked at Susan. "You and Michael deserve more alone time."

* * *

26 Togginham St. – London

ALEXANDRA CLARK

Andy Milluzzi's laptop depicted a one-square-mile zone surrounding *The Triarchy*. "Your troublemakers have eleven cameras, not ten, feeding signals to the security cabin."

Each device lit-up in turn on the screen. "All the onshore cameras are radio-frequency driven. That's easy to commandeer. The challenge will be the hard-wired devices on the yacht. I'll have to board her to install some helpful toys."

"How will you pull that one off?" I asked, already knowing Andy had an answer.

"The vendor has alerted the head of boat security to a possible flaw in the software. They are expecting a tech from headquarters to show up and do the update. My friends at the firm gave me credentials and have forwarded my picture and a bio to the captain."

"What if they do an image search, Andy? You're a pretty well-known face in tech circles."

Andy fanned a set of credentials like a deck of cards. "A face who was recently hired as chief of security for the company. The press release went out today. More kudos to Director Taylor. I wish I had his address book."

Anastos shook his head in awe. "When the US government says it will help out, they deliver."

I circled a finger in the commander's direction. "What about your gang, Commander? We can't do this without their contribution."

Anastos retreated to a kitchen cupboard and retrieved a small canister of Tatlı Briki, one of the more refined brands of Turkish coffee.

"You'll carry three of these, Ali. Each contains an aerosol canister of fentanyl, enough to kill the entire ship's compliment in less than five minutes. It's our improvement over the stuff the Russians used on a group of terrorists who took over a theater in Moscow. Unfortunately, it also permanently neutralized about two hundred of the audience members, too."

I recoiled. "You've been keeping those in this flat?"

"Benign until activated. I'll show you how when we're a little nearer to our target."

There were still many questions. "So, all I have to do is get past the wave runners, avoid whatever shipboard armed security will likely be walking around, find where these three dirt bags are sleeping, activate the canisters without killing myself in the process and sneak back off the boat alone and undetected?"

The three stared at me as if I was an idiot. Lee shrugged. "It was your idea. You have to figure out at least some of the logistics."

I was disliking my brilliant plan more and more with each new revelation. "Why don't we just get Terry Taylor to provide a couple of Navy Seals and stick a demolition charge near the engine room? Simple and provides a nice bit of fireworks we can all watch from the safety of that guided missile cruiser in international waters."

Anastos took a Guinness from his refrigerator, holding it up with a questioning expression that asked if we wanted some, too. Nobody bit.

"This was approved as a covert mission, Ali," the commander said after taking a long drink from his bottle. "It sends a powerful political message that our nations are not only united in our resolve to live without a Triumvirate but have the capability to penetrate the most secure defenses to take them out if a new trio tries to emerge."

I was backed into a corner. I could feel the drug addict's adrenaline rush. "OK. When do we do this thing?"

The commander looked at his watch. "Andy is out of here in about ten minutes. Corporate jet direct." Anastos gave Andy a mock frown. "Don't get used to all this luxury, Andrew."

The commander continued his lecture. "Our resident genius will be on *The Triarchy* before dusk. We leave for Ankara tonight. You'll board her tomorrow night, Ali, do your thing and we'll all be back in London the next afternoon."

I stared at Lee, realizing that this might be one crazy idea too many. "You saw what I was like when I thought I had lost Jessica, Liyanna. Will you be as much of a sniveling mess if something happens to me?"

Lee winked. "Are you kidding? I'm famous. I can have any woman, gay or straight that I want."

I knew she didn't mean it and tonight in some Turkish hotel we would each work through our fears in the most intimate of rituals.

* * *

JESSICA RAMIREZ

When my senses returned. I felt the press of a half dozen zip ties against my wrists and ankles. A dog collar encircled my neck, chained to the base of a toilet. Someone stuffed a washcloth in my mouth, taped tight with duct tape circling twice around the back of my neck with just my nostrils for an airway.

My memory was working just fine now. The layout of the space confirmed my hypothesis. I was enjoying Excalibur's hospitality on the cold tile floor of her bathroom at the Sentinel Hotel, totally naked, but apparently unviolated.

It didn't take long for the ideas I explored on the treadmill to resolve. Susan Molinero had the perfect escape plan. She would let her enemies kill me, convince Sandra Sullivan she was me, have the good doctor carve my face into hers, and hide out in Paloma in the perfect disguise: a cop.

* * *

26 Togginham St. - London
ALEXANDRA CLARK

The doorbell ring tone pinged the commander's cell for a second time. He frowned, pulling a pistol from the silverware drawer. "Not expecting anything or anyone."

The screen revealed a breathless FedEx driver carrying a thick square box.

Anastos keyed his phone's microphone. "Can I help you?"

The frazzled face read the tag on the box.

"Delivery for an Officer Alexandra Clark."

Anastos looked at me. I shrugged. "Not expecting anything."

"It's from someone named Jessica 5537."

The tension broke. "Take your piece if it makes you feel safer, Commander. Jess sent us a going away present."

* * *

The Nines – Portland

Michael Wright was stunned by the attention the woman gave him as the elevator ascended to the rooftop restaurant at The Nines. The moment they were alone, she pressed his body against a corner.

"I've been thinking about your proposal, Michael. Perhaps being the wife of an FBI agent isn't so bad, after all."

Michael liked the proximity. All his senses switched into high gear. He knew what was ahead and wanted to make a memory of this moment. He reveled in the aroma of her hair, the curve of her hips and the unaccustomed sweetness of her breath.

Someone had prepared for this moment with a mint. Jessica hated mints.

"What changed your mind, baby?"

"You did. In the car yesterday. And last night in your bed. I wouldn't mind adding that to my daily fitness routine."

The word "baby" was always a trigger with Jess. An objectifier her cop brethren liked to toss as hand grenades in the path of the few female officers who hung in at Paloma PD. Now the word seemed to turn up her heat.

The floors ticked off. The ride was short enough for this beautiful woman to get her message across and long enough for Michael to process it.

"Let's not tell Gina just yet," he said, brushing his lips against hers and moving his attention to the left side of her neck. He could feel her shiver as he found a hot spot and the laceration that wasn't part of Jessica's carotid geography. "And maybe I'll tell her to get her own lunch and take the afternoon off so we can negotiate details."

The elevator door slid open, revealing the panorama of the famous rooftop bistro. Michael Wright let his lunch partner walk ahead of him to the hostess stand, feeling the vibration of his cell in his pocket.

As he expected, it was Gina with the intel he already confirmed. He had a text prepared and ready to send in response, even before he finished reading hers.

That's not Jessica. I think you are dining with Excalibur. Be careful!
G

* * *

26 Togginham St. - London
ALEXANDRA CLARK

"By protocol, I should have our guys check this for explosives,"

Anastos said as we stared at the box in the center of our round table.

"Says the man who had enough poison to kill everyone within a square mile in his coffee pot." I ignored him, pulling the quick release strip to reveal the contents.

Inside was a square package with Joey Price's handwriting on it encased in dry ice, a cell phone, and a note.

Dear Ali,

Michael's people told Chief O'Brien you didn't mean to quit. You know how he bends over for federales. So, you're officially a cop again. Promotion to detective, too.

Oh, the people I have to sleep with to do things for my best friend!

X's cell phone is in this package. Use it to contact the Tri-guys when you're ready to send them to hell.

Go forth and kick ass, partner.

Love,
JRam

Chapter Forty

The Sentinel - Portland

The Albanian had a cousin. His job was to find out where Excalibur was staying, should his relative fail to kill her in the hospital parking lot. Discovering the man dead in the trunk of the Crown Vic amplified his resolve.

A forum spun up on the dark web where friends and family of X's victims shared intel about her likely whereabouts. Several posts mentioned a hotel in Portland, Oregon, called "The Sentinel," with postscripts telling the group that assets were on their way to exact revenge.

The cousin didn't have a gun. But he did have a knife. As a former army medic, he knew just where to cut to make death both painful and slow. With competition on the way, time was of the essence.

Emerging from the fire exit on the third floor he saw a black housekeeper pushing her cart toward him from the far end of the hall. His eye contact convinced her to pause next to the room where his target should be.

He watched her touch a magnetic key against a door handle, before propping it open and returning the credit-card-sized device to a cup atop the cart which held a small inventory of replacement soap bars. The woman dragged a vacuum into the room. He soon heard its whir, thankful for the noise that would cover his surgery, should X be in the next unit.

With the manual dexterity of a close-up magician, he retrieved the key, pressed against the door handle and heard the soft gears of the lock mechanism release.

The Albanian stuck a shoe against the jam to keep the door slightly open. He redeposited the key in the soap cup and slipped inside.

* * *

The Nines - Rooftop Restaurant

"What changed your mind, baby?"

Michael tossed the trigger word at his companion again. Jess would have chewed off his head for using it twice in less than ten minutes.

The girl tilted her head slightly, her brown eyes misting as she stared. "This whole horrible adventure. I want Sandra Sullivan to give me my Jessica face again, so I can just be a decent cop and a worthy wife."

She pressed a hand on top of his own. "I've been pretty selfish, Michael. I see that now. I apologize for whatever anger I may have expressed in the past. Please know that all that matters to me now is that we are together. I want to please you as no other woman has ever pleased you. I want to have your children. I want to be your wife, now and forever."

So perfect was the vocal impersonation that Michael felt pressure grip his chest. These were the words he hoped Jessica might someday say. In his heart of hearts, he was coming to the realization that perhaps she never would.

The Beretta pressed against his belt, a reminder that this woman was not the love of his life and was very capable of ending it.

"What kind of wedding would you like, Jess?"

"The biggest church you can find, love. I want a train the length of a football field and a diamond the size of a golf ball."

"On an FBI agent's salary?"

"Oh, I expect to fully kick in my half. I've been saving for this all my life."

Michael's culinary and coital appetites vanished. He at last understood Jessica's reticence. The situation had to feel right for everyone involved. Michael realized that until his impetuous marriage proposal in the Phoenix hospital room, she had likely not even considered matrimony.

Their discovery of one another was just beginning. They both needed time to be sure a long-term relationship would be mutually beneficial.

A waiter appeared, welcoming them in the usual way. "Would the lady like a beverage before lunch?"

Susan Molinero batted her brown eyes and gave the server a salacious smile. "A gin martini, please. Without olives."

Jess hated gin.

* * *

The Sentinel - Room 216

The Albanian was stunned by the sight; his quarry bound hand and foot, a dog collar around her neck chained to the base of a toilet.

It made no sense. None of this assignment made sense. The relative he swore to avenge deserved to die. There was dancing in the streets and few tears at the man's funeral. But family blood had bonds that supplanted convention. The woman's face was identical to the image he held in his hand. She had likely killed his cousin. He was the angel of death. Providence had presented him with a compliant victim, "tied up in a bow," as the Americans liked to say. Do the deed and get out.

* * *

JESSICA RAMIREZ

I felt sorry for the guy. The look of confusion on his face at seeing his target so neatly presented would have made me laugh if these damn zip ties didn't hurt so much.

He ripped the duct tape from my face. That hurt. And he pulled out the gag to get a good look at me.

Retreating to the doorway, the man studied a photograph with the intensity of a cartographer inspecting a lot line for an impatient real estate broker, eyes bouncing back and forth between the picture and me.

Satisfied that the two things he saw matched, he produced the knife. We're not talking about a jackknife or a switchblade. This was one big Crocodile Dundee, "That's no knife... This is a knife," kind of knife. It was long and thick with razor-sharp serrated edges, able to bisect everything from prime rib to pop cans.

The thing was designed to slice my stairway to heaven and there wasn't a damn thing I could do about it.

Have you ever been in a totally hopeless situation where your I-don't-give-a-shit attitude kicks in and your flippancy generator switches on?

Well, that's where I was. Buck naked, totally helpless with this Mediterranean-looking dude standing in the bathroom doorway, admiring his blade as if it were an inflatable sex toy.

I swung my bound legs over the edge of the bathtub to moon the guy. "Is it true what they say about the inverse relationship between big knives and small genitalia?"

He didn't acknowledge the taunt. I surmised I had surpassed his command of English vocabulary.

"Hey, Bongo. Are you going to do what you came here to do, or are you going to make love to your knife all afternoon? Let's get on with this, I have an appointment with my next life."

It must have been my tone of voice. The guy's attention broke free from his weapon and he gave me his best misogynistic glower. "You kill my cousin?"

I had an idea. It turned out to be a bad idea. "No. That was my twin sister. She tied me up like this because our mother liked me best. Cut me loose and I'll show you where she is."

No comprehension. "An eye for an eye," he said, probably sharing the last morsel of his English.

My killer swung the blade from an upward display-mode to a downward-facing, I'm-gonna-cut-out-your-living-guts position, squeezing the leather handle to conjure up whatever dark gods he worshiped.

His eyes narrowed and he growled the final words I expected to hear.

"Time to die, Excalibur."

* * *

The five suppressed gunshots came in quick succession. The aim was perfect. My assailant's head bucked to the left. Red droplets sprayed from an ever-widening exit wound with each successive blast as his melon bounced against the bathroom door. The metal blade fell from his grasp. It sang like a tuning fork when it hit the tiles. The man's body toppled forward into the cramped space.

There wasn't enough room in this toilet for the two of us, as the cowboys used to say. His corpse landed, post-coital missionary on my nude form, his head resting between my boobs as the blood drained from where his left temple used to be into the dark depths of my cleavage.

Gina Manson materialized in the doorway, still crouched in

firing position, smoke rising from her hot gun barrel like the lazy upward curl of the ash end of a cigarette.

"Who taught you how to use a gun, kiddo?" I asked.

She just stood there, jaw working with no words coming out. It occurred to me that the image of the two of us on the floor must be the stuff of post-traumatic stress.

"First time you've killed someone?"

She nodded.

"You did good, Gina. Now do me a favor. Grab this boy's blade and cut me loose. I'm gonna need a shower."

My savior found her voice.

"Make it a quick one, Detective Ramirez. Your twin is lunching with Agent Wright, and I think they both know who is who."

Chapter Forty-One

Bodrum, Turkey

B lack-clad security, complete with full-coverage head gear ferried Andy Milluzzi to *The Triarchy* on a gleaming, twin-engine launch in the scorching afternoon sun.

Andy tried to imagine how hot it must be beneath the heat-sucking ebony gear the team was forced to wear. His encyclopedic mind made note of the gender, size, and build of each person. Two at the docks with machine guns, two escorting him in the launch, side arms visible in Kydex holsters, and another pair, standing on the launch deck at the stern of *The Triarchy*, armed with matching automatic weapons. As he expected, the two snipers scanned the inlet from the sky bridge.

Detective Clark would have her work cut out for her.

The newly credentialed director of client technical support stepped aboard. A man dressed in traditional sailor-white shorts and button-down shirt with the stripes of the First Mate studied Andy's identification. He spoke perfect English.

"What happened to your predecessor, Mr. Milluzzi?"

"You know The Valley, Mr. Booth. Everyone is always poaching talent."

Booth allowed the microscopic hint of a smile. "You do your homework, Mr. Milluzzi. Not many know me."

"The Firm shares your concern for security, sir. As you know, each solution is custom designed. Competitors have bounties in circulation for any information about our code. We need to know who the stewards of our interests are with the same level of granularity."

Booth's distrust returned. "We paid a substantial price for reliable software. Updates have come to us on portable drives via bonded courier. Why this in-person visit? And why now?"

Andy hoped his preparation would pay off. "Each system we deploy is comprised of two primary elements, software and hardware. Within the hardware is firmware which allows the device to communicate with the server. Unfortunately, the manufacturer of your on-board cameras does not prioritize security to our standards." Andy produced a clear plastic bag. "This is a temporary fix until we can provide you with better camera hardware. The risk is minimal. I recommended we press for early delivery of replacement devices so we would not need to disturb you twice. But our president directed us to deploy these countermeasures now. He was quite insistent."

Booth processed the information before speaking. "That's Clay. You've said exactly what he told me when we talked."

Andy bowed in embarrassment. "I'm sorry, Mr. Booth. But our CEO's name is Paul, not Clay. And he spoke with one of your three guests, unless the briefing he personally gave me is incorrect."

The smile was bigger this time, but not by much. "Good. I apologize, Mr. Milluzzi, but you understand that we had to be sure you were who you said you were."

Andy bowed again. "I understand, sir. I don't want to inconvenience you any longer than necessary. I have the appropriate schematics and the entire process should take less than an hour. May I begin?"

Booth raised a hand toward the bridge. "By all means. Naturally, you will have an escort, to assist you with anything you may need."

Andy smiled. "Naturally."

* * *

The Nines - Room 608

Michael Wright had no idea where Jessica might be or what steps Gina might be taking to find her. He only knew he needed to buy time for events to transpire. When Susan turned out the lights and pressed him toward the bed in his suite after their lunch, he had two choices. He could kill her now and risk whatever countermeasures she may have had pre-planned for the eventuality of her death or keep her on the hook until he had more intel.

Michael rationalized the second option was best for all concerned. Excalibur's memory was priceless. In the right psychological hands, she could solve perhaps one-hundred cases. She was worth more alive, than dead.

But could he do what needed to be done?

Michael sat dutifully on the edge of the mattress. Tiny shafts of afternoon sun painted the far wall, casting a shadow on the topography of Susan's shirt as she slowly undid each button.

The last of the porcelain circles pulled free. Susan shed the khaki shirt she selected from Jessica's closet after changing out of the workout clothes. Michael was surprised to discover that it was the only layer between his eyes and Susan's body.

"Why darkness instead of daylight?" he asked.

Susan pressed his shoulders backward onto the mattress. She climbed aboard and began to undress him.

"It heightens the other senses, baby. The sounds, the smells, the touch." She circled his lips with her tongue. "And the taste."

And you can't see the nuances, Michael thought. *Where is your scar?*

He memorized every square inch of Jessica's anatomy. No surgeon's knife could duplicate that detail.

When Susan finished her work, Michael felt vulnerable and helpless. He had zero interest in this romantic interlude. And after his near-death experience with Vega in Phoenix, he wasn't in the mood to take another one for the team. In fact, what was centermost in his mind was slipping the Beretta out from under his pillow and putting a bullet in Excalibur's forehead.

"What's the matter, Agent Wright? Afraid you'll be dominated by someone who could just as easily kill you as defile you?" Susan straddled her prey. "Show me what you've got."

Testosterone shot through Michael's metabolism. The challenge was clear. And there were no more secrets. His heart rate increased.

"How well did you do in entomology class, Michael? Remember the bug species where the female ravishes her mate and then devours him?"

Michael grabbed Susan's face, pulling it within inches of his own. "I dare you to try."

* * *

Room 601

JESSICA RAMIREZ

I'll self-censor the string of expletives for young eyes who may find their way to this tome. That FBI boy couldn't resist sex with a killer.

Let's get up to the minute. It's downright creepy to shower in the same room where a dead guy has bled out. I had to use his back as a floor mat and do the high wire thing to dance out of Susan's bathroom. Gina brought me clothes. That woman deserves the Attention to Detail award for thinking of everything.

She didn't say much in the car back to our hotel. I don't blame her. You can't know what it's like to take a life, even a deserving dirt bag, until you've pulled the trigger.

But to her credit, she got her mojo back in the elevator. "Agent Wright got a make on X the moment she walked in the room. They lunched at the hotel restaurant. My last fix shows her in Room 608."

With the day I'd had, you couldn't blame me for an attitude. "Has she seduced him yet?"

Gina faced the elevator door like a statue. But her eyes slid in my direction. "I'm afraid we'll be able to tell very soon."

Which brings me to the now, sitting before one of those huge concave computer monitors, watching my fiancé bonk the woman intent on killing me.

Gina hid her eyes with a palm. "I'm sorry, Detective Ramirez. I wasn't sure what might happen, so I put a camera in the room, just in case we needed evidence later."

Michael made a move I knew well, eliciting some verbal delight from his partner.

I rolled my eyes, "Well, at least we know she can sing the high notes."

Gina tried to ground me. "Let's think this through, Detective. All he knew was that you were missing. He was certain I would try to find you. If he let X go, she might return to where they took you and kill you."

Another wail emitted from the computer speakers.

"Sounds like she may die of pure delight," I muttered, twisting Michael's engagement ring around my finger as I focused on the proceedings. "Looks like she studies yoga."

Gina winced. "What should we do?"

"What firepower do you have in here?"

"The Sig I carried when I... I shot the man who was about to kill you. And there's a Smith & Wesson M&P thirteen-shot in my backpack."

"I'll take the Smith. We'll let the scene play out and then I'll kill them both... Jesus, does Michael have to act so damn excited about all of this?"

I gave a glance to Gina. "What would you do if a guy you were supposed to marry was playing Pornhub with an assassin?"

A gleam the size of Rhode Island brightened her eyes. "Got anything valuable in Room 608, Detective?"

"I think we've shared enough adventures for you to call me Jess."

Gina produced a butane cigarette lighter from her butt pack. A thumb twirled the flame setting to high.

She handed me a room key.

"They are in the suite's bedroom. I'll disable the chime I installed on the door. Take this little baby in there and warm up one of the sprinkler heads where you can slip back out without getting too wet..."

I was on her wavelength. "And the water pressure will trip the fire alarm."

"And," Gina continued, "you'll have a dozen firefighters breaking down the door about three minutes later."

* * *

On Board The Triarchy

A black clad soldier that could have been his twin handed Andy's escort a printout with a woman's face on it. The Russian exchange was beyond Andy's understanding but one word didn't need a translation.

"Excalibur."

The face on the print-out belonged to Alexandra Clark. Andy kept his focus on his work.

"What exactly are those little ring things?" The voice behind the black mask sounded East European.

"They scramble any unusual firmware code that may try to send itself to the server," Andy said. "And your security chief will get a notification that the unit is compromised."

With two units left to modify, the questions from Andy's handler got more specific.

"I thought CAT-6 cable was shielded from nearby electromagnetic signals."

Andy flipped the tiny circular device open for inspection. "Ahh. Someone who knows his network gear. Take a close look. See the little pin in the center? It perforates the outer shield without endangering the connection. Pretty slick, eh?"

"How does it alert us?"

Andy smiled at the soldier. "You're one of the security nerds, aren't you?"

If it was possible to blush beneath the sweaty heat of a black cotton ski mask, the handler did just that. "I'm new. They think the timing of your visit and the proximity of your last assignment to the town where their target once worked is more than a coincidence. I'm supposed to make sure it's not."

Andy radiated empathy. "I got that same stuff during the interview. Now it all makes sense. Right place. Wrong time."

He clicked the ring around the network cable at the base of the second to last camera.

"I think my bosses are more scared of a system failure and what that would do to referrals. If it were me, I'd wait the two months for the new cameras."

The handler pointed to the last camera. It was attached to the windshield on the fly bridge, between the snipers.

"You've focused only on your work. You have not asked me any questions and it seems as if you want to get off this boat as fast as you can. Is that the modus operandi of a spy?"

Andy felt a tiny trickle of sweat drip off the end of his nose. It wasn't from the heat. He laughed, loud and long enough to attract attention.

"Just the habits of a nerd who would rather be playing Roblocks in an air conditioned hotel room than standing on a boat in the hot sun snapping rings around wires." He held out a palm with the last ring centered in it. "Look, I can show you how to install this thing, so if your supervisor decides to remove them, you can do it."

He handed the last ring to the new guy. The kid looked up at the flybridge and shivered. "I hate heights. The ladder is over there. I will wait here. The men with guns are just as mean as they look. They know what you are doing and why. Just keep quiet, get the work done and we'll get you on your way."

Andy shook the kid's gloved hand. "If you ever want a job on dry land, look me up."

The Nines - Room 608
JESSICA RAMIREZ

The security in these hotel suites is downright lousy. Entering the room was a breeze. The shenanigans in the bedroom continued at full volume. I thought there was some danger the bed might break.

Above the entry I saw the tiny fire sprinkler head, complete with its straw-like orange trigger. The butane ignited on the first twirl of the flint. I was able to keep one foot in the doorway to facilitate a quick departure as the blue flame licked the thin piece of plastic that held back the water. In less than five seconds, I heard a pop and the exhalation as the small air pocket that kept the water pressure at bay whistled out of the sprinkler head.

I was out the door and back in Room 601 in time to see Michael and Susan soaked in an ice-cold torrent from the fire control system.

Susan was smarter than I realized. She was dressed and gone before Michael could put the pieces together.

I spat another obscenity and gave chase. But when I opened the door, the hallway was deserted. I rolled the dice and went for the fire stairs but picked the wrong end of the hall. By the time I sprinted to the other side, I could see the light from the exterior door on the ground floor dim as it shut.

Way to go, Jessica. She's on the loose again and it's all your fault.

Chapter Forty-Two

Parkim Ayaz Hotel - Bodrum, Turkey 2300 hours

ALEXANDRA CLARK
I had my pound of flesh, Excalibur's cell phone and some shakey proof that security on board thought I was Susan Molinero.

The only option was to let them know I was coming.

Lee objected. "Excalibur's picture is all over the dark web, Ali. They will out you the moment you're on board."

I didn't want a fight to be our last memory of one another, so I didn't press too hard. "I wish there was another way. Anyone have suggestions?"

Anastos, Andy and Lee looked at one another. Nothing came.

"OK. I'm going to make the call. Commander, I'll hike down the road to the extraction point we agreed on, in case they have GPS tracking when I turn this phone on. I will text you when I'm out."

"I have a position with a view of the boat, Ali," Anastos said.

"Give Andy a signal on one of the security cameras and I'll ping those snipers for you to make 'em think you've got friends."

I tried to smile. It was hard. "Better than nothing. Can you hear stuff on those monitors, too, Andy?"

Good ole Andy grinned at me. "Just watch your language, Detective. I'll be listening."

Tom Anastos signaled to my favorite nerd. They quietly slipped out of my room, leaving Liyanna and me alone together.

"I'm gonna shag you all night long when I get back," I said.

"Monaco," she answered. "And then two weeks in Scotland. I want you to meet my family."

I laughed. "And then we'll go to Paloma, and I'll introduce you to MY family. A lesbian lover AND a black chick. It will be fun watching my father have a stroke."

Lee softened. "Jess is alive, Ali. You damn well better stay alive, too. I watched you mourn, and I don't intend to follow in those footsteps."

We embraced for a long time. It wasn't long enough. When I left it was hard for both of us to see through the tears.

* * *

Liyanna Evans found Andy sitting alone on deck chair, illuminated by the reflections of the pool lights. She was sure he could tell she had been sobbing.

Andy motioned to the chair next to his. When she sat, Lee became aware of Anastos' absence.

"Where is The Commander?"

Andy flicked a pebble into the pool, disrupting the soft ripples created by the filtration pumps.

"Deploying some of his own magic."

Lee pounded her thigh with a fist. "I wish I had magic to deploy, Andy. I have a bad feeling that Alexandra is not coming back from this mission." She spit on the pool deck. "Bloody Triumvirate. I'd kill them myself if I could get close enough."

Andy Milluzzi leaned forward in his chair.

"What if you could?"

* * *

The Nines - Room 601

JESSICA RAMIREZ

Gina Manson's more spartan quarters were now our accommodations. The suite was ruined. The bulk of the Portland FBI office followed the firefighters. Then came the call from Director Taylor. Michael was off the case and we didn't even have to cough up the video of his escapades with Susan. He was recalled to D.C., due in the Associate Director's office in forty-eight hours.

The man my mother wanted me to marry sat on the edge of Gina's bed, head in hands, wearing a bathrobe, the only thing dry enough that fit. His hair still glistened from the sprinkler head shower and his mood was dejection.

Despite his idiot behavior, I actually felt sorry for him.

"You can tell your boss I own this, Michael. I knocked over the dominos that let X get away."

Gina piped up. "It's my fault, Agent Wright. The idea was mine."

Michael looked up at us. "I was the agent in charge. I was supposed to protect you both. And look what happened? Twenty-some dead since I engaged, the love of my life defaced. And I had that woman in my arms. My assignment was to execute her. I had her. And I let her get away. This is complete and utter failure."

I tried to give Michael some perspective. "You saved my life, probably three times during this little adventure. Points for that."

"Yeah," Michael answered. "But no points count unless Excalibur is dead."

We heard the knock on the door. Nobody tensed up. Our adrenaline reserves were shot.

It was an agent from the Portland FBI office with some clothes for Michael and orders for him to relocate to a much less ostentatious motel closer to the bureau's Oregon outpost.

If it was possible to look more pathetic, Michael pulled it off when he came out of the bathroom. Dressed in poorly fitting slacks and discount-store shirt, he held out his hands to frame the scene.

"This is what a loser looks like."

I was beginning to lose my patience. "Well, at least you're taking it like a man."

The cow eyes told me I struck a nerve. "Perhaps I'm not the man who deserves you, Jessica." And then to Gina, "You two can keep the room until tomorrow. There's a plane ticket to get you home, Gina. Jess, I guess it's back to Dr. Sullivan's place. I hope she can give you your face and a bit of the life I've taken from you."

With that romantic soliloquy, Michael Wright walked out of our hotel room, likely certain he was also walking out of my life.

Bodrum Castle

Begun in 1402 The Petronium, The Castle of St. Peter or simply Bodrum Castle has had many residents. From the Knights of St. John to the Ottoman Empire, its walls have provided refuge. Its ramparts stood watch over the Agean, an early warning system until the castle was abandoned after World War I.

Today it is home to the Bodrum Museum of Underwater Archeology. And naturally, Tom Anastos knew a docent with the keys.

The Commander navigated the ancient promontory to his sniper's perch in the English Tower and the one window that gave him a perfect view of *The Triarchy*.

Despite an increase in suicide bombings, backpacks were still part of many a tourist's wardrobe. Tourism equaled liquid capital and not one of the people he passed on his way gave him a second glance.

They might have thought differently if they watched him unpack a miniature arsenal. The Anzio 20mm rifle had a maximum firing range of nearly three miles. With its night vision sight and armor piercing 20mm rounds, keeping an eye on the two snipers on *The Triarchy*'s fly bridge would be easy.

The harder decision would be whether or not to deploy the newer, smaller Javelin anti-tank missile. The top secret shorter brother of the weapon busting Russian tanks in Ukraine broke down into pieces so small that only the most sophisticated expert could identify it.

When Anastos received his final briefing from a now very much involved MI6 Director, Mo Gerhardt, his last order was to ensure that *The Triarchy* never left port with The Triumvirate alive. Everyone on this mission, including The Commander was expendable.

Anastos perched the rifle's tripod on the brick sill of the window well. The Javelin was within easy reach if he needed it. He prayed to the karma gods he would not.

* * *

The Bodrum Inlet
ALEXANDRA CLARK

I wondered how long the information MI6 planted connecting my face to Excalibur's would fool The Triumvirate's security team? A beat-up Fiat picked me up at the agreed upon place. In five minutes, I was riding the launch toward *The Triarchy* with a submachine gun pressed against my back. The full-coverage black uniforms were especially effective in the darkness. Nobody spoke.

The launch tied off at the sea deck of the immense yacht. The soldier with the gun pressed me toward some stairs. But not before searching me for weapons, inspecting my bag and carefully studying the square box, still encased in ice, and the trio of Turkish coffee containers with death inside.

At the bottom of the stairs, the man I recognized as Booth from Andy's description stopped us. We were square in the eyeball of a security camera.

"What did she bring?"

The muffled voice behind me grunted. "A refrigerated box and three containers of Tatlı Briki."

"Gifts. A token of gratitude," I said.

Booth ignored me. "Take it all up and throw it overboard," he commanded. "Then return immediately."

The soldier relieved me. Over the hum of the generators, I could hear the bag splash into the docile waters of the inlet. The fresh press of the weapon against my back was confirmation that the soldier had returned.

It was time to do something. "I have delivered what your bosses have asked," I barked. "Pay me."

Booth raised a fist but caught himself. "Watch your mouth, woman, or you'll join your trinkets in the Aegean with a bullet in your head."

"Try it, Mr. Booth. You don't think I would come aboard without backup. Right now, there are six rocket-propelled grenade launchers trained on this vessel. My own snipers have your boys in their crosshairs. If they don't see me on that launch with a briefcase in ten minutes, you and everyone aboard will provide the city with an appropriate fireworks display."

Booth looked to the soldier behind me. "See anyone else?"

"No, sir," was the muted reply.

Booth whispered instructions into a hand-held radio. He held the photo printout of my face next to the real thing. "You have three associates, Ms. Excalibur. Two women and a man. They arrived at twenty-one-hundred hours and are staying at the Parkim

Ayaz. I have assets headed there now to liquidate them all. As usual, you evaded us. But your greed delivered you into our hands."

I did the best I could to smile. "In sixty seconds, the snipers will land on the deck above us, dead."

Booth produced a reptilian smile and pressed a button on his Rolex. "Let's count it down together."

The Nines

JESSICA RAMIREZ

Gina and I sat wordlessly in a corner table at the hotel bar. The margarita tasted terrible. My trusty geek girl had the good sense to let me drink and think. And I did.

I thought about the chain of events that brought me from a small, Illinois river town to the Colorado rapids at the base of the Grand Canyon. I thought about the UK night sky and the approach of the London Eye Ferris wheel as a disabled helicopter I held onto for dear life lost altitude. I thought about the innocents who died when Susan destroyed my apartment building and the Paloma gang bangers Michael gunned down when X hired Antonio to do her dirty work. I thought about smashing Vega's skull against the rocks and the sizzle of burning flesh as two men, one innocent and one guilty were electrocuted and met their maker.

I thought about the three women who shared my last name, who buried me for dead, the surgeon who tried to save my face and gave me the face of a monster instead. I thought about Ali and Lee and the look of love I could see whenever their eyes met. I thought about that same look Michael gave me and how I was unable to give it back.

And I thought about Susan. It was naive to believe that a caring friend at the right place and the right time might have shown her the way to a completely different existence. Whatever her past, she was beyond redemption. Susan's crimes would have to be judged by a higher power.

Whether or not I loved Michael Wright, he had done what he thought best to protect me, rolling backup since the night he shoved Ben Batavia into a corner and threatened to beat his ass if he ever abused me again. I owed him for that, and for a hundred other things I probably still didn't know about.

I contemplated the half-consumed fishbowl of tequila, cointreau, salt and lime, swirling it to watch the ice cubes perform a synchronized swim routine.

"You know something, Gina?" I said, startling my drinking buddy. "It's a good day to die."

A cloud overtook Gina's features. "Do you need to talk with Dr. Sebastian, Jess?"

"Not me," I said, lifting her cell from the table. "What's our private text line to Excalibur?"

She gave it to me. And this was our text exchange.

Susan. This is Jess. You know by now that Michael has been recalled. And I know your exit strategy. You can't do it without killing me. Tell me where you are, and I'll give you that chance. But only if we are alone. If I get any sense that you have backup, mine will track you to the ends of the earth and I will carve that pound of flesh out of your guts myself.

I hit send. The wait felt like an hour, but Gina told me it was less than a minute.

The text included a set of map coordinates east of Puyallup Ridge Lookout. The satellite view revealed a single cabin above the tree line. She ended the message with the word,

"Midnight."

Chapter Forty-Three

On Board *The Triarchy*

ALEXANDRA CLARK
The two shots were barely whispers. The thudding bodies above us got Booth's attention.

A phalanx of black-clad soldiers appeared at the top of the stairs. Booth barked at them in Russian. Mine was good enough to decipher orders to replace the snipers and return to their posts.

"Seven minutes," I said. "Get me my money now, or we'll all meet again in hell."

Booth turned toward the bowels of the vessel. "Follow me." He stopped us outside a pair of mahogany doors and made a signal to the security camera above it.

The doors slid open with the silent whisp of their starship brethren. Booth flicked his wrist. My soldier guard ushered me inside.

Three men sat in leather chairs with their backs to us. They gazed at a wall of flat-screen television sets, each set to a different channel. The only sounds were those of the ship's support systems.

I could feel the dehumidified cool of the air-conditioning tickle my neck.

"Well done, Susan," an Asian voice said. "You frightened Booth. That is not an easy accomplishment."

"You brought us the pound of flesh," said a Russian. One of the screens replayed video of Jessica's Paloma apartment complex exploding. "And video proof of the completion of your assigned task."

"The money, Booth," said the third in a distinct, clipped East Indian accent. "And the usual safe passage to shore."

The tickle of the machine gun barrel told me my singular encounter with The Triumvirate was over.

I turned. The doors swished open. With Booth in the lead carrying the suitcase, I walked toward the stairs. As the mahogany doors slid shut the East Indian added, "The MI6 misdirection was a nice touch Alexandra."

When I heard the click of a lock securing the conference room, Booth turned toward me with a suppressed semi-automatic in his right hand.

"The usual safe passage, Officer Clark."

When he lifted the weapon to fire, I heard the cough of a silencer and saw a red dot appear on Booth's forehead.

The soldier's muffled voice took on a familiar Scottish brogue. "What was that you said about shagging me all night long?"

"Andy's idea?" I said turning to face the remarkable, ebony-uniformed woman I would love for the rest of my life.

"All us blacks look alike," Liyanna Evans said. "It only took a minute to find someone my size, neutralize them and borrow their wardrobe."

"Got the tea?"

"You know I do."

"And the location of the ventilation system?"

"That was your job."

I slapped my forehead, "Oh damn! I knew I forgot something."

For a nano-second I had her fooled. Not long enough to enjoy the moment.

"Take us there, luv," Lee said. "Grab the briefcase with the money and let's get off this bloody boat."

* * *

The Fiat was waiting at the dock. Lee and I got in the back seat. She put a gun to the driver's head. "Go exactly where I tell you to go or you're a dead man."

"You wouldn't kill one of the good guys, would you?"

Up came the mask revealing Andy Milluzzi's grin. "Direct to the airport," he said, pointing in the direction of the dark ramparts of Bodrum Castle. "per Commander Anastos."

"What shall we do with that briefcase full of money, luv?" Lee asked.

I contemplated the thick aluminum container. "I think it's an appropriate contribution to Jessica's retirement fund. I wonder if the department will match it... like a 401K?"

The tiny car peeled away from the inlet, toward a maze of streets in the direction of freedom.

Chapter Forty-Four

On Board *The Triarchy*

"I still think the Clark woman could have been useful," the East Indian said, fingering the remote control to change the image on one of the conference room's flat screens.

"And she came alone," the Russian said. "Brave, very brave."

The Asian sipped his tea. "Not alone, my friend. There were others."

"Do you think they succeeded?" the Russian asked.

The Asian reversed the video of the Paloma explosion, watching it for the hundredth time.

"Success is not defined in a single lifetime, comrade. This is where our philosophies diverge. In my country, events progress with deliberation. Your people want riches now. That leads to dangerous decisions with long-lasting impact. We believe sustainable wealth and power are the product of generations."

The East Indian jumped to his feet. "How? How did they do it?"

The Asian sighed. "Poison. Even now I sense its presence."

His agitated partner pounded on the huge doors. "Let us out! Let us out!"

The Russian lifted his crystal glass, studying the clear perfection of its contents. "Excellent vodka. I wish Prokofiev was still nearby to procure it for us." He turned to his Asian compatriot. "Have you identified a successor?"

"Yes."

"I have not. It is good to let the cream rise to the top."

The third man continued to pound on the mahogany. It's sheer thickness absorbed the energy.

"And our Indian friend?"

The Russian sipped his drink, savoring its sharpness. "Obviously he has no successor. I doubt he has the confidence of his people."

The pounding barely registered beyond the confines of the conference room. The Asian calculated that the bulk of the security team on deck were likely huddled near the cooling vents for relief from the heat of the evening. Already dead.

Chapter Forty-Five

East of Puyallup Ridge Lookout

J ESSICA RAMIREZ
Susan was true to her word. I did not detect a single human along the dark winding road to her cabin. It weaved a path upward through dense forest until the altitude could no longer sustain the trees. When I began to second guess the road map that replaced my trackable GPS phone, a small orange dot appeared near the top of my windshield. It grew into a small square cabin, framed against a black sky painted with thousands of tiny white diamonds.

Adjacent to the cabin, my headlights revealed the same MTT420R crotch rocket I rode in pursuit of Tony DeSalvo on the afternoon when this adventure began. The months since felt like years.

Thinking about it lifted my shields and waves of fatigue pulsed in time with my heartbeat. Every punch I ever endured throbbed. The tiny incisions that turned a broken face into that of a killer radiated pain. The many suppressed memories in my emotional wheelbarrow threatened to spill over into sobs of sorrow, shame, and regret.

I forced myself to concentrate on the person inside the cabin. Tonight, she would either pay for hundreds, perhaps thousands of deaths, or walk free from this place with an exit strategy and another notch on her barbaric belt of cruelty.

I gave Susan the courtesy of a knock.

"It's open."

The face I was accidentally given by a benevolent surgeon balanced her pistol in firing position from the comfort of a wooden chair at the end of an oak table. A tiny orange blaze in a small fireplace was the only illumination.

Susan Molinero inspected me, nodding in approval. "This Dr. Sullivan is pretty damn good, Jessica. I will avail myself of her services after you're dead. She'll do anything to give the girl she defaced her identity back."

"And then you'll kill her, too?" I asked. "Just as you killed her innocent daughter?"

"You know me, Jessie. I don't like leaving a trail."

I moved my hand away from the Smith & Wesson Gina Manson provided, holding them both up where my adversary could see them.

"Let's make a deal, Susan. Since you're the professional and I'm just a small-town cop, I'm already dead. I'll put my gun on the table at the same distance you've put yours. We'll talk. And when it's time, you say 'go.' The fastest draw leaves here alive."

Overconfidence and arrogance walk hand in hand. I figured Susan Molinero had plenty of both.

The table was long enough for six. Susan took the man's spot befitting our Mexican household. I knew she did that to piss me off.

My former classmate placed her weapon two feet away and motioned for me to sit. I mirrored her position at the other end, including flipping my Smith so it was accessible to my dominant hand.

"You'll have to learn to shoot left-handed, Susan."

She reversed her gun to accommodate a south paw. "Ambidextrous, Jessie. Didn't you read my middle school bio? I thought cops did their homework."

I forgave myself for that error. It wasn't that long ago that I couldn't remember my name.

"What happened to you, Susie? What turned you into a killer?"

"Come on, Jess. That's Police Academy 101. Mass murderers all struggle with normal relationships. You knew me. I had none."

"You had Roberta."

"Every so-called friend in my life served a purpose. Bertie did me a favor by planting doubt in your head about my death. Even at age thirteen, I was adding useful cards to my hand. Bertie was just another Queen of Hearts, tossed on the pile. In poker, the cards you can't see are the ones that can kill you."

"And Diana?"

Susan shook her head. "Poor Diana. I warned her to watch out for that bitch of a partner of yours. I told her Clark was smart. Smart enough to figure out the poison play, and switch glasses. Smart enough to swap clothes so I would put a bullet in the wrong head."

Susan's eyes caught the dancing fireplace flames painting reflections on the far wall through the diamonds on my engagement ring. "Nice jewelry, Jessie. Somebody is working very hard to get laid."

I slipped Michael's ring from my finger. It was the first time it had been off my hand since I found it at Sandra's house. "You know what he's like in bed. You might as well try this on, too. If you kill me, you'll probably have to get it resized. Those fingers look fat."

Susan studied the piece. It occurred to me that if I weren't such an honorable person, I could have shot her dead right then. She slid the glittering band onto her ring finger. It fit perfectly.

"Thanks, Jessie. I prefer this to pulling it from your bloated corpse."

Susan walked the high wire of a high-functioning psychopath; not much different from Tony DeSalvo at the core. But wise enough to turn a sickness into a profession.

"What's the gasoline for, Susan?"

"I torch the place after you're dead. This little box is the only thing on earth in my name, so the authorities will assume, and I will escape."

I needed to know about Sandra Sullivan's daughter, the body Rick Meredith found in Susan's bed. A dead innocent with dreams and potential that would never be realized.

"Why Lucy, Susan? She truly idolized you. Probably a first. Could you find no compassion for that kid whatsoever?"

"Your boyfriend and his brothers were getting too close, Jessie. I needed a plausible exit. Lucy Sullivan had a useless life. She did us all a favor by giving the world's most revered instrument of death the chance to continue to serve."

My face flushed. The rise in my temper felt good. I knew Michael wanted the redemption of killing her, but I had no intention of giving Susan even the most microscopic chance of continuing her path of death and destruction.

Reading other people must have been one of the cards she held. Her eyes narrowed as she smiled.

"Let's not kid one another, Jessie. You and I aren't that much different. I'm well paid by powerful people to rid the world of their enemies. You are underpaid to do the same thing. Only you must overcome a broken justice system and incompetent associates. I always win. You almost always lose. But when we snuff a dangerous flame, we're both doing the world a favor." She held up two fingers. "Vega, Prokofiev, need I say more?"

Behind my fury was a tiny grain of regret. "I wish I had been nicer to you in school, Susan. Perhaps if you had more of the right friends, we might have ended up working together."

Susan placed her hands flat on the table. "We're getting close to 'go,' aren't we, Jessie?"

I followed suit. I had only one card to play: the speed with which I could draw and accurately fire a gun I hoped it would be enough.

"I pity you, Susie. But I have no regrets about killing you."

Susan's focus on me was total. A lifetime of thoughtless disregard for the value of a human being created a killing machine good for only one purpose.

"You were one of the few who were nice to me, Jessica. I'm sure you don't remember. But I never forgot it. Antonio was picking on me in middle school and you intervened. That's why you didn't die the moment you walked through that door. It's ironic that I hired "El Asaltante" and his boys to kill your family. It felt good to learn that he died in the process."

I knew about Michael dispatching Tony's gang buddies, but not about their leader's death. Despite his own dark path, I felt a pang of grief.

"Your doing?" I asked.

"Through one of his rivals, Jessica. Fifty dollars. Too little to add to my bill."

Susan wiggled her fingers on the table. A smile I had seen in my own mirror spread across her face. "Thanks for sticking up for me on the playground that day, Jessie. See what kindness buys you?" She shot a nano-second glance at an old-style analogue clock that hung on the wall. "Ten minutes."

I rarely give up on a human being. But I had lost any hope for Susan Molinero's rehabilitation a long time ago.

Tonight, I would become Karma's instrument, or its victim. One of us was about to die. My fear was gone. My concentration complete. I prayed to my father before entering the house. I was ready. It was time.

"Goodbye, Susan. Say the word."

* * *

Gina Manson couldn't keep her mouth shut. Michael Wright was grateful for that. But she wrestled with her conscience for too long. He cursed the darkness slowing his progress.

As Michael's SUV skidded to a stop in front of the cabin, he heard a pair of gunshots.

He was uncertain if the relationship he had built with Jessica Ramirez over the preceding three years had a future. After his ultimate infidelity, Michael wouldn't blame her for going her own way.

As he thought about it, he realized that was the only way Jess ever went.

A dim, rectangular glow appeared between the pair of windows at the front of the cabin. A woman emerged, tossing a lighted match into the darkness .

She walked halfway to the SUV before turning to watch the flames lick the exterior. The woman stood there, as if in reverence for a funeral pyre as the bright orange bier was consumed.

When only embers remained, the she nodded, turned, and walked toward the passenger side door.

In the darkness, Michael Wright could not tell if she still wore his ring.

The woman looked straight ahead, seemingly unaware of his presence, lost in some far-away place with her only her thoughts as companions.

Michael dropped the SUV into gear and slowly threaded his way back down the mountain toward an uncertain future.

He noticed blood weeping slowly from a wound in the woman's right shoulder. She did nothing to stem the flow.

The face was the same. But whoever walked out of that cabin was a stranger. At a loss for words, Michael finally stumbled through, "Where can I take you?"

He knew both Jessica's and Susan's voices as well as his own. This one was different. Unfamiliar.

"Take me to Dr. Sullivan. I want a new face."

Chapter Forty-Six

Portland **Research Hospital - Four Months Later**

Alexandra and Liyanna delivered the news of Jessica's existence in person to the Ramirez household. Maria fainted. Mama praised God. Mamacita just smiled, as if she had known it all along.

It took some time, but two million dollars in United States legal tender found its way into untraceable securities on an air-gapped computer with Jessica Ramirez's name on it. Thank you, Commander Anastos. Jess would probably argue with Ali about the ethics, but Alexandra Clark had seen The Triumvirate face-to-face. Her partner had earned that money and the financial freedom it brought.

Chief O'Brien quickly acceded to Director Taylor's request to reinstate the detective, now captain with full back pay and benefits. The FBI combed the ashes near Puyallup Ridge. They ran the cremated human remnants they found through DNA testing, using Excalibur's brother as a match. The results were inconclusive.

Taylor also kept his promise to Michael Wright. All sins were forgiven. And yet, one transgression remained. The agent kept his distance from the Portland Research Hospital. This was a sin only she could forgive. Her silence spoke volumes.

Superstition bloomed around the mysterious deaths of everyone on board a yacht known as *The Triarchy*. When no entity would claim her, the Turkish government towed the vessel and the bodies it held to an undisclosed section of the Aegean and scuttled her.

* * *

The last of the twelve procedures only required a minor anesthetic. Most patients would have been thrilled with the surgeon's earlier artistry, but Dr. Sullivan wanted this one to be perfect. With a lifetime of family photos as her guide, the hospital staff marveled at the transformation.

Despite entreaties, the patient refused all visitors, except for Dr. Sebastian. She never left the confines of the private room Dr. Sullivan paid for. A treadmill and weight machine were installed. The patient spent her days strengthening her body, mind and spirit, working out like a fiend followed by long, deep conversations with her psychiatrist.

No mirrors were allowed, and window blinds were kept shut so the patient never saw her reflection.

The day before the final surgery, she asked for one person to be present when she awoke. Terry Taylor provided a private jet as transportation.

After tying off the last of the micro sutures, the surgeon nodded to the anesthesiologist to switch from the twilight drug to pure oxygen.

She motioned to the outsider. "I want you to be the first person she sees when she wakes up."

The patient's eyes fluttered. The lids lifted and her eyes focused.

"Recognize anyone?" Sandra Sullivan asked.

The patient nodded.

"Do you know who you are?"

Another nod.

"What's my name, partner?" Alexandra Clark said as tears streamed freely down her cheeks, falling like raindrops on the patient's surgical gown.

The voice was hoarse but strong. "You're getting me all wet, Alexandra."

"We told your family you were alive. But all this denial-of-visitors behavior is making some people wonder who walked out of that cabin."

"Who's we?"

"My wife and I."

"Lee said yes?"

Ali held up her left hand. An austere golden band circled the ring finger.

"Someone in Portland wouldn't answer my calls, so we got married without a by a justice of the peace without a maid of honor. We are saving an ostentatious London wedding for later on... The sacrifices I make for friendship."

The patient let her eyes close. "Congratulations."

"Ready to go back to work?"

The patient shook her head. "I'm done. They win. I've had enough of everything associated with that life."

Alexandra shook the patient's chin to rouse her. "That's not the woman I know. Before you get to see the doctor's artistry, I need proof. Did Dr. Sullivan put my BFF's face on an assassin?"

"Look who's talking. Seventeen dead on a two-hundred-million-dollar yacht. Takes one to know one."

Alexandra Clark drilled her gaze into the patient's eyes. She racked a round into her Glock, pointing the weapon toward the ceiling for effect. "Prove it to me, hot shot. Something only you and I know. Get it wrong and I swear to God, I'll become

Karma's avenging angel and kill you right here on this operating table."

The patient's smile came slowly. It was exactly the smile Ali knew by heart.

"5537," Jessica Ramirez said. "Go get me a mirror."

THE END

Acknowledgments

Jessica Ramirez is based on the life and work of Lt. Traci Ruiz, police officer extraordinaire. Traci's adventures don't approach the theatrical magnitude of those I created for Jessica, but she's impacted hundreds of lives along the way and shares many of Jess' best personalty traits.

Alexandra Clark is a composite of many good friends, in and out of law enforcement. Cindy Bird-Boyd's personality was a central influence. Shelley Appelbaum gave me Ali's character name. I dedicate Jess' partner to her.

Andy Milluzzi, Tom Anastos, Mo Gerhardt and Savvy Schmidt are all real people. Of course they don't do the jobs I created for them, but each has a special energy that imbues the characters who share their names. I'm grateful for their willingness to let me celebrate them in print.

Sandra Sullivan and Assunta Sebastian are two author colleagues who helped me come up with a name for Susan's altar ego. Their rewards were strong supporting roles in the story. I hope I communicated their awesomeness within the context of the cast members they helped portray.

FBI Associate Director Terry Taylor is based on a fellow drummer who grew up to be a high school principal. Appropriate training for a top cop.

Gina Manson and Emma Sutro are nods to two more author friends, Penny Manson and Marie Sutro. Both write much better than I. Hoping my showcasing them in a positive light earns a decent pair of book reviews.

Many of you know my friend and brilliant writer, James L'Etoile. It was fun giving him a cameo as Ali's early love interest. And superlative writer Rick Meredith made the huge mistake of inviting me to bunk at his place during a book tour. I rewarded him with instant death in the story after his character is sent to be one of Jessica's protectors.

Layanna Evans' character was a gift from the noted techno-thriller author Louise Dawn. I wanted Ali to fall in love with somebody special. Louise proposed a mixed race Zulu-Scottish cop with South African roots. Perfect.

Fans of Jessica's previous adventures will recognize Chief O'Brien, Captain Ben Batavia and the exquisite Dr. Joey Price from Chasing Vega and Chasing The Captain. Reader acclimation brought Joey to Paloma to play a role in this story.

Dawn Elick, the Special Assistant to the President is in loving memory of my dear friend Dawn Elick Hosmer. We lost her to cancer as Karma was in its final birthing stages. The world is diminished without Dawn. I hope her brief but powerful scene might point you in the direction of reading her own exceptional prose.

NSA Director, Mike Wolthuis is a tip of the hat to a close Michigan friend. He would make a great leader at that agency.

Stories like Chasing Karma naturally must take some liberties with the space / time continuum, proper police procedure and some of the technical aspects of the weaponry the characters use. Anything too far outside of believability is my own fault and not the fault of my physician - crime author friend D.P. Lyle, top cop trainer Bruce Sokolove and a dozen other law enforcement professionals in the US and the UK who consulted with me as I crafted this book.

Special love to the extraordinary author S.M. Freedman. Shoshona read the galley and pointed out three crucial opportunities to improve the story. She's brilliant and I pay attention. The finished product is significantly better thanks to her assessment.

Joan Turner Nichols edits my stuff. Bobbye Marrs creates Jessica's book covers. Kerry Schafer is more than just a business manager. Her imprint on the positive aspects of my writing took Karma to a higher level. It also helps that she has psychotherapy skills in her past. She helped keep me centered when life tried to knock me out of alignment.

Most of us authors believe our most recent publications will be our last, especially when plot lines seem to fall apart and characters demand to take the story in directions we had not anticipated. The support of the author community kept me going through the arduous process of creation.

I don't know what I did to deserve Dänna Dennis Wilberg in my life. Outside of my wife and family, no one person has been a bigger cheerleader. She is an accomplished writer and an award-winning movie producer / director and television personality. Her Grace Simms and Suzanne Cash stories are great reads. She has a gift for popping into my orbit at moments of self-doubt with a kind word and a gentle push. I couldn't ask for a more supportive colleague in The Craft. May we all be as richly blessed.

Story consultant Dawn Alexander's whispers can be felt throughout Chasing Karma and Stephie Walls gift for creating powerful, moving scenes was a touchstone as I tried to help Jess wrestle with the hand grenades I kept throwing at her throughout the book.

Special thanks to the incomparable Pam Stack. She dragged me back into the talk-show biz. Over sixty Authors on the Air interviews, exposed me to immense talent and new friends.

I try to channel Lee Goldberg's intensity, Boyd Morrison's felicity with the chase, the wonderfully addictive storytelling styles of Danielle Girard, C.L. Taylor, Megan Abbott, Tori Eldridge, Matt Coyle, Walter Mosley, Gregg Hurwitz, Rachel Howzell-Hall and Hallie Epheron.

Real cop, Pete Stipe was on my mind while writing this story. His memoir touched my heart at just the right moment. Jess' descriptions of life in her world channel my friend and author Craig Pittman's joyfully jaded journalistic outlook.

Mystery/Thriller writers are kindred spirits. I hope I can someday repay my fellow travelers' many kindnesses, their candid, caring feedback and their blind faith that Chasing Karma would turn out to be something worth reading.

This is the part where writers thank patient families who endure our long absences when we write, listen to early drafts of unfinished work, and generally put up with us. My adult children, Shelby, Brandon, Casey and Stephanie show incredible patience with a dad who is still trying to find his way at age 68. My beautiful wife, Colleen contributes the spice in both Jess and Ali's personalities. She believes I can do anything. I've mined that character flaw for forty-four years and hope to keep riding the wave for as long as she'll have me.

There is no story without readers. A toast to you for sticking with this tale to the very end and reading the acknowledgements. Thank you for buying Jessica's books, the ultimate encouragement for people like me to keep trying to tell better tales.

Karma flexes her muscles in strange ways. I hope she smiles on each of you as we keep trying to figure out the next chapter together.

Terry Shepherd - Jacksonville, Florida - January, 2023

Also by Terry Shepherd

Chasing Vega

Chasing Cody

Chasing The Captain

The Corona Ripper

Learn more about Terry and sign up for his newsletter at
TerryShepherd.com.